worth the TROUBLE

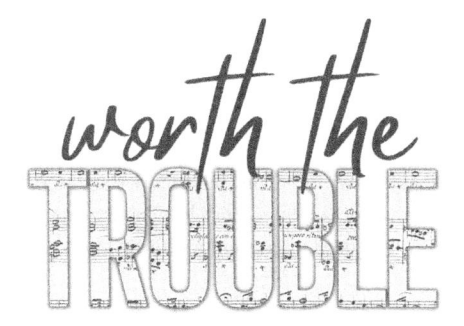

EVA SIMMONS

Copyright © 2023 by Eva Simmons

All rights reserved.

No portion of this book may be reproduced in any form without written permission from the publisher or author, except as permitted by U.S. copyright law.

This novel is entirely a work of fiction. The names, characters and incidents portrayed in it are the work of the author's imagination. Any resemblance to actual persons, living or dead, events or localities is entirely coincidental.

Editing by Kat Wyeth (Kat's Literary Services)

Proofreading by Vanessa Esquibel (Kat's Literary Services)

Cover Photography by Ren Saliba

Cover Design by Eva Simmons

ISBN: 9798395313379

Playlist

Somebody—Memphis May Fire
Ain't No Rest for the Wicked—Cage the Elephant
Howlin' for You—The Black Keys
Heroin—Badflower
The Bird and the Worm—The Used
The Red—Chevelle
Calling All Cars—Senses Fail
Faces—Scary Kids Scaring Kids
Whirlwind of Rubbish—Toydrum, Gavin Clark
Seven Devils—Florence + The Machine
Handlebars—Flobots
Way down We Go—KALEO
Trip Switch—Nothing But Thieves
Dark Things—ADONA
Mr. Sandman—SYML
Vermilion, Pt. 2—Slipknot
Impossible—Nothing But Thieves
Play With Fire—The Rolling Stones
Wrong Side of Heaven—Five Finger Death Punch
I Wanna Be Your Slave—Maneskin
Arcade—Duncan Laurence
Blindfold—Sleeping Wolf

Hollow—Belle Mt.
Devil's Advocate—The Neighbourhood
Creep—Kina Grannis
Skinny—KALEO
Paralyzed—NF
Lover, Please Stay—Nothing But Thieves

You can find the complete playlist on Spotify.

For the broken boys who need to be reminded there's still a heart worth loving beneath the scar tissue

1

Rome

"It's been seventeen days since I've fucked someone. Pat me on the back and call me celibate."

My comment almost knocks Noah out of his chair he's laughing so hard, but perfectly uptight Eloise just rolls her eyes.

"You're disgusting." Eloise frowns, pushing her long brown hair off her shoulders and letting it fall down her slim back.

"What's wrong, princess?" I cross my arms over my chest. "Figured you'd be proud of me."

That's not why I actually said it, but it's too easy getting a reaction out of her—and everyone else for that matter. So I just can't help myself.

One off-the-wall comment is all it takes to knock people off balance. And if no one knows what to expect from you, they never expect anything specific.

Exactly how I prefer it.

"Rome, man." Noah walks over and slaps a hand on my shoulder. "Your dick's going to fall off if you aren't careful."

"Fuck you." I toss his hand to the side as the band takes their seats in the interview room, and I claim a chair at the end. "Being careful is for boring pricks like you assholes. I'd be more concerned with my dick hating me for only screwing one chick for the rest of my life."

Noah shakes his head and shares a look with Sebastian.

I'm tempted to tell them to fuck off. It wasn't that long ago they were more than happy to indulge in nameless blow jobs and free pussy.

Not that either of them seems to remember that at the moment. Because it all changed when the dominos started falling. And first to go down was Sebastian.

As the lead singer, Sebastian should be drowning in tits and orgies with random women, but something about Cassie and her pink hair got him all twisted and monogamous. And the way he's eyeing her right now as she stands in the corner talking to Adrian tells me it's just a matter of time before he loses all good sense and puts a ring on her finger.

Idiot.

She's pretty and all, but one woman forever? No thanks.

Next to abandon me was Noah, which really pissed me off because he was my wingman for years, and I never thought I'd see the day. His pretty-boy smile and down-to-earth surfer look brought women to their knees—literally. But then he met Merry, and his tatted-up wife made him a bigger punk than Sebastian.

Last to fall, surprisingly, was Eloise. And while I usually wouldn't give a shit because she never partied with me anyway, she had to go and take Adrian with her. He's always been uptight, being our band manager and all, but at least he'd still go out with me. And now, he'd rather be stuck to her side when he isn't working.

I shouldn't be surprised since it was no secret that he was obsessed with her from the moment he started managing the band. But I kind of hoped they'd never finally do the inevitable.

Now it's just me—the only true rock star of us left.

Why they gave it up for relationships confuses the fuck out of me. But here they are, looking over at me with judgment in their eyes like *I'm* the crazy one for celebrating the perks of fame.

At least it's better than when they look at me like I'm next. Like one wrong step and my dick will fall into the pussy it's going to want to bury itself in forever.

Fuck. That. Shit.

Never going to happen.

Just because I've been on a bit of a dry streak lately doesn't mean there's a leaf turning over. I'm just so fucking bored after this last tour and can't seem to get my head back on straight from all the shit that happened.

The tour might have started fine. World tours are always my favorite because I get to sample every beautiful thing as we circle the globe. But after a while, something felt off. Add in the shit that happened with Eloise and her stalker, and I was more in the mood to murder someone than fuck them.

So here I am.

Seventeen days without getting laid.

That's got to be some kind of record—at least, for me. Maybe after this interview, I'll hit up a strip club and get my dick wet just to prove I'm not losing my shit.

Noah leans toward me in his chair and knocks me with his shoulder. "You okay, man?"

"Always." I grin and try to bury whatever doubt just crept in.

He nods, but his eyebrows pinch, and I don't like that he doesn't seem to believe me.

Of everyone in the band, I'm closest to Noah, and the dude can read me better than anyone. Like right now, when he ties his shoulder-length blond hair back as he assesses whatever he's seeing on my face. He knows something's up, and he's right.

I've felt off for a while now. Demons are a bitch like that. Following you around whether you're smoking, screwing, or sleeping. I used to think if I just did a little bit more of anything I'd be able to silence them.

Fuck me, apparently.

The reporter sits down on the chair in front of us. Her knee-length pencil skirt rides up as she crosses one leg over the other and smiles. She's got big lips and innocent eyes, and she's pretty in an uptight, prissy kind of way that I usually find hot because it's so much fun to mess it the fuck up.

But again, nothing.

What the fuck is wrong with me?

Through a wall on the far side of the room I hear music playing, and I recognize the song: "Ain't No Rest For the

Wicked." It immediately makes my skin crawl because every word is like an anthem I'll live and die by.

I heard it enough growing up for it to become a part of who I am.

My dad would play it on repeat when he was too tired to beat the shit out of me. Like he was trying to nail the message to a post in my brain. At least it was one of his lesser forms of punishment, and coming from a man whose brand of education was extremely specific—and often hurt like hell—it was the better option.

And effective.

The song ends, and I wonder if there was music at all or if I'm just hearing things. But then, the song starts over from the beginning, loud enough to draw Eloise's attention this time, so I know it's not in my head.

Just what I need when I already feel off balance—thoughts of my father added into the mix.

Maybe I died and I just haven't realized it yet. After all, I've got *perdition* tattooed on my stomach because I've known since I was old enough to know anything that it's where I belong—in a constant state of suspension.

Most people wish for heaven and fear hell. I'd take either over the purgatory I've spent my life in. Chasing a high until it finally breaks me.

When I was real young, I still believed that everyone reached that point in their lives when shit turned around. I truly believed the universe would decide one moment I'd suffered enough. It's that same dumb thinking that convinced me my father would one day reach a point where he'd get tired of using me as a punching bag.

The day he broke his knuckles on my face, I saw the truth.

I suffered plenty and nothing saved me.

Nothing would.

There was no magical event that would change my life unless I was the one willing to do it. So I did—with the band and with my music. I sold one pound of flesh at a time, and now, I'm being mentally crucified for enjoying the perks of it.

The song starts over.

It starts. Fucking. Over.

"Rome?"

My eyes snap back into focus on the reporter sitting in front of me, and I feel the eyes of the rest of the band.

"What was the question?" I lean back in my chair and cross one ankle over the other, trying to pretend I'm bored so she doesn't notice me crawling out of my skin.

The reporter pushes her glasses up her nose, and her sweet brown eyes dart to the paper in her hands. She's nervous. The tick as she flips between the pages gives her away. She probably hopes I don't see it. But that's the problem, I see everything. Even when I don't want to.

"What made you fall in love with music?" Her eyes dart back up to me.

I bring my hands together and pop my tattooed knuckles. "You mean besides the pussy?"

A blush spreads like a wildfire on her neck because it's too fucking easy for me to get a reaction. It's what I'm good at—pushing people to their limits. Finding the line that keeps them comfortable and forcing them one step over it.

I'd pretend to give a shit, but what's the point? I do what I want, I say what I want, I fuck who I want.

Over the reporter's shoulder, Adrian shoots me a glare, telling me he's not impressed with my comment.

Guy is such a buzzkill lately. You'd think getting regular pussy would put him in a better mood, but apparently not. He's always stressed out and hyper-aware of everything I do.

Play nice, he told me as I walked into this interview room. Like I'm a child who needs watching. Sitting here now, I can feel the imaginary leash around my neck tightening.

Not sure why when I've been good lately—boring even. Acting like a grown-ass man trying to help these punks start a record label. Lately, they've had nothing to worry about. I'm not in the mood.

You're losing your mind.

"I'm sorry—" the reporter stutters.

Her eyebrows pinch and it's cute. But still, my dick feels nothing. Something is definitely wrong with me.

"Joking." I force a smile, noticing Adrian's shoulders relax from across the room, even if he knows it's a façade.

I'd like to flip off everyone in this room and tell them all I didn't become a rock star—the Riff King—to play nice. But I'm not in the mood for a lecture later, so I hold my forced grin.

"Cage the Elephant," I answer the reporter's question. "Their music got me into it."

"The band?"

I nod. "Listened to a lot of music growing up, but something about them—consider me inspired."

The reporter is satisfied enough with my answer to smile and move on to Eloise for the next question. I gave her what she was looking for—something that sounds nice on paper, even if it's not the truth.

The real reasons I got into music wouldn't be feel-good enough for her story, so I doubt she'd actually want to hear them.

What I don't tell her is that music is the only home I had growing up. Because housing, people, schools, and belongings were interchangeable. They could be given and taken in a heartbeat.

But songs stayed. In my head. In my bones. They gave me a place to live—to disappear into—when everything else fell apart.

Music was what kept me sane. It's what kept me from telling Dad to just pull the trigger already when he put his rifle to my head.

I didn't need possessions or friends or a roof as long as I had the beat. I didn't even need a family. Or so I thought. Until Sebastian and Eloise bulldozed into my life and took me in as some kind of unofficial stepbrother and bandmate.

They grew up in a rough enough situation themselves that they didn't need to ask what was wrong to know something just was.

They invited me to crash at their place once, then twice, then every night. They gave me a spot in the world before I knew what having one meant. And they gave me music. If for no other reason than that simple fact, I'll always owe them.

But I'm not telling this prissy reporter any of that shit. She can accept my candid response and move on to the next question—which she does.

The string of interviews is endless. If it weren't for Eloise and Noah, I'm honestly not sure how we'd survive it. Sebastian looks just as bored as I am, on top of being distracted by Cassie laughing and flipping her pink hair over her shoulder in the corner.

At least the reporters don't notice or care because they go on with their questions like it's any other day. They accept my half-assed responses and fall for Noah's smiles and Eloise's rock princess act.

Fuck all this noise.

When the interviews finally wrap, I feel like I'm barely able to sit still.

Hopefully, tonight is the night I can get out of my head long enough to break this seventeen-day celibacy streak because a bottle of whiskey and a couple of strippers are the only thing that sounds halfway decent at this moment.

"Who's down to go out?" I ask as the band walks outside.

Cassie has already wrapped herself around Sebastian and he's twirling a pink tip from her blonde hair around his finger, so I know he's not in.

"Missing tour life?" Cassie nudges my arm which, from Sebastian's glare, he doesn't appreciate.

"Always."

Except for the first time ever, that might be a lie because I'm not.

"We're headed home." Sebastian squeezes Cassie against his side.

"Figured. I'm asking those of us who aren't pussy whipped."

Problem is, the glares that surround me are proof there's no one left. Noah and Merry bailed straight after the interviews ended, and Sebastian and Cassie barely decline my invitation before walking away.

Now I'm left with Eloise, who's standing here frowning.

"We're headed home too. Sorry. Long day." She wraps her arms around Adrian, looking so small tucked under his arm.

Unlike the guys in the band, I think Eloise actually does feel bad about bailing and leaving me alone.

"Yeah, yeah." I plant my hand on her head and shake it, trying to lighten the mood.

I might purposely guilt Sebastian and Noah about ditching me for their chicks, but I like seeing Eloise happy after all these years, so I don't want to do that to her.

She swats at my hand as she pulls away, trying to fix her hair, and Adrian wraps his arms tighter, kissing the top of her head.

"Not sure why you're worried about your hair when Adrian's just going to mess it up later." I laugh when it makes both of them glare at me.

"Be good, Rome." Adrian ignores my comment and points a finger at me. "If I get a call from jail tonight, I'm not picking your ass up until morning."

"Like they'd arrest this face." I tip my chin up and grin. "Go fuck your girl and stop worrying about me."

Eloise shakes her head, but Adrian just pulls her toward the car.

"Have fun," she says.

"But not too much, right?" I yell after them.

Adrian laughs. "Exactly."

Eloise giggles and they disappear into the night, leaving me standing here alone once more.

Like always.

In my head, I swear I hear the same song from earlier kick up again, but there's only silence. I close my eyes and take a deep breath, clenching my fists at my sides.

Big things are about to happen—the band is starting our own record label. We're growing our brand.

I've gotten everything I ever wanted and more. I made shit happen. So why does it feel like a clock is ticking down and something's about to snap?

My phone buzzes and draws me back into my body. A few of the guys are already at a club, begging me to join them.

Good, something to do. Because if I sit in my thoughts much longer, I might be tempted to finish what my father started years ago when he tried to beat the life out of me. And that wouldn't be very productive.

2

LILI

ONE, TWO, THREE, FOUR.

Five, six, seven, eight.

The instruments might as well be playing my ribs like harp strings. The moment they start, my limbs follow. To anyone watching, my movements are measured, effortless. But inside, I know the truth. I hear the counting.

One, two, three, four.

Five, six, seven, eight.

It's just me and the musical heartbeat.

The strings are playing, tugging. Pulling me limb by limb across the stage and reminding me there is still feeling in my bones.

One, two, three, four.

Five, six, seven, eight.

Ticking.

It never really stops, except maybe when I'm sleeping because then I fall into those dreamless sleeps I've had as long as I can remember. Like my life, quiet and focused. No interruptions.

My body moves on instinct with little instruction.

One, two, three, four.

Five, six, seven, eight.

I sweep my leg up as my back bends, and I feel the stretch in my already cramping hamstring, but it doesn't prevent me from doing a full split in midair. The music owns my body, and right now, it's listening.

I am—

"Lili."

The music cuts out as my feet hit the stage and reality rushes back.

My feet are throbbing and my whole body aches. We've been at this for hours with little progress. Not that anyone notices or cares. They'll work us until we collapse, splash some water in our direction, and then require more.

My eyes cut to Pauline, who is waving me forward as she talks to one of the stagehands. I look over at Rico, my dance partner, and he just shrugs.

"Thought we had it that time," Rico says, walking away and pushing his sweat-drenched, long dark hair off his face.

He hops off the stage and reaches for some water, pouring it down his throat like he's dying of thirst.

"Apparently not," I mumble, making my way toward Pauline, who is perched between two men.

There are so many scarves, beanies, and ripped jeans. It's ridiculous.

I'm barely down the steps at the front of the stage when the vultures start to circle. Someone reaches for my hair and another starts dabbing my cheeks with shimmer.

There's an endless line of people prodding, primping, tugging. I barely notice anymore. My body hasn't been my own for as long as I can remember.

All I feel is the constant pit in my stomach and a sick feeling I'm not sure I'll ever get rid of.

Pauline waves the vultures off me when I reach her, and they scatter like mice.

"Lili." She slides her glasses down her nose to give me the full effect of her disappointment. "You're drifting again."

She waves a finger in the air, and her eyes follow it as it swivels in circles. "Drifting," she repeats, slower this time, her finger twirls once more before coming to a dead stop.

"I hit my marks." I'm sure of it. After all, I was counting. Not off by even half a second. "Every single one."

"Lili, my love. My darling." She stands wrapping her bony hands over my shoulders. "You are a butterfly."

"Thank you?"

Pauline shakes her head. "No."

"No?"

"The butterfly flutters. Flapping, flapping." She waves her arms at her sides like she's embodied the insect, then slaps her hands at her sides and stares at me. "I need a fish. I need liquid."

"Liquid," I repeat, but I'm more lost than ever.

Pauline is eccentric in the most extreme sense. One day we're being compared to animals at the zoo. The next, we're meant to be the elements, raging on the earth. None of it makes any sense—except to her and Gail, her assistant.

I'm here to dance, which used to be simpler.

Why is everything in my life suddenly so complicated?

Pauline flows her arms out to the side in waves. "Liquid, my darling."

The familiar pounding between my eyes starts throbbing. "Got it."

I've been dancing my whole life and in the industry most of it. I know better than to argue or question her because no one cares to explain themselves to "*the talent*". Something my mom has been sure to remind me of again and again, while she parades me around like her own personal show pony.

I'm honestly not sure who's more controlling, the dance company or my mother.

I glance over Pauline's shoulder and sure enough, Mom is frowning at me from across the room. Try telling her this is simply a rehearsal—not a live show. According to her it's equally important I don't fail at either. As she always says, one wrong step and someone will be there to take my place.

Perfection, nothing less.

It's why she refuses to give me even an inch. She monitors where I go, what I do, what I eat, when I sleep. My life has belonged to her and dance for twenty-two years, and I'm not sure the day will ever come when that will change.

It doesn't matter that I'm a world-renowned modern dance princess. To her, I'll always be fighting that line between acceptance and disappointment.

Pauline dramatically fans her face, drawing my attention back to her.

"Gail." Her shrill voice sends a shiver down my spine, but her assistant comes running. "We're done for today. Get my things."

She walks off without so much as a glance in my direction, yelling to the room, "Tomorrow, three thirty," before disappearing backstage.

Mom takes that as her cue to dart toward me. I'm tempted to disappear into the crowd before she gets to me, but it would be a temporary fix. There's no escaping this woman.

"Lili Chen." Mom stops in front of me, clutching her purse.

If she was capable of frowning, I'm sure that's the expression I'd be faced with right now, but Mom is stoic at all times. The queen of indifference. Happy, irritated, unaffected—they all look the same on her.

After all, she was a Tennessee beauty queen, so she's mastered the art of when to put on a performance. She comes from a long line of Beaumont beauties, as her hometown calls them. She's a people pleaser to the core, only once wavering from expectations by marrying my father, and in the process, disowning her family.

Something I don't think she's ever openly talked about. It would be improper—something a lady should never be.

Besides, she doesn't seem affected by it as much as I would expect. She immersed herself in Dad's world and grew accustomed to his family and the newfound access to excessive amounts of money. What started as love quickly turned to greed, because although he was the only one she would show any glimmer of affection to, it was scarce.

At least her love for him existed. My birth might as well have been a business transaction, given she raised me more as her prodigy than her daughter.

When I was a little girl, she'd sit me down to brush my hair. She'd watch me in the mirror as she lectured me about how to be successful in the world. She'd remind me why it's important to maintain appearances and how she was thankful I was pretty. Beauty was something I was going to need to rely on if I wanted to go somewhere with my dreams. Or so she said.

Men don't want women to be smart or vocal.

They want trophies.

Sadly, I clung to those moments when it was just the two of us. No matter how dark her words were. I'd pretend it was how she loved me since it was the only way she knew how to. Lessons of survival instead of nurturing.

Maybe she did me a favor. But now I've reached a point where numbness is all I've got left, so I'm not sure what the point is.

"What was that?" Mom's eyes skim me over in assessment.

She never looks at me like a daughter she loves. Instead, her gaze is detached and cold. I'm a project. But I'm not sure if she considers me a good one or a mistake she's still trying to correct.

"Dancing." I roll my shoulders back and brace for her impact.

Her eyes snap to mine. "It was pitiful. You can do better unless you're ready to hand over your career to Angelica or Simone."

Little does she know her threat sounds like a dream come true right now. I might have spent my entire life working up to this performance, but I'm exhausted, and her comments aren't helping.

"You can't rely on a rehearsal for practice." Mom tips my chin up and focuses on the circles under my eyes, seeing straight through my makeup. "I've told you again and again you need to be dancing at least two hours a day."

"That's what I'm doing."

"Make it three, then." She narrows her gaze, brushing her hand over her slicked-back blonde hair to make sure not a strand is out of place. "And I'll have Milano cut your calories by another hundred."

"Mom—"

She pinches my side, and I wince. "You're looking fluffy, and you've only got four weeks until your performance."

"I've lost five pounds." I frown.

"Either way." She shakes her head. "Maybe you should move back into the city for the next few weeks. Galivanting in the forest is no way to prepare for the biggest show of your career. You don't even have a proper practice space."

"The entire living room is empty; I've got plenty of space to practice. We talked about this. I need some alone time to clear my head before the show."

My fingernails dig into my palms at the thought of Mom insisting I listen to her, and I'm relieved when she doesn't.

I'm twenty-two, so she technically shouldn't have a say in where I live or what I do. But she's managed my life more than she's parented, and it's a role she didn't relinquish just because I grew into an adult.

Besides, we both know she could veto any of my own decisions by simply hanging the threat of my career over my head.

Or worse, she could use *him* to do it for her. My spine stiffens at the thought.

Mom might not be much of a parent, but I'd like to think she's at least invested enough to care the slightest. She's the one who has been there every step of the way and made my career flourish. She made all my childhood dreams come true.

The trouble is that some days I wonder whose dreams they were in the first place. Not to mention, the rift chasing them formed in our relationship. Something further solidified by Dad's death.

He was the light we shared, and when that went out, everything else did as well.

It's been difficult, but I've learned to accept it. This is my life.

And it's also why, for my own sanity, I'm not moving into the city as she wants me to. I need the clean air, the trees, and the distance. I need a little freedom to remember why it is I'm doing this.

There's no finding that in the middle of a city.

"I'll practice more," I say, diverting her attention. "And Milano can update my menu starting tomorrow."

I'm already starving and tired at the thought of it, but if it will allow me to keep what little power over this situation I have, I've got to make the sacrifices that will appease her.

Mom nods. "You will. And, Lili, no distractions."

"No distractions." I force a smile and hope it looks genuine.

I'm not sure what it's like to actually smile anymore. The ability to feel joy faded with my loss of tears, and my body's constant state of hunger.

Mom looks me over one final time before turning and walking away. No hug, no goodbye.

I should mind.

But where we look opposite in appearance, I sometimes wonder if we're the same person inside. Marble statues polished to perfection. Something she willed into existence through years of conditioning and influence.

Once Mom is gone, I make my way to the dressing room to shower and change. I tie my wet hair in a knot on the top of my head and try to hurry.

If I hang around too long, the rest of the performers will try to convince me to join them for dinner. And although my stomach hurts from hunger, the last thing I should be doing is pissing Mom off by consuming extra calories.

"Tomorrow, darling." Rico grabs my hand as I slip past and plants a kiss on the back of it.

I force a smile and nod, ready to be dragged into his conversation, but he's already distracted by one of our backup dancers and is draping himself around her. So I make my way outside.

I'm relieved to be met with the cool night air. The days have been blistering hot in the middle of summer, and something about the heat wave makes it hard to breathe.

I start toward my car and appreciate the quiet of the city this late at night. The bustle of the streets when I arrived at midday has calmed, and only a few people mingle on the sidewalk. Even though the dance studio is downtown and in a busy area, in this moment it's calm.

I'm accustomed to being surrounded by people, but it doesn't mean I prefer it. Hence why I was drawn to renting Eloise Kane's house in the first place. In the middle of nowhere with no one crowding me.

My phone pings, and I pull it out of my purse, frowning when I see the name on the screen.

Milano: I'll drop off a new set of meals tomorrow.

Mom worked fast apparently. My stomach growls, and I can't remember the last time I had a meal that wasn't planned, weighed, and carefully calculated. I bury the thought and type back.

Lili: Thanks :)

At least in a text, I can use emojis in place of real expressions. Through the screen, it's easy to pretend I'm still pleasant and happy.

Tucking my phone back in my purse, I look up just in time to run into a solid wall of muscle.

"Woah there." A deep laugh cuts through the dark night.

I blink, as strong fingers grip my arms and steady me. The man standing in front of me grins and any words I have get stuck in my throat because his smile is so raw and uninhibited that it catches me off guard.

He should look like danger with his tattoos peeking out of every ridge of his clothing. But the carefree grin that stretches his cheeks draws light all the way up to his dark eyes, and I can't deny the genuine freedom in his smile.

Then there's his stare, fixed on me and magnetic. I can't help but feel the sands of time slowing the longer I stare into his eyes.

Or maybe it's a beat ticking. A pendulum. A dance.

One, two, three, four.

Five, six, seven, eight.

I hear it. I *sense* it in him.

One, two, three, four.

Five, six, seven, eight.

"You alright, sweetheart?" The stranger quirks an eyebrow and looks me over once more. "Dangerous time of night to be walking around distracted."

3

Lili

I'm no stranger to looking confident men straight in the eyes and holding my ground. In the dance world, I've been put on display for some of the most powerful men around the globe.

Billionaires, presidents, and princes.

I've been paraded around, fawned over, questioned. I've learned how to stare men in the eye while balancing delicacy and confidence. I know how to stand in a room with them and be unaffected.

But something about the man in front of me stirs something foreign.

Maybe it's the fact that he has the kind of stare there's no escaping. Dark, infinite, echoing. Or maybe it's the third eye tattoo on the center of his throat watching me like a bad omen. But my confidence is faltering.

I take a step back and break his gaze just to be safe. I don't like that all it seems to take is one look for him to let himself inside my head without knocking. Like he's tapping the ice. Hairline fractures spreading.

"Sorry." I brush past him, keeping my eyes up this time so I don't run anyone else over.

"That's it?" he says with an amused laugh that's almost haunting. "You could at least tell me your name, sweetheart."

Stopping with my back to him, I take a deep breath and count.

One, two, three, four.

Five, six, seven, eight.

I swear there's static in the air. It's pulsing, pulling me in all directions when I'm usually perfectly collected.

I should keep walking because, as Mom reminded me, the last thing I need right now are distractions. But something about this man with his overconfident laugh and third eye tattoo inches under my skin, and I have this unexplainable need to prove myself.

"I'm not your sweetheart." I spin to face him.

Bad idea.

He's a foot away, and even though I'm fairly tall, I have to crane my neck back to look him in the eyes. His tattooed arms are crossed over his chest and his smirk ticks higher as he rakes his teeth over his bottom lip again.

He narrows his eyes and I feel the game playing in them. One he seems confident he'll win. His eyes skim me like he's sizing me up and wants to take whatever he sees in me for himself.

Little does he know that would require me to have something of my own in the first place.

"What?" I snap when he doesn't say anything.

I'm usually soft-spoken, so I'm not sure why he's drawing this edge from my tone.

"You're a dancer?" His eyes pause on my leg warmers.

I grip my purse, not liking how he seems to be mentally evaluating me and writing a list of assumptions in his brain. "Maybe."

His dark stare flicks back to mine. "I must be in luck then because I'm feeling lonely."

"Lonely?" I repeat it like a question because I'm not sure what he's talking about.

But then he sweeps his gaze over me before shooting me a suggestive smile, and I realize exactly what he's saying.

"Did you just insinuate what I think you did?"

Somehow this man has the uncanny ability to bring my blood to a boil in the span of one minute. Because I'm pretty sure he actually thinks I'd strip for him.

"It was worth a shot." He shrugs one shoulder.

"For your information, I'm not *that* kind of dancer." I tip my chin up.

He grins. "Noted."

Every response is casual and nonchalant. Like he's pushing buttons simply for a reaction. Saying whatever he has to in order to get one. The smile crossing his cheeks shows me he's satisfied he did. And every gesture I offer in return he takes as a challenge.

"So if you're *not that kind of dancer*, what are you?" he asks, almost mocking.

"What are you?" I throw his own question back at him, even if I know I shouldn't.

His eyebrows pull together at my question, but I'm not sure why he seems confused. "Flattered you're curious."

"It's called making pleasantries." I roll my eyes.

Did I really just roll my eyes?

I know better than to let people gain any kind of reaction from me. Annoyed or otherwise. And the way his grin widens means he caught the reaction and he's feeding off it.

"Rome." He tips his chin. "And you are?"

"Lili."

He nods once, and I'm not sure why I feel nervous all of a sudden.

"And what do you do, Rome?" I cross my arms over my chest, mirroring him, or protecting myself from him. Who knows, except that I can't escape the flutter that kicked up when I said his name. Even if I don't appreciate that he seems to enjoy bothering me for his own amusement.

Rome laughs loud. He tips his head back like he needs to make more space for it. I'm not sure why he thinks everything I ask is funny, but it's grinding on my nerves.

When he catches his breath, he shakes his head and looks at me once more with those eyes that might as well be oblivion because they drag me to a place where there's no escaping.

"I play music," he says.

"Anything I would have heard?"

He smiles. "Apparently not."

I'm not sure what he means by that, but it feels like a jab. It's no secret that I've always been a little sheltered, so I'm probably not familiar with whatever genre Rome's music falls into.

"Are you in a band?" Now I can't help myself because I'm genuinely curious.

He nods his head. "Enemy Muse."

"Interesting name." I tip my head the slightest. "It's a dichotomy."

"That it is." He winks, and it shoots straight through me.

I roll my shoulders back and hope he doesn't notice I'm feeling off balance.

It's just hunger, anyway. People don't tilt me off my axis; I don't allow them that kind of power. It's the lack of calories after a long day. That's all. I'll get home, eat my final meal of the night, and everything will settle.

"Well, it's nice to meet you, but I should get going."

I move to step around him, but he wraps a hand around my elbow, making me pause. It's not that his grip is hard, if anything, he's barely holding on. But his calloused fingertips on my skin freeze me in place.

"It's barely eight." His eyebrows pinch.

I'm sure to him it sounds early. But the fact that it's almost eight means I'm already behind on my schedule. Food this late won't sit well, and with the drive home, there's no way I'll be in bed before ten. Which means I'll no doubt wake up tired, and Mom will once more focus on the circles under my eyes.

No distractions.

But that's what Rome is. A giant distraction. It doesn't take me knowing much about him to see that.

"Exactly." I pull my arm from his grip and step around him. "I'm already running late."

Instead of leaving it at that, Rome falls in step beside me as I make my way to my car.

"Got a hot date or something?"

"Is that your not-so-subtle way of asking if I have a boyfriend?" I lift an eyebrow at him but don't stop walking.

He shakes his head. "No, I already know you don't have a boyfriend."

"How's that?"

"Let's just say I've got a sense about these things."

I roll my shoulders back. "Whatever you say."

"Am I wrong?"

Without even looking at him, I feel him smiling. He knows he's not wrong, I'm just not sure how he does, so I don't bother responding.

"Now, about that date…" Rome drags the word out.

"Who says I have a date?" I'm not sure why I keep entertaining him with questions, but they spill out like he's hooked me up to some kind of machine that drags the reservations from my bones.

Rome eats up the space in front of me and stops so suddenly I almost run into his chest. "You could."

I tip my chin up and try to hold onto my resolve. "Maybe I do."

It's a flat-out lie. I can't remember the last time I even went on a date. Six months ago, maybe? I haven't wanted to since… *him*.

Besides, I've got bigger things to worry about than another person's feelings. But Rome doesn't need to know any of that.

"Then ditch them," Rome says nonchalantly. "Hang out with me."

"You want to be my date?"

He laughs, but it's darker this time. "Sorry, sweetheart. I don't date. But it doesn't mean we can't have a little fun."

I'm not sure why I'm even still talking to him. Every assumption I've had about Rome since the moment I plowed into him is proved true each time he opens his mouth. He clearly thinks something of himself and has no problems flaunting it.

"Charming." I frown. "But I'm going to pass."

"You're not attracted to me?" He forces a pout that's so fake I can see his grin buried in it.

"What does that have to do with anything?"

"Good to know you are then."

I cross my arms over my chest. "I didn't say that."

"You didn't disagree either." He cocks an eyebrow, and I swear his eyes darken. "I'll accept the compliment."

"I'm sure you will." I purse my lips, biting back much more I'd love to say.

A pang deep in my stomach starts to ache, and I hope it doesn't show on my face as I clench my jaw and bury it.

"So about tonight?" Rome leans closer and even though we've been standing a foot apart, my head swims at the sudden nearness. He smells like apples and spice. Like the edge of fall and winter when the earth cools and your body craves the warmth of a fading summer. The thought alone is enough to make me shiver. "Promise I'll make it worth your while."

He's so close I feel his breath at my ear, tickling my skin. And even if I make a living dancing with men on stage, the static from Rome reminds me just how long it's been since I've really felt another human being.

I turn my face to his, and I swear there are mere inches between my mouth and his full lips. I expect him to pull back, to give me space, but he stays in my bubble and smiles. He swallows and the bob of the third eye on his throat watches me.

There's nothing reserved or cautious about a man like Rome. He invades everything he touches and demands to be noticed.

A car horn blares nearby, and it makes me jump, pulling me from whatever trance I'm lost in. I step back and take a deep breath of the cool night air, but it does nothing to replace the hint of apples lingering in my lungs.

"Have a good night, Rome." I nod my head once, snapping my spine upright and walking past him.

"You too, sweetheart," he calls after me.

But I don't look back at him or his third eye that sees straight into the pit of my soul. I don't face his disarming smile or admit to myself how his presence brought me to the edge of where I'm normally comfortable and nudged me past it.

I keep walking, breathing, counting.

One, two, three, four.

Five, six, seven, eight.

All the way to my car, I count. And even if I feel his eyes on me, I don't turn back because there's no point. Rome is nothing but trouble. He's dangerous and everything I don't need in my life right now, even for a night.

No distractions.

4

ROME

MOST PEOPLE LISTEN TO music for the lyrics. They need the song to be defined for them in carefully spelled-out sentences so they can relate. They need the singer to tell them how they should be feeling by drawing it out in pretty fucking pictures.

When I listen to a song, half the time I ignore what the lead singer's saying. Not because I don't give a fuck, but I don't need it.

I'm hearing the beat, the rhythm, the vibrations.

Like life, music is up for interpretation, from the lyrics to the drumbeat. It paints different colors for each listener, mutually heard and uniquely experienced.

The song stirs, and I hear every individual instrument working together, playing along with them in my head.

I might have never been the smart kid in school, but I always understood music. I could pick up just about any instrument and play it because sound spoke to me better than words did.

The beat picks up, and I lace my fingers together behind my head. I close my eyes and feel the hum of the guitar as the strings ride out a wave long after the guitarist stroked them. I hear the heartbeat of the bass and the energy of the drums.

I see blue and violet so deep and dark they're nearly black. An ocean at midnight with a full moon hanging in the sky above it. I smell the salt and feel the depth of it. I get lost in the rhythm of the waves.

If only it could take me away.

"What do you think?" Adrian's voice cuts in as the song ends.

My mind snaps back to my body, and I open my eyes, leaning forward to rest my elbows on my knees.

Adrian mutes the microphone to the sound booth so the band can't hear us talking and spins in his chair to face me.

When we decided to start our own label, we underestimated the amount of work involved. While Adrian and Eloise have been focusing on the business end, Sebastian and I committed to finding talent.

Except Sebastian is off somewhere right now probably fucking Cassie for the thousandth time or doing something equally pathetic. So today's auditions are up to me.

"They're good." I rest my chin on my knuckles and watch the band through the glass.

I can feel their nervous energy as they fidget and pretend to be productive while they wait for our thoughts. But there's also excitement buried underneath. They're practically itching with energy.

One word and I can grant or destroy their dreams.

Luckily for them, they've got the talent, and they're the first band this week to actually capture my attention.

"Let's bring them in for Sebastian." I lean back, lacing my fingers and popping my knuckles. "We'll move forward if he's also onboard."

Adrian nods. "You got it."

"That's all for today, yeah?" I stand up, anxious to get out of here.

It's not that I don't enjoy finding new talent, but this is the first band today I've actually liked, and beyond that, their music resurrected something in me that won't quite settle.

"That's it. You out of here?"

I nod, grabbing my leather jacket off the back of the couch.

"Hold up." Adrian stands, scratching the back of his neck and dipping his chin. "You doing all right, man?"

"Peachy as always." I smile. "Why? El worried or some shit?"

"Something like that." Adrian crosses his arms over his chest. "But be straight with me. As nice as it is not dragging your drunk ass out of strip clubs every other day, it's not like you to stay in."

"You keeping tabs on me? I'm flattered."

Adrian shakes his head because the guy knows how to see past my bullshit. The more a person tries to get in, I deflect, distract, and grin at them. There's nothing to see if they're too busy staring at the bullshit.

"I'm good, promise." I shrug. "Recouping from that last tour. Bitches almost broke my dick I was getting so much pussy."

"I'll leave out the last sentence when I report back to Eloise." He frowns. "Besides, when's the last time you've needed time to recoup?"

Adrian looks me over, but I don't drop the grin, hoping it's enough to get him out of his head about this.

I'm not sure what it says about me that the band gets worried when I'm not dipping my dick in a new pussy every night, but it can't be a good sign. Not that I really care about their opinions.

It's no one's business that I enjoy fucking women like they're my own personal advent calendar—a different chick every day. Sex is my stress relief, my calm, my peace. And I don't repeat women for a reason. I'm not looking for a relationship.

Problem is, ever since the shit that went down at the end of the last tour, my dick and my head aren't in the same mental space for the first time in years. While my cock would like to get lost between some random stripper's legs and forget whatever's itching to get out from inside me, my head is flat-out uninterested.

I barely fucked anyone those last couple of weeks on tour, and since we got back to Denver, my sex life has become all but nonexistent.

Twenty-one days of nonexistence to be exact. Almost a fucking month. If my dick doesn't sue me for neglect, I'll be surprised.

That's it, tonight I'm fucking someone—*anyone*—just to prove a point.

"I'm hitting up The Velvet Room with a few buddies tonight." I plant a hand on Adrian's shoulder. "So stop thinking about my dick and worry about your own turning against you for forcing it to endure a lifetime of repeat pussy."

Adrian narrows his eyes and they're nearly murderous. "Watch how you talk about Eloise."

It's just too much fun to piss Adrian off. Eloise is like a sister, so I'm glad they've found each other. But I don't get it, and I'll use every chance I can to remind him of that fact.

After saying my goodbyes to the band, I head out of the studio and hop on my motorcycle. I may live around the corner from Adrian, but I pass my driveway and keep riding.

I need the air, the sounds of the road. I need to clear my head.

I'm not usually thankful for living in the middle of nowhere, but right now, it feels good to be on an empty road with nothing but trees as my witness. If I weren't so good at burying my feelings, I'm pretty sure this is what would be considered a meltdown because I haven't felt like myself in too long now, and I'm tempted to drive until I disappear.

It's been six years since we became famous, and I buried everything in my life that happened before it. Six years of pretending the person coming to the surface lately doesn't still exist. Six years of enjoying anything and everything I could get my hands on.

Years of the band watching me spiral and waiting for me to snap out of it, when all it took was one moment.

Finding out Eloise was raped flicked a switch inside me. It reminded me of the real roots that grow when you've been a victim. It reminded me of all the shit I've been hiding from.

And now here I am, stuck in the wide-open space of Denver, left alone with the demons in my head. While the band is in no rush to head back out on tour, I'm not sure how long I can stand sitting here with my thoughts kicking me in the temples.

Maybe I'll take Adrian up on his offer to send me to LA to check out a few bands. I can chill with my buddies at Twisted Roses and get some new ink. Anything to get me out of my head.

Turning another corner, I realize I'm halfway to Denver, and I really don't know why I'm heading to the city. I don't meet up with the guys for another few hours, so I was going to smoke a joint and take a nap.

But as I'm about to turn my motorcycle around, I spot a car on the side of the road up ahead with its hazards on and immediately smile.

A black BMW 8 Series is pulled over, and it's a car I've seen before, with a familiar figure bent over the hood as she talks on her phone. I swear this girl is looking for trouble. She's oblivious to her surroundings and distracted just like she was the first time I met her.

I roll to a stop on the side of the road in front of her car and her eyes flick up at me, widening.

Damn, Lili is pretty. Ink black hair that falls nearly to her waist. Her dark, skintight, itty-bitty dress draws attention to her petite figure, and her empty skin begs to be carved up with tattoo ink.

Fuck me.

I'm pretty sure if my dick could talk, he'd actually say that to her. Because when she stands up straight and rolls her prissy shoulders back, all I want to do is bend her back over.

Apparently, I wasn't going crazy that night a few days ago when I ran into her on the sidewalk. She really is that fucking beautiful. I chalked it up to the fact that my dick is willing to sink into just about anything right now because I don't get hung up on girls. But there's something about this one.

It's those eyes. Darker because of her thick lashes and not afraid to look straight at me.

She's soft but fearless. Curious but introverted.

A *dichotomy*.

"You," she says as I slip off my helmet.

"Well, hello again, sweetheart." I grin, not missing that it drags her attention for the briefest moment.

She tips her chin up. "Still not your sweetheart."

"And I'm *you*?" I climb off my bike and walk up to her.

"Oh, that's right, you're probably used to people bowing at your feet." She starts to roll her eyes, but almost as if she catches herself, she stops and narrows them instead.

"Am I?" I tilt my head and try to read the irritation on her pretty heart-shaped face.

Something about the fact that I'm riling her up makes me want to do it more.

"You are Rome Moreno, right? Or should I say, the Riff King?" She crosses her arms over her chest, and it pushes her small tits into perfect mounds.

"You looked me up?" I smile and get so close I'm definitely in her personal bubble. "I'm honored."

Lili holds her ground, not blinking. "Don't be."

"Keep telling yourself that if it makes you feel like less of a stalker." I lean in because I can't help myself. I need another hit of the scent that hasn't left my head for days.

She smells as expensive as she looks. Like pears and sugar and wine. Like all the things a man like me isn't allowed to taste, but he can't fucking help himself.

Something about the fact that she's delicate and sweet. Uptight and prissy. It makes me want to rile her up. To dirty her. To bleed her purity and replace it with sin. I want to fuck the polished defiance out of her and make a mess.

But that's a dangerous thought because Lili isn't like the girls I go for. Lili's the kind of girl you wine and dine before you take her to bed. The kind of girl you hold doors open for. The kind of girl who expects things.

While I'm not the kind of man you expect shit from. I fuck you and leave you, and you thank me for it.

So why does this chick get under my skin?

"You lost, sweetheart?" I look around at the empty road, then back at her.

She shakes her head, and all it does is kick up that sweet scent of hers. "My car died."

"I can see that." I step in closer. "But why were you out in the middle of nowhere at this time of day? It'll be dark soon. You like tempting danger?"

Lili narrows her eyes at the innuendo in my tone. Nothing gets past her. She's smart—smart enough to know better than to trust me.

"It's not the middle of nowhere." She tips her chin up in defiance. "I live out here... for the time being anyway."

And that's when it hits me. Eloise's little house guest. The dancer renting out her place. *Off limits*, if I remember correctly.

I can't help but grin at the challenge.

5

Lili

Of all the days.

Of all the people.

It would figure I'd be standing on the side of the road staring at *him*.

Rome Moreno.

Yes, I'd googled him after our literal run-in the other day. And while I expected him to be trouble from that interaction alone, I wasn't prepared for everything that popped up on the screen when I typed his name in.

He's famous to the point that I now understand why he seemed surprised I didn't know who he was. But I live under a rock and have my whole life, so I've never heard of him or his band, Enemy Muse.

Not that it's a bad thing, apparently. From everything I've read, Rome is trouble. Reckless, wild, sleeping his way through the female population. It would be gross if it didn't make me feel a little sad for him. Because while I'm sure he enjoys himself, I get the impression that's not the only reason he puts on this endless show of not giving a shit.

"You're the dancer renting Eloise's house." Rome smiles.

Eloise Kane.

Another thing I learned when I was stalking him online. Apparently, the woman who is renting her house out to me is a member of his band.

I nod and Rome smiles, sending a shiver down the full length of my spine. And once again, I can't tell whether it's because he's standing this close or if my body senses the danger that I assume follows him.

"Guess that makes us neighbors then." He winks, once more shooting me his blinding grin.

"Neighbors?" I purposely picked a house in the middle of nowhere. I didn't even know I had neighbors.

"Her property backs up to mine, as luck would have it," Rome says.

"Not sure that's what I'd call it."

The universe must be messing with me. I'm in Denver preparing for the biggest show of my career, the last thing I need is Rome Moreno that close to my doorstep. Not that it should matter. If anything I read is true, he's never had a shortage of women chasing after him, so why would my doorstep matter to him?

My phone pings, and I frown when I look at the screen. Wonderful, my mom is already at the gala and is wondering where I am.

"Something wrong, sweetheart?" Rome looks down at my screen.

"Are you going to continue calling me that?"

He shrugs one shoulder. "Probably."

I pinch the bridge of my nose, feeling the familiar throbbing already settling in between my temples. Mom won't care that I'm running late because my car broke down. She'll just use it as another reason on her endless list of why I should be staying in the city with her instead.

Even in my head, I sound like a teenager being pushed around by my parents. It's embarrassing.

"I'm running late, and the tow is still thirty minutes out," I say reluctantly.

As much as I would rather have the help of anyone other than a tattooed rock god, he's all I've got in this moment. Besides, my mom's wrath is worse than dealing with Rome.

I think.

"I'd be happy to offer my services." Rome bites the corner of his lip and gives me a once-over.

He hums and it draws my attention once more to the third eye tattooed on the center of his throat.

"You're one of *those* guys, aren't you?"

"What guys?"

"Waiting around just so you can jump at the opportunity to save the damsel."

"Not something I've ever been accused of." His stare lands on me again, and I'm caught off guard by the gold shimmer in his eyes. "Would you like my help or not?"

I look over my shoulder at the empty road that disappears into to the deep forest. As much as I'd like to prove my independence, I'm out of options.

"Please." I turn back to face him.

His eyes shine as his grin widens. "So polite. I like it."

"I get the impression there isn't much you don't like." I roll my eyes because Rome seems to have the uncanny ability to edge me to the limit of my irritation.

"Was that a joke? Cute." He tilts his head to the side. "But you're wrong, there's plenty I don't like."

I'm tempted to ask him what, but I stop myself. The last thing I need is to show any interest in a guy like Rome Moreno. Knowing him, he'll take it as an opening to get up my skirt.

He pulls out his phone and types something before tucking it back into his pocket.

"Leave the car. My guy will get it back to El's house." He walks up to me and plucks the keys from my hand, hitting the button to lock it and tucking them in his pocket.

"Your guy?"

Rome ignores my question and tips his chin at the road ahead. "Where were you headed?"

"The Rose Theater for a gala."

"Fancy." He shakes his head and chuckles.

My ribs constrict as I clench my fingers.

Everything about Rome is unpolished, so there's no way he can understand the world I'm forced to live in to make my dreams a reality. But I don't appreciate the fact that he seems intent on making fun of me about it.

"If it's too much trouble—"

"It's not." He takes a step toward me, and I have to lift my chin to meet his gaze. "Hop on."

He pushes something against my stomach, and I look down to see him handing me his motorcycle helmet.

"Wait, what? I'm not getting on that," I point to his bike, "in this."

I sweep my arms down, drawing his attention to my short black dress.

Of all the dresses Mom could have had delivered for tonight's event, she had to pick this one. Something short and tight, no doubt an attempt for her to show off what good shape she keeps me in at all times. I'm uncomfortable enough standing here in it, but Rome's eyes running the length of my body makes me shiver.

His stare pauses on the hem that hits me mid-thigh, and his head tilts as his stare darts back up to me.

"Why not? Skip the panties today, sweetheart?" Rome smirks. "Promise, I won't mind."

Did he really just say that?

I swear he finds amusement in drawing out a reaction. Or he just has absolutely no filter.

Probably both.

"I didn't skip anything." I cross my arms over my chest.

He leans in until his mouth is by my ear and his breath is tickling my neck. "Even more intriguing."

Sucking in a sharp breath, I have to take a step back. This close, Rome is too overwhelming, smells too good. He fogs my head with a constant mix of intrigue and irritation, and it's got me on edge.

I grab the helmet out of his hands before he can say anything else filthy and walk around him. "Let's just get going."

With the helmet strapped under my chin, I stand and wait for him to sling his leg over the bike, not missing that he's chuckling.

"Don't you need a helmet?" I ask him as the motorcycle roars to life.

It sends vibrations through the forest. Veins of energy sweep the ground and climb my bare legs, making my insides flutter.

"Only have the one." He shrugs, looking at me over his shoulder.

"You could die."

The corner of his mouth ticks up, and I almost think he took that as a challenge.

"I'll be fine, sweetheart. But I appreciate your concern." The bike roars as he faces straight ahead. "Now hop on."

I've never been on a motorcycle before—or done anything remotely dangerous.

Being a dancer means I have to take care of my body if I want to maintain my career. On top of that, my life is carved in crystal. My parents came from money, as did their parents, and their parents. I was brought up to respect the fruit of many generations. To talk quietly, to act like a lady, to follow directions, to not talk back.

To be careful.

I know better than to put myself in the line of danger. Yet, as I take Rome's hand and accept his help as I climb onto his bike behind him, I can't help that my heart is racing.

My legs straddle him, and the wideness forces the hem of my dress dangerously close to my hips. My butt is barely covered, and I can't ignore the fact that all that sits between Rome and me is my flimsy, lacy underwear.

The bike rumbles as he pulls forward, and I feel it all the way up my core. Heat rushes my cheeks, and I'm thankful Rome can't look at me right now or it would give him one more thing to make fun of me about.

It's not my fault I've gone too long without an orgasm. It's not as easy for me to let down my guard with people as it seems to be for him. While he sleeps his way around the world, that's nowhere near the case for me.

Besides, it's not like Rome is the cause of the blood rushing between my legs right now. It's the bike rumbling beneath me, the heat of a man—any man—between my legs. It's the scent of a fading summer and the craving for warmth in winter.

I refuse to believe the inferno building in my center has anything to do with Rome Moreno.

"You all right back there?" Rome yells.

I realize I'm gripping his waist for dear life, and I loosen a little at his comment. We're probably not going that fast, but it feels like we're racing through the forest. Or maybe that's my heart in my chest.

"I'm fine," I lie.

He doesn't need to know that I'm actually terrified. That my life has been so sheltered that this is the most excitement I've had as far back as I can remember. He doesn't need to know that for the first time in a long time, I feel something other than empty.

I close my eyes and rest my head against his solid back, trying to steady my breathing, letting my body lean with his as he winds along the road. I relax and hand my control over to him, as I'm used to doing with people, even if with him it feels different.

It's freeing.

Speeding down the road, nothing between me and the air. Just Rome and me.

One wrong move and we could be blood splatter on pavement, but for some unknown reason, I trust him.

The hum of the road and Rome's steady breathing calms me, and I melt into it. I allow myself to feel the warmth of being wrapped around him. I let my hands hold him and find comfort in it.

He's lean, but solid muscle. And I can't help but wonder just how far his tattoos go. From the pictures online, they appear to cover him almost completely, and I can't help but wonder what each one of them means, if anything.

Things I shouldn't want to know.

When we roll to a stop, I finally lift my head, and I wonder if he finds it odd that I've all but cocooned myself around him for the entire ride. If so, he doesn't say anything.

"Here we are." Rome steadies us with his feet on the ground.

"Wait." I look around, reaching to slip the helmet off my head. "This isn't my house."

"Pretty *and* smart," he says almost mockingly. "It's my house. I'm assuming you don't have a spare car and you're going to need some way to get into the city?"

He holds his hand out to the side, the same way he offered it to me when I climbed on the bike, and I take it.

He doesn't even look back at me as I climb off and adjust my dress, so as not to flash him.

In fact, for having such a dirty mouth, Rome hasn't been anything other than physically appropriate. He always maintains a safe foot of space, even when he leans in. He never touches me, even playfully, and he averted his eyes even after making the joke earlier about my underwear.

Obscene as Rome is, there's almost an air to him that hints he's secretly a gentleman. It's puzzling.

"So this is where you live?" I look over the large house that stands in front of me. It's modern with sleek lines and wide windows. If a house could feel like a person, his house feels like him. Mostly hidden by the trees with a tall fence around the property so that an outsider can only see the sides he wants to show them.

"This is it." He climbs off the bike and takes the helmet from me as we walk toward the front door.

Each step feels like a warning. After all, what sane person follows the lion into his den and expects not to be eaten?

Although maybe I have it wrong. Maybe everything I've read about Rome is just that—rumors. Maybe he really is a gentleman.

But as soon as the thought crosses my mind, Rome swings open his front door and I step directly into a wide open living space. And right dead center are two built-in stripper poles.

I had it right the first time. If this were a fairytale, Rome wouldn't be my hero. Not by a long shot.

6

ROME

Lili's eyes dart from me to the two poles in the middle of my living room, but she doesn't say anything.

I've never thought much about the fact that I committed one hundred percent to my house being a bachelor pad. It's who I am. The poles in the center serve their purpose as a statement so that any woman who enters gets a clear picture of exactly what I offer: fun, freedom, sex.

If they're looking for love, they've come to the wrong place.

It's why I don't usually bring girls like Lili back here. She's too uptight and prissy to be standing in a home built for debauchery. But as she steps further into the room and skims her fingertips over the back of my black leather couch, I can't help but wonder what it would take to break her of her perfection. Because I'd love to bend her over and fuck her dirty.

"I'll grab my keys, and we'll get going." I breeze past her before my brain continues down the dangerous path it's barreling.

As much fun as it would be to see what it takes to get Lili on her knees, I know better than to fuck someone with her kind of expectations. She's the type of girl who ends up with some guy who wears suits for a living and has boring vanilla sex with her on a perfectly curated schedule. The kind of guy who will give her a nice house and a couple of kids. The kind of guy who'll stick around for more than five minutes.

That's not me.

I make my way into the kitchen and grab the set of keys for my Range Rover out of one of the drawers. By the time I make it back into the living room, Lili's sitting on the couch looking like there's a stick up her ass with how upright she is.

Her chin is tipped up in defiance, and I'm getting used to this look on her. Stubbornness has always been a huge turnoff for me because I'm bullheaded enough for myself, but she wears it with the kind of confidence that makes me question things.

Sitting, her dress rides further up her thighs, and I have to try not to remember what it felt like to have her legs spread wide open behind me on my bike.

"You built this house?" Lili asks as I walk further into the room.

I nod. "A few years ago."

Her eyes skim the room again, and I'm not sure anyone's taken in my home the way she is, pausing at every piece of art and furniture. Granted, most people who come here show up to party and forget about shit, so they don't really care much about their surroundings.

"Do you like living out here?" Her eyes flick from the window to me.

"Not particularly, but I was outvoted."

"Outvoted?"

I circle the couch and drop down beside her. Throwing an arm over the cushion behind her, I'm pretty sure her back stiffens even more.

"When we hit it big, the whole band built houses out here. I'd prefer a penthouse in the city or some shit, but those assholes wanted space." I shrug.

Lili runs her hands up and down her thighs. "Are you all from around here?"

"Fairfield." No matter how long it's been, that city name still comes out through gritted teeth. "California."

"Do you go back often?"

I tilt my head to the side, trying to remember the last time I've had a conversation with a woman that wasn't going to lead to sex. But that's why I don't spend time around women like Lili. The last thing I need in my life is people asking questions or wanting to know things about me.

It's unnerving, so I do what I do best, say something rude or obscene to push her away.

"You're a curious kitten." I grin, waiting for annoyance to paint Lili's face.

But Lili doesn't break my stare, she doesn't frown or show much of a reaction. If anything, her eyes work like cogs in a wheel, spinning, as she tries to read me.

"You do that a lot, don't you?"

I hitch an eyebrow. "What?"

"Deflect to avoid letting people in."

I'm not sure when she turned to face me, but she is. Overconfidence bursting out of such a tiny body. Wide sweet eyes that are secretly devilish and trying to see through my bullshit.

"Guess you'd have to know me to get the answer to that." I lean forward, bringing my elbows to my knees.

Her stare finally breaks as I cross my arms over each other, and for the briefest moment, they trace some of the tattoos on my forearms.

I'm sure she sees the scars. The tattoos only hide them so much, and while Lili is distracted in most situations, she seems keenly observant in others. And right now, her stare draws the pain to the surface.

Growing up like I did, it's easy to forget your first wound or your last. It all bleeds together and most of it gets blocked out for self-preservation.

But there's only so much one person can bury and forget, and Lili's stare focused on my arm has my skin burning with memories.

The house is quiet, meaning one of two things. He's either not here or too drunk to be stumbling around. The stench of smoke as I turn the corner indicates which, and I find him slouched in his chair in front of the television.

He's watching it with the sound turned all the way down, and he probably doesn't even realize it. His head is tipped back, and his eyes are shut, but the cigarette is firm between his fingers, so he isn't asleep.

The empty whiskey bottle on the side table tells me I need to get the fuck out of here before he sees me.

"Rome." *His voice is tired and scratchy, filled with disgust like it always is.*

Too late to run.

Too late to hide.

Doesn't matter anyway. The devil has a way of finding you.

I step into the room without saying anything because one word is all it takes to tip the scales against me, and I'm never sure what word will set him off.

He opens his eyes and tips his head to the side to look at me.

They say the eyes are the door to a person's soul but that's assuming a person has one. Maybe that's why my dad's eyes are so dark and empty because all they lead to is the void I'm not sure was ever anything more than the black hole he lives in.

I've never seen him happy, never even seen him smile. If there's evidence he ever has, I'm sure he burned the pictures.

"Where the fuck were you?" *Dad snaps.*

The air snaps.

The tension snaps.

Everything around me clicking, like the sound you hear on a roller coaster as you ascend the first hill. A slow clenching of teeth as the pinnacle gets closer. Knowing it's only a matter of time before you go over the other side, and the ground gives out, making your stomach drop.

With each step, I feel the teeth of anticipation counting down.

Dad looks me up and down as I stop beside the chair he's sitting in.

"I was at work." Instead of adding 'because you weren't', I shut my mouth. No use poking the bear unless I'm in the mood to get hurt.

Not that it'll stop him.

Dad peels himself up to a sitting position, and it doesn't matter that I'm finally almost his height or filling out my T-shirts, he's got more over me. Cold indifference. Violence he knows I won't reciprocate.

Not because I don't want to, but because you can't beat a man at his own game when he's got no soul. And while I like to parade around like I don't give a shit, it's not actually the case. Because I might hate this motherfucker who gave me life, but I won't go down for him either.

I'm smarter. I'm patient.

I'll get out of here someday.

Dad's gaze runs over my face, and he grimaces. I'm surprised he even looks me in the eyes when he usually avoids it. Says I look too much like her and it's not fair when I'm the reason she's dead.

"Sure you were." Dad stands, coming to his full height.

Unfortunately, being drunk doesn't make him off-balance or sloppy. That, I could deal with. Instead, all it does is fill him with more rage.

He faces me and pulls his cigarette between his lips, taking a long drag and holding the smoke in while he stares me down. Cold eyes that don't reach anything resembling a person.

When he finally releases his breath, it clouds the space between us, and I try not to react to the smoke filling my nose and mouth. But he reaches in and lands the burning end of the cigarette on my arm as he does.

It sizzles through my skin, and I choke on the smoke-filled air at the surprise of it.

Grabbing my arm, I hold where he put the cigarette out on my skin and remind myself not to feel it. Not to validate the pain by acknowledging what it does to me.

Dad smiles, but it isn't amusement, it's sick satisfaction.

"Don't be late again," he says, pushing past me.

The now burned-out cigarette falls to the floor as he passes. I hold my arm and close my eyes, blocking out the pain and focusing on something else—anything else.

Someday he'll get what he deserves, and I can't fucking wait.

"Rome?"

I blink and I'm brought back to Lili sitting in front of me. She's leaning in, giving me a hit of her sweet perfume.

"You went somewhere just now," she says, but her tone is level. Her words are a fact instead of an accusation.

She's right, not that I'll admit it. It's been a long time since the memories have managed to make their way out like that, and it's unsettling.

"It was nothing." I shake my head and smile, throwing dirt on the demons trying to get out.

Lili looks like she wants to ask more to figure me out, but instead, she surprises me by relaxing slightly. Like it comforted her to watch me break around the edges. I'm not sure how to take that, so I shake it off instead of thinking too much about it.

"What about you, sweetheart?" I change the subject. "I assume there's not much in the middle of nowhere for you. Why choose to rent El's house instead of just staying in the city?"

Lili's gaze drops to her fingers, and she grips the hemline of her really short dress and clenches it like she's trying not to let me see whatever thought she just had.

I get the impression she's used to showing off a certain side of herself, and it comes apart a little around me. And I kind of like that I break through her cracks and get hints at someone a lot less sure of herself underneath.

"I don't mind the drive when my car is working." Lili's eyes flick up to meet my gaze. Deep pools that hide all the things she doesn't say. "And I don't mind the quiet. Most of the time I prefer it, actually. At least then I can still pretend there's some of me left."

I'm not sure what she means by that, but deep down I get it at the same time. If her life as a dancer is anything like mine when it comes to fame, I'm sure she spends most of it living on display.

"We should go." Lili stands so fast I'm surprised she doesn't fall over in her heels. "I'm already running late."

I'm not sure why she went from relaxing to suddenly being in such a rush, but I nod and stand without saying anything.

She's right, *we should go*. I need to get her out of here. Lili in my space is a bad idea. She doesn't belong with her questions that dig too deep and her eyes that see too much.

I'm not sure what it is about her that draws out the darkness in me, but I feel the veins bubbling under my skin. Memories and smoke and blood begging to show.

Girls like Lili are nothing but trouble. And not the kind I'm used to getting in.

7

Rome

Nothing good comes from sitting around in one spot too long. Too much time to think—to marinate. I try to ignore the pressure building between my temples, but like a kettle on the stove, it increases every day.

It's never been this difficult for me to distract myself from the shit in my head. In the past, I'd drink enough whiskey to light a match to my thoughts and enjoy watching them burn. But that's my problem. They always leave ashes behind, waiting for the wind to kick up and blow them around. And the longer I sit here, I feel the tornado swirling.

Maybe it's that we have no immediate plans to head back out on tour. Maybe it's just years of bodies finally floating to the surface. All I know is I'm over it.

"Where are we at with signing Manic Idols?" Sebastian glances up from his phone and leans back, looking at Adrian.

Adrian closes his laptop. "Waiting for their attorney to get back on the final review of their contract."

"Do you expect any curveballs?"

Adrian shakes his head.

"Good." Sebastian's gaze moves to me. "What about Girl vs Hate? You said they're good."

"You'll like them." I pop my knuckles. "They've got potential, and they remind me of us when we got started."

What used to seem like yesterday feels like a whole other lifetime right now. Back then we were kids chasing music, skirts, and highs. And now, here we are, acting like actual adults and giving a fuck about what we're doing with our lives.

When did we grow up?

Half the band is sober, and almost all of them are settled down. We're starting our own label and taking on real responsibilities. Knowing if it goes sideways, it impacts other people. They're putting their careers in our hands and trusting us not to screw them sideways.

Sebastian looks back at Adrian. "When are they coming back in?"

"Thursday. El said Magnum Records is also interested, so we need to move fast if you want to sign them."

"They won't entertain Magnum." I laugh.

Sebastian's eyes pinch, and Eloise looks up from her phone for the first time during this conversation.

"Just trust me."

Girl vs Hate is the first band we've seen that has really caught my attention. They've got a quality unlike the others. I can't put my finger on what exactly draws me to them, but I feel something stir in my bones when they play. And the raw, real quality makes something perfectly clear to me—they aren't looking for a label like Magnum. They came to us for a reason, and I'm sure they'll wait.

"All right. Well, that's all I've got for today." Adrian plants a hand over his laptop. "El and I are going to touch base with Noah once he and Merry get back tomorrow, but things are looking good."

I nod, standing up. When did my life start feeling so fucking domestic? Not too long ago my responsibilities consisted of sweating onstage for thousands of screaming fans and fucking them to keep them happy. Here in Adrian and Eloise's kitchen, we're building an actual business.

"I heard Sage and Jude were in town," Sebastian says, following me around the kitchen island.

"You heard right," I say, looking over at Eloise. "Coffee?"

She nods, so I grab a mug and pour myself a cup. I'm pretty sure I haven't had a full night's sleep since the tour ended. While most people find the long nights traveling the globe difficult, it's calming for me. I love the motion of the road and how it puts my nightmares to sleep.

But when I get back home, the quiet of my house sinks in. The voices kick up in my head. And I can't seem to keep my eyes shut without facing the reason I let my music take me away.

"You went out with them, and you didn't get arrested?" Sebastian leans his hip against the counter and smirks at me.

Adrian circles into the room and takes the pot of coffee from me as I bring my mug to my lips.

"One time." I take a sip. "And I'll never live it down."

Sebastian shakes his head. "Twice—"

"That you know about." Adrian crosses his arms over his chest and lifts an eyebrow at me.

Fucking Adrian, knowing all my shit because he's the one who cleans up all my messes.

"That I know about?" Sebastian tips his head back and laughs. "And here I thought getting caught with those hookers would have taught you something."

I shrug a shoulder. "That was a misunderstanding, and you know it. I don't pay to get my dick sucked when there are more than enough lips willing to do it for free."

"Lovely." Eloise rolls her eyes, leaning into Adrian's side when he wraps an arm around her.

She looks up at him and he kisses her on the forehead. It's simple, boring, unimportant... but I get a tight feeling in my chest.

"I want the dirt," Sebastian says, looking between me and Adrian. "When else have you been arrested?"

"Fuck off." I laugh, not telling him because it's more entertaining to annoy him.

It's not really that interesting anyway. While my buddies from LA have done time for real shit, I mostly just get myself into trouble. Fucking where I shouldn't, snorting what I shouldn't, being where I shouldn't.

Can't help myself.

"Fuck you, man." Sebastian waves me off. "If you and the guys didn't get locked up, what did you do? Bingo night at the senior center?"

"Jealous?" I smirk. "And no, we checked out the Velvet Room."

"Heard it's nice."

I nod my head.

The Velvet Room is everything you'd expect from a high-end strip club in Denver. Classy tits and nice booze, the perfect place to entertain. So when Sage and Jude rolled through town on business and made time to finish up a tattoo on my thigh in the process, I treated them to the city's best pussy.

And the Velvet Room was crawling with the perfect distractions to finally get me out of my head.

It should have worked.

The VIP room. Prettiest chicks in the state—maybe even the country.

Ass.

Alcohol.

Coke.

All my favorite fucking things. But while the guys were more than happy indulging in everything the club put in front of us, I was checked the fuck out.

I'm starting to think this last tour broke me.

I look over at Eloise, who's lost in thought as she sips her coffee and stands next to Adrian. Every time I look at her lately it sends my brain spiraling, and I wonder if anyone notices.

There are very few people in the world I care about on a personal level—her being one of them. And to think that someone messed with her. That someone forced themselves on her. I might have kept it together on the outside, but inside is a tunnel vision of red that still hasn't faded.

Maybe it's that I know what it's like to have someone rip your soul out of your body. Maybe it's that I understand the scars that come with true violation. But I can't kick the mess of shit that stirs every time I'm reminded what she's been through.

And unlike me, she's somehow so strong through all of it.

While my demons made me turn to debauchery, she turned to celibacy, and I can't help but question what it says about me that I've lost all sense of control.

How many drinks, women, drugs, or distractions is it going to take? Because when I look in the mirror, all I see are the same eyes staring back at me as that punk kid my father used to beat the hell out of. Except now, he's buried in tattoos and pretending they hide him.

Those thoughts circle like vultures in my head.

Which is why it's now been twenty-five days since I've touched a woman. And yes, I'm still fucking counting.

At this point, I'm not sure if the fact that I haven't had sex for nearly a month is self-inflicted punishment or me trying to prove something. But even if it's pointless and means nothing to anyone, I can't seem to break this lame-ass celibacy streak.

Write it on my tombstone—*Rome Moreno, The Riff King, died turning down a stripper's willing pussy in favor of going home with blue balls.*

"Hey." Eloise bumps my arm with her shoulder, and I realize I've been drifting off again.

Sebastian and Adrian have moved to the other side of the kitchen and are digging through leftovers, but Eloise is staring at me with a pinched expression.

I wrap my arm around her and give her a hug.

Eloise is the kind of person who makes you feel accepted no matter how fucked up you are. She's seen me at my absolute worst and still treats me the same as her own brother. It's something I appreciate.

"You okay?" She blinks up at me. "Something seems off lately. What's going on?"

Her eyes search my face for clues, and even if part of me would like to hand them over to her in reassurance, it doesn't come easy to me.

"Adrian didn't deliver his report the other day?"

El shakes her head. "He said what you wanted him to say, that you're fine and all that. But I know you and I worry."

"Yeah, yeah. I know you do, *Mom*." I plant my hand on the top of her head and tussle her hair until she wiggles away.

Adrian glances over long enough to catch her smacking me in the chest and smirks before going back to his conversation.

"You know I'm always good." I tuck my hands in my pockets and lean against the counter. "Shit's just off since everything that happened on tour. It stirred things up, I guess. Figured you'd be proud of me tamping it down and shit."

I grin, but it doesn't erase her worried expression.

"I'm glad to see you not getting into trouble." Her eyes assess me. "But I know you Rome and tamping it down isn't your thing."

She's right. She knows she's right. But I have no answers to give and it's irritating.

"I'm fine. Give me a week and I'll be fucking every chick in the city again."

Eloise rolls her eyes.

"Hey, I've been meaning to ask you." I smile wide and try to divert the conversation. "What's up with your pretty little house guest?"

"No." Eloise's tone is as flat as her expression.

"No?" I laugh, and it's loud enough to draw Adrian and Sebastian's attention. "Why not. She seems sweet."

"You didn't." Eloise is shaking her head.

Adrian walks up beside her. "Didn't what?"

"Rome, please tell me you didn't." She's so flustered she ignores Adrian's question.

"Hmm, let me think." I bring a finger up and purse my lips, seeing how far I can push this to piss Eloise off. At least if she's focusing on being mad at me, she won't be trying to get inside my head.

"Rome!" Eloise slaps me on the arm, but I catch her wrist in my hand.

"Chill, princess. I didn't touch her... exactly." I grin, remembering Lili's legs wrapped around me on my motorcycle. "Her car broke down, so I gave her a ride."

"I'm sure you did," Sebastian snorts, helpful as always.

I narrow my eyes at him. "Not that kind of ride."

WORTH THE TROUBLE 67

Why do I feel strangely defensive about what he said? Who cares if I bent her over the hood of her car? She's a chick, and I bang enough of them to not give a shit who knows what I did with who. Except, I don't see Lili like that.

Fuck me.

Turning back to Eloise, the anger has faded from her face, and it's replaced with something I can't quite read.

"Don't worry, princess. She's not my type." I shrug. "Too many expectations."

"God forbid." Eloise frowns.

Instead of reassuring her, I keep my expression passive. After all, I mean it.

I think?

Lili with her uptight personality and eyes that see through all my shit is the last thing I need. It doesn't matter if I can't stop picturing her ink black hair spilling across the pillows on my bed. She's got attachments, expectations, and shit I can't live up to.

"Seriously?" Sebastian laughs. "There's a chick on this planet you're not trying to bang?"

I shrug.

"Never thought I'd see the day." He smacks me on the shoulder, but I flip him off.

"Both of you need to stop talking about her like that." Eloise frowns. "She's a person, not... whatever it is this is."

"Yeah, yeah." I shake my head, setting my coffee mug down on the counter. "On that note, I'm taking off."

Eloise narrows her eyes at me. "Leave her alone, Rome."

"Of course, princess." I wink, and the frown on her face means she doesn't believe me.

Do I even believe me? Because as I walk out of Eloise and Adrian's house and hop on my bike, I can't help it. And instead of turning down my street, I keep going until I hit another driveway.

Call it curiosity.

Call it obsession.

I *said* Lili was a bad idea for a guy like me. I *said* I wouldn't seek her out. But I'm fucking destructive.

8

Lili

Mom frowns. And while her disappointment should be disheartening, it's a relief. Coming from her, a silent reaction is better than a vocal one because then I can interpret it however I want to.

Her lips press into a thin line as she stands with her arms crossed over her chest and waits for me to finish my routine. It doesn't matter how hard I practice, or if I hit every mark, she'll find something wrong, as she always does.

It's never good enough—*I'm* never good enough.

Each crease on her face makes me miss my father. How he was the only one with the ability to soften her. Not that he was particularly warm toward either of us. But he at least acted like there was love behind his actions instead of burying everything in cool indifference as she does.

Both my parents were raised with money and status, even if from very different worlds. And they tried to ingrain in me the same beliefs they shared. Children are to uphold generations of legacy. Love is unimportant.

Which is why, to them, I've never been more than a tool used like their wallets to demonstrate their class and power. As long as I could dance, I had worth, and if I wasn't going to get their love, I was going to get their respect.

After all, I was built to dance and molded to be successful with it. Give a girl enough practice, a strict diet, and specific admiration and it becomes all she'll live for.

I wasn't raised to be soft and warm. I was raised to put on a show.

Arching my back one final time and kicking my leg straight in the air, I feel my entire body burn. I'm tired, hungry, and drained, but Mom showed up insisting on "*checking in*" before tonight's rehearsal, so I have no choice but to let her see how I'm doing.

As I swivel and plant both feet back on the ground, I fan my arms out and come to a stop in the center of the living room, once more facing her frown.

"Hmph." She narrows her eyes.

"I'm ready," I say, straightening the hem on my cropped tank top. "See?"

"You'll be ready when Pauline says you're ready." Mom's tone is clipped, dropping her gaze to scan me once more before straightening her expression. "At least you're following Milano's diet."

Hence why I'm always starving.

But I don't dare say that, instead responding with a single nod.

My updated diet is even worse than my last one. Barely any calories, much less carbs. I'm honestly not sure how

I'm functioning. My body aches and my stomach twists like it's curling in on itself.

It's nothing new. I've been conditioned to handle restriction since I was seven, so I'm a professional at pretending I'm unaffected. I wasn't allowed food, so I thrived on Mom's acceptance instead.

The corner of her mouth ticks up in approval, and I take it as the only crumb of appreciation she'll offer.

"Be there early tonight. I don't want any more mishaps like at the gala," Mom says, turning to leave.

"My car broke down."

Mom looks over her shoulder and narrows her eyes at me. She didn't ask a question, so I shouldn't have bothered trying to respond, but it flew out without thinking. Something that's been happening more and more recently.

"Early." She punctuates her statement as she turns and walks away, and I follow her to the front door, opening it for her.

"Oh, and Lili, Rico will be your date to dinner with the Jacobsons on Friday. It's already been arranged."

"I don't need a date."

Mom doesn't bother looking at me or addressing my comment. "The Jacobsons have invested a fortune in this show, and nothing looks better than their star performers getting along."

Getting along, as in, she wants them to think there's more happening between us. Nothing sells tickets like whispers of love blooming.

At least if she's going to pimp me out to anyone, it's Rico. He's just a friend and we enjoy spending time with each other. She doesn't need to know there's no chemistry, except for what we have on stage. If it makes her happy to think there's more, and it keeps her from setting me up with guys who might expect something, I'll take it. Plus, it doesn't hurt that Rico comes from an equally prestigious family, so we understand the pressure each other is constantly under.

"Rico's father—" Mom stops short at the sound of an engine rumbling toward us.

The air might as well fill with static at the familiar sound sending shivers through me. I close my eyes and feel it, wishing it's all in my head because of all the times Rome could pull up to the house on his motorcycle, he had to choose the moment my mother is standing at the front door.

Opening my eyes, I realize it's not my imagination. He's rolling to a stop like it's a statement. I'm not sure if he's moving in slow motion as he peels his helmet off or if my brain is pausing on how to handle this moment because time stills.

Rome's wearing ripped jeans, straddling a bike with so much power I swear I can still feel it between my legs. His tight T-shirt grips his biceps and shows off his ink-laced arms. He's danger, and everything I can't seem to stop thinking about.

His dark eyes meet mine and a smirk climbs his cheeks as he gets off his bike, sending my mom into motion. She positions herself between me and him with her shoulders pulled back.

"What do you want?"

I rush around her before Rome can open his mouth. Because in the handful of times I've met him, I know whatever he'll say will just cause trouble.

"Rome, meet my mom, Katherine Chen." I step aside and wave my hands between them. "Mom, this is Rome Moreno. You remember Eloise, who rented me this house? Rome is in her band, and she mentioned he was stopping by to fix the... the...uh..."

"Stereo?" Rome finishes, with an amused expression.

We both know it's a lie. But anything is better than trying to explain why a tattooed rock star just showed up at my house on his motorcycle.

Why is he here, anyway?

"Yes, the stereo has been acting up," I say, turning back to Mom. "And you know I need it for practice."

"It seemed fine just now." Mom glares, her gaze moving between Rome and me.

I shrug. "It's intermittent."

Mom mulls it over, giving Rome a final unimpressed once-over, likely deciding he's beneath her and not worth another moment of her time, as she turns to me. "Very well. On time tonight, Lili. No excuses."

With that, she walks away and gets in her car. No hug. No goodbye. Just my mother. It isn't until she starts down the road that I feel my shoulders finally relax. Which is the exact moment Rome chooses to chuckle, drawing my attention back to the solid wall of muscle standing in my driveway looking like a walking distraction.

"Rome." I narrow my eyes at him, crossing my arms over my chest.

He dips his thumbs in his pockets and scans me over, making me realize I'm standing in front of him in nothing more than a cropped tank, skin-tight shorts that might as well be underwear, and leg warmers. Not unusual attire for a dancer, but around him, I feel completely exposed.

"Afternoon, sweetheart." He grins.

"Still—"

"Not my sweetheart, I know. Keep telling yourself that." He winks at me.

Jerk.

"Why are you here?" I turn to walk back into the house, only realizing my mistake when Rome follows me and closes the door behind him.

Nothing good can come of spending time alone with him. It feels too good when it shouldn't.

"I'm fixing your stereo." He leans against the wall and crosses one ankle over the other, watching me circle the kitchen to grab some water.

"We both know it doesn't actually need fixing." I take a long sip, hoping it can cool the fire in my chest.

Rome grins. "Your plumbing then? Need someone to clear out your pipes?"

"Is everything an innuendo with you?"

He shrugs, not answering.

Outside, his eyes were almost golden, but under the dim kitchen lights, the darkness drinks the gold.

I take another sip of water and wish Rome would blink or look away because his gaze is intense enough that it's difficult to stare at him for too long. As if he reads my mind, he breaks his gaze and scans the room.

Setting down my glass on the counter, I make my way back into the living room, wrapping my hair up in a tight ponytail so it doesn't get in my way.

"Practicing?"

I spin, not realizing he followed me, and he's standing right in my bubble, catching me off guard.

"Why are you here, Rome?" I ignore his question because he still hasn't answered mine.

There's no reason for him to show up in the middle of the day, even if I have imagined it a few times. We aren't friends.

But here Rome stands, in my living room with barely a few feet between us. And I'm reminded how dangerous it feels to be around him. Because my thoughts are murky and my skin tingles.

Rome takes another step forward and I step back, unable to help it. He closes in on me, and I try to keep my distance until my back strikes a wall, pinning me in place in front of him.

Stopping, he plants a hand on the wall beside my head. But he doesn't lean in closer or touch me. He doesn't need to because I feel every inch of air between us. His eyes are fixed on mine and his expression is unlike anything I've seen on him.

Vulnerable, maybe?

He swallows hard, and I'm reminded of the third eye on his throat always watching, even when he blinks. Reminding me that when Rome is in my space, there's no escaping.

"Why did you lie to your mom?" Rome asks, once more ignoring my question.

"My mom?"

He nods, eyebrows pinching, and I almost think he seems genuinely curious about my answer.

"You should be thanking me," I say under my breath. "I saved you from the wrath of Katherine Chen."

"You think I can't handle your mom?"

I shake my head, but the darkness in his eyes makes me think that maybe Rome is one of the few people in this world who wouldn't be affected by the force that is my mother.

"Either way..." I switch gears, not entertaining whatever thought flashes in Rome's mind. "The last thing she needs to think is that I'm out here getting distracted."

"Is that what I am, Lili?" Rome leans in the slightest bit. "A distraction?"

Something about my name rolling off his tongue is more disarming than him calling me sweetheart.

"I think you know you're a distraction, Rome," I challenge him. "Hence why you still refuse to answer my question."

"Just because I haven't answered doesn't mean I'm refusing." Rome shrugs, his eyes dipping to my throat as I swallow. "Maybe there's no answer. After all, I was hanging out with the band, then I was headed home. But somehow, I ended up here. Why is that?"

Rome shifts, and I swear if I breathe in my chest might brush his. Part of me wants to—wants to feel him like I did on the back of his bike. And something about the inch of space he leaves is torture, which he must know because the grin that paints his lips is downright wicked.

Tipping my chin up, I dare to face him. To stand toe-to-toe with this tattooed rock star who takes up residence in my head when I don't have room left. I tilt my face and we might as well be sharing a breath.

I stand off with a man who I get the impression is used to people bowing down and giving him exactly what he wants.

I lick my lips and don't miss that even if he doesn't break my stare, he swallows at the movement.

I don't know why Rome Moreno is at my house, but I know it's for nothing good. His scent is addictive, and his body turns good intentions bad. Then there's the fact that he makes me feel at ease when I know I should be keeping my guard up. Somehow, he's my kryptonite.

The good girl inside me crumbles to pieces. She's tired, and starving, and desperate for a taste. It could be that my mom's visit set me on edge. Or that years of being told what to do makes me want to go rogue. But with Rome standing in front of me, it's a dare I can't resist.

I can't help that I rake my teeth over my bottom lip just to draw a reaction, or that all this man makes me want to do is challenge him.

His gaze drops to my mouth, and I feel us both pause around a truth neither of us wants to accept.

"You're here because you can't help yourself," I say, knowing it's bold but also that I'm right. For whatever reason, I've caught the beast's attention, and I can't help but want to feel what it means to be his prey. "What do you plan on doing about it?"

9

ROME

When I left Adrian and Eloise's house, I didn't plan on showing up at Lili's doorstep. And even when I did, I didn't intend on coming inside or standing here with her pinned against the wall tempting me with her presence.

But here I am. Playing with fire when I know all it does is leave more ashes.

Ashes that are blowing around at the moment and clouding my judgment. Because no matter how wrong Lili feels, she's the closest thing I've felt to *right* in a long time, and I can't figure out why.

So why haven't I leaned in? Why haven't I closed the gap? What the fuck is wrong with me?

I blame her eyes. While her body is barely clothed and she's leaning in like she's begging to be unraveled, her eyes hold her innocence. A hint of fear mixed with determination. She wants to play the game to see how far she can push me, and while I'd love to prove she's not prepared for it, I'm more curious as to why.

Fuck.

I step back, and Lili melts against the wall with an exhale.

"Is that a challenge?"

"What if it is?" Lili says, out of breath.

For being as uptight as she is, there's a sassy tongue hiding beneath her perfectly polished exterior, and I don't know why she's wasting her time giving me an invitation.

"Why?"

It doesn't make sense. There's no doubt in my mind Lili can get any guy she wants, and she doesn't seem the type to screw around. But here she is throwing herself at me when she's spent every other interaction pushing me away.

"Isn't this what you do?" She waves her hand between us, seeming flustered all of a sudden. "Or are the tabloids wrong?"

"They aren't."

She winces at my statement, but there's no point beating around the bush. I've banged my way through women around the world a few times and made no apologies for it.

Except, my words feel like a half-truth because *this* isn't what I do at all. Usually, I use them and walk away. I don't think about them when they aren't around and show up at their houses. Whatever has me circling Lili like a buzzard is fucking with my head.

Lili stands with her arms at her sides. Frustration written all over her face. Her skin is flushed pink and on display in her itty-bitty outfit. She's so damn tempting, and yet, I can't seem to disconnect my dick's desire to drive into her with the nagging warnings going off in my head.

Lili is trouble.

She'll want more from me.

I'll just mess her up.

"Your reputation is no secret." She looks hurt by her own statement, but I don't know why. "You've been with lots of women."

"What's your point?"

"So, it's just me you aren't interested in then?"

She tries to brush past me, and I realize she thinks I haven't made a move on her because I'm not attracted to her, or don't want her, which isn't the case. I turn and grab onto her arms, pulling her back to my front, and loving how she takes in the sharpest breath at the feel of my body.

I drift my fingers up her arm and find the base of her throat to feel her pulse racing.

"Don't. Say. That," I warn her.

She turns her face to the side and looks up at me over her shoulder, tipping her chin up in defiance. "Why? Not like you'll do anything about it."

A taunt and she knows it.

Snaking my other hand up her side, I draw my palm along her smooth skin, up her body, and over her perfect tits, not missing that she presses her ass against me at my touch. But I don't encourage her by squeezing them or playing with her tight nipples, I move all the way up to her neck, wrapping a hand around her throat and pulling her tighter against my body.

"Has no one warned you not to tempt the devil?" I tilt her head so I can bring my mouth to her ear. "You might not like what you unleash."

I squeeze the column of her neck gently. Not enough to take her breath, but to make her work for it. Because something about the idea of being the beginning and end of this girl is appealing.

"I'm not some breakable thing, Rome." Lili lets out a long exhale. "I can handle it."

"Is that really what you want, sweetheart?" I release her throat and move my hand up to graze her full lips with my thumb. "Do you even know what you're asking for? Do you want me to fuck the sass out of your mouth before I fuck the fight out of your pussy? Because that's what I'd do. I'd fuck you dirty and shatter that perfect glass tower they've locked you away in. Do you want me to ruin you just because you're bored and looking for trouble?"

She's breathing so hard she's panting. Like she can't catch her breath. I'm tempted to shove her to her knees and stick my cock down her throat because I don't play games. But something about this delicate creature in my hands makes me pause. She smells like pears and sugar and things I'm not supposed to taste.

For good reason.

"Don't mistake me for a gentleman because I'd rather destroy you than save you." I move my hand once more to her throat and she tips her head back against my chest, breathing hard. "Or is that what you want?"

Her hands move to my sides, and she rests them on my thighs, pressing her body fully flush with mine. But instead of reaching for more, she closes her eyes and sinks into my hold like she trusts me with things she shouldn't.

"I don't know, Rome," she says, and it's almost a whisper. "Maybe I just want to feel something again."

"You want to use me?" It should make me happy because that's all I'm good for.

So why does it feel a little like a knife twisting for the first time in my life?

"No... I..." Her eyes open and she searches my face, seemingly coming to a realization. "Rome, I'm sorry... I..."

The spell broken, I let her go and take a step back. "It's fine. I shouldn't have done that."

She paces the room, redoing her ponytail. "It's just the show is coming up, and my mom was here this morning. It's one event after another. And then you showed up. I don't know what I'm doing."

Lili cuts off her ramble and plants herself on the couch, which is sitting at the edge of the living room, leaving a wide-open space she probably practices in.

She buries her face in her hands and it's the perfect opportunity for me to get out of here, but for the same reason I found myself showing up at her doorstep, I walk over and sit down beside her. I lean back and stretch my legs out.

For someone who always has something to say to break the tension, I'm coming up empty.

"I didn't mean to insinuate what I did." Lili looks up at me.

I drop my hands to my lap and realize she's sitting up straight as a pole again.

"You know..." Her eyes dart away, nervously. "I'm not saying all you do is get around or anything."

"I do though."

Her eyes snap back to mine, but it isn't disgust I find in them, it's something undefinable and far more dangerous.

"I've fucked my way around the world more than once, sweetheart."

She chews the inside of her cheek, not blinking as she assesses what I'm telling her. I'd like to dig into her pretty little head and hear what she thinks about my comment, which isn't something I can say I've thought about another person before. Her lips part and the sweetest exhale leaves them.

I can practically see her coming to her senses. Her expression shifting as she realizes what she almost let me do—what I wanted to do more than anything in a long time. I watch Lili's face change as she rebuilds her composure, burying whatever was stressing her out earlier and collecting herself. I watch her morph once more into the girl who is way too good for me.

"Feel better?"

She takes in a deep breath and nods. "Sorry—"

"Don't worry about it." I plaster a smile on my face that hurts a little more than it should right now. "Happy to help."

Lili shifts in her seat, looking far too innocent all of a sudden. So I change the subject.

"This where you dance?" My eyes move to the empty space that takes up most of the living room.

Her shoulders relax with my question, and some sick part of me finds relief in the fact that I have the power to calm her as much as I seem to be able to wind her up.

"Yes." She glances around at the furniture all pushed against one wall. "Although, I guess it makes for an odd entertaining space when there are guests."

"Screw 'em." I shrug. "Your house, your rules."

She quirks an eyebrow at me. "This coming from a guy with stripper poles in his living room."

I tip my head back and laugh, hard. And when my gaze falls back on her, I appreciate that I'm met with amusement instead of disgust.

"What can I say, I appreciate the arts." I wink, and the faintest blush climbs her cheeks.

"I'm sure you do, Rome Moreno."

Something about the way she says my full name. How she's small but infinite. How she's delicate without being the least bit fragile. She's a force to be reckoned with.

"Need proof?" I lace my fingers together and cup the back of my head. "Dance for me and I'll show you just how much I appreciate the arts. You're supposed to be practicing anyway, aren't you?"

Lili's head tilts, and I wait for a perfectly punctuated *"fuck you"* to fall from her lips. But instead, she rolls her shoulders back and stands up.

"I'll tell you what," she says, sashaying to the center of the empty space, before running her foot in a semi-circle along the floor like she's about to glide over water. "You tell me one real thing about yourself, and I'll dance for you."

"Something real?" I'm honestly not sure why she cares, which has me both curious and on edge.

Lili holds a finger up in the air, pointing it in my direction. "And not some rehearsed response you give in interviews."

"Been spending time on the internet stalking me again?" I grin.

She rolls her eyes, immediately seeming annoyed that she let me see her do that. "Don't flatter yourself. I'm in the industry—or a similar one anyway. I know how it is to only show them what you want to."

"Fair enough."

We might come from different worlds, but we're no doubt faced with similar devils. Being in the spotlight means everyone seeing you and no one *seeing you*, all at once.

"I'll tell you something real." I lean forward, resting my elbows on my knees, watching her as she kicks a leg up and stretches, making me wonder why I didn't fuck her against the wall earlier. "But then I want something real in return. Not a performance. I want to see you dance how you'd do it if it was just for you."

This is dangerous territory. Drifting to parts of the ocean that look too close to the Bermuda Triangle. I'm saying shit I know better than to say to a chick because I don't need attachments.

Lili nods once, and I feel her defenses slip away, even if only for a moment. Breaking my stare, she walks over to a side table and grabs her phone off it, starting to flip through, pausing only to glance in my direction.

"So, Rome. Ready for your question?" Her teeth run over her bottom lip.

"Fire away." I don't lean back or relax. Instead, I can't help but stay hyper-focused on her.

She scrunches her nose at something on her phone screen. She's tapping her toe on the ground and biting her thumbnail, and I wonder what got to her just now. But then her eyes meet mine and she seems to catch herself fidgeting, so she stills as she presses play on her music.

I feel her question in the air before a word gets out. Weighted. Dangerous. Her hands slide up her body and into her hair, before tugging the hair tie out and letting her black hair fall like silk over her shoulders.

"What makes you happy, Rome Moreno?" Lili asks, tossing her hair tie onto the couch and making her way back into the center of the room.

I laugh, assuming I must have heard her wrong, because of all the things people want to know about me—where my scars come from, why I hide them, why I'm a detached asshole—what makes me happy isn't one of them. But Lili stops in the center of the room with a flat expression on her face, and it makes my smile fall.

"What makes me happy?" I repeat her question and she nods in response.

Leaning back, I stretch my arms over the couch and think about it because I'm not sure I've thought about the answer to that question in years. I know what keeps me satisfied, what keeps me going, what drives me.

But happy?

I look her dead in the eyes and can't help the weight that forms on my chest. "I'll tell you when I find it."

It's the truth, and a sad fucking realization.

Lili looks me over, probably deciding whether my answer is bullshit or not. The song kicks up and she closes her eyes, taking in a deep breath as she tips her head back. Her neck rolls, showing off its length, and reminding me of when I had my hand wrapped around it.

Everything about her is elusive. How she starts to sway like her body is made of ribbons. How she takes up the full space of the room with her movements. Her dance is flawlessly imperfect because it has no rhyme or reason, while still making perfect sense to me.

It's her, unfiltered, in a way I believe she is when she's not chained down by her profession.

The song she chose is something instrumental and soft, like Lili. No lyrics except the ones she makes as she starts to move with it. And I swear, I've never understood a song more than I do right now.

I've never understood a person like I do her in this moment. She dances and I shouldn't like it as much as I do, but I can't tear my gaze away.

10

LILI

As if surviving in a world of dance professionals isn't unbearable enough, the parties are the cherry on top of the bullshit. Stuffy, fake. My skin is already crawling, and I just walked in.

"Drink?" Rico looks down at me and smiles.

Sometimes I wish I saw him as something more than a friend. He's handsome in a textbook kind of way with strong features and a smile that knocks you off your feet. But even in his blinding presence, I feel nothing.

I nod, and he brushes his hand over my lower back before disappearing into the crowd, leaving me in a room full of vipers alone.

Without scanning the faces, I feel them watching me. To them, I'm something I'm not. Interesting, pretty, a dancer for their entertainment. I'm a prize to win.

Mom is standing with a group from Eden, my dance company. She smiles at something one of them says and I'm sure it looks genuine to those who don't know her. But I do. She's simply playing nice to get on their good side as they set up my next dance tour.

I'm still in the middle of prepping for the performance of my career and she can't help but already be thinking about what's next. I'm exhausted thinking about it.

From across the room, I meet Mom's gaze and she frowns, likely disappointed to see me standing alone instead of parading myself around in front of everyone. But then her eyes fall over my shoulder and her annoyance turns to something much more menacing.

"What are the chances?" I hear his voice behind me at the same time as a shiver runs the length of my spine. The kind only Rome Moreno seems capable of pulling out of me.

My eyes are still locked on my mom, and the darkness in her eyes becomes clear to me as she assesses the man standing over my shoulder.

She might have believed he was at my doorstep for a valid reason, but there's no way she'll let this slide. I can already feel the questions revolving in her head as her gaze moves between us.

Mom shifts and I sense her about to head in my direction, so I spin on my heels and brush past Rome, trying to ignore the devious smile stretching his cheeks.

"Why are you here?" I ask, already feeling him following me through the crowd.

I need to escape—to anywhere.

I might have let Rome get in my head a few days ago when it was just the two of us in my living room, but that can't happen again. If anything, it was a reminder of the madness that follows him. How he uses women as commodities and people for amusement. Whatever this thundering is inside me, it's going to have to settle down because I'm smarter than to get stuck in the middle of the storm that is Rome Moreno.

"I could ask you the same thing." Rome reaches for my elbow as he follows me through the crowd, but I pull it away.

Finally reaching the edge of the room, I spin to face him, realizing immediately what a bad idea it is as I look up into his devilishly dark eyes.

They're almost as disarming as his appearance tonight. While I've only ever seen him in T-shirts and jeans, he's wearing a custom-fitted tux. Tattoos peek from his collar and at his wrists, giving him an edge he wears well.

I've seen plenty of men in suits, but not the way he wears it. Somehow, he manages to look almost as provocative as if he were wearing nothing at all. Which is something I should not be thinking about.

"Why are you here?" I ask again.

Rome ticks his head to the side and my gaze follows, until it lands on two familiar faces I remember from my online search of him and his band—Eloise and their band manager, Adrian.

"Micah Jacobson produced a charity show for us a couple of years ago. We were invited."

The world feels like it's shrinking. The last place I'd expect to see a rock band is at an event thrown by a higher-up in the dance community, but here he is, proving there's no escape as long as I remain in Denver.

"Small world," I say, meeting his gaze once more.

Rome smirks. "That it is."

His eyes skim me, and while I've felt eyes on me all night, none strip me like his. And not in a way that feels sexual because he doesn't stop at the dip of shimmery green fabric that lands beneath my belly button in front or the slit that hits me mid-thigh. His eyes rip through the surface of this façade and slice to places it's not safe for me to let him see.

"You're beautiful, Lili," he says, looking me in the eyes.

Something about the softness of his tone paired with his genuine gaze takes the fight out of me.

"Thank you." I nod, waving my hands up and down at him. "You're not so bad yourself. The Riff King in a suit. Who would have seen it coming?"

Rome leans in closer, bringing his lips inches from my ear. "Don't let appearances fool you."

He pulls back a step, but it doesn't make it easier to breathe because anywhere he is, feels consuming.

"There you are." Rico moves around Rome and stops at my side, snaking a hand around my waist.

I don't miss that Rome's gaze drops to Rico's hand on my hip, and I swear his jaw clenches. But just as I'm about to introduce them, another person catches my attention.

"Rome, you're not going to believe who I just ran into..." The brunette bombshell stops right in front of me, at Rome's side.

His eyes cut in her direction, and his expression softens, almost like he's happy to see her.

"Natalia Carmichael," the brunette finishes. "What are the chances?"

She laughs freely as she wraps her hands around Rome's arm, exuding the kind of comfort that extends beyond good friends. Her head tips back as she looks up at him, and it sends her dark waves cascading further down her back. She's short but curvy in all the places I'm sure Rome appreciates.

My opposite.

While I'm small and cold, she's warm and inviting. And even if jealousy isn't something I'm used to feeling, a knot tightens in my throat.

What did you expect? Him to be here alone?

He's Rome Moreno.

But something about witnessing it in the form of this woman on his arm is unsettling.

The brunette's eyes move to Rico and me as she rubs Rome's arm up and down. He hasn't pulled his hands from his pockets to return the gesture, but he doesn't seem surprised by it either.

"Ines, this is Lili," Rome says. "And..."

"Rico." He introduces himself as Rome's gaze slides to him, and from the excitement in his tone, I don't think he's sensing the same tension I am. "Big fan, man."

Rico reaches out his hand and Rome shakes it, but his expression is missing his trademark grin.

"That last album was killer," Rico praises him, apparently more familiar with rock music than I was when I first met Rome.

Rome nods, looking him over, before his gaze once more finds me, like he's trying to piece us together and decide what he thinks.

Rico leans in close and brushes my hair off my shoulder. "Your mom's looking for you."

"When isn't she?" I say, finally breaking my stare on Rome and trying to ignore what feels like daggers shooting out of his eyes. "Nice to meet you, Ines, and good seeing you, Rome."

Before he can respond, I cut him off with a nod and tug Rico away.

"What in the ever-loving world was that?" Rico asks under his breath as we disappear through the crowd.

"Rome Moreno."

"Oh, I'm aware," Rico says, and I look up to see him grinning. "But I never thought I'd see the day."

"What? Meeting a rock star?"

Rico laughs. "No. Seeing Lili Chen with her panties in a twist over a guy who would give her mother a heart attack."

"I don't have my panties in a twist," I huff.

"Sure you don't." Rico pats my shoulder. "Keep telling yourself that."

***

The night is already dreadful and boring, but Rome's presence makes it nearly unbearable. He's everywhere I look with the brunette Jessica Rabbit hanging from his arm. And to make matters worse, it's obvious I can't stop staring at him.

Every time Mom catches me glancing in his direction, she makes a comment about *the guy who was fixing my stereo*. Something Rico finds highly amusing once he hears the story because he knows it's total bullshit.

My gaze finds Rome once more over Mom's shoulder, where he's directly in my line of sight. It's a spot he has permanently affixed himself this evening. And while he seems to give no thought to the bombshell rubbing herself against him, I don't like whatever it's stirring inside me.

My stomach tightens every time he smiles, and it's bordering on painful.

It's hunger—that's all.

It's the only thing that makes sense.

After all, I skipped dinner for this event and Mom brushes off the food trays every time the waiters circle near us, so it's the lack of calories getting to me. My stomach twists, and I can't help but clench Rico's arm from the sudden sensation.

"You feeling okay?" He dips his mouth near my ear.

Mom smiles proudly at Rico's closeness, like she's imagining sweet nothings he's whispering, when it's nowhere close to the truth.

I shake it off. "I'm fine, just tired."

It's not a lie. I've never been a good sleeper, but the stress from the upcoming show paired with a recent cut to my carb intake has made it nearly impossible.

"Actually..." I pat his arm. "I think I'm going to take off."

"This early?" Mom's posture straightens, and she frowns at me. "You've barely made your rounds."

"I have. Twice," I remind her. "It's getting late, and I need my rest for tomorrow's practice."

There—I throw the one excuse at her she won't argue with. As much as she lives for a party to parade me around at, she'd rather I perform well on stage. Her nod of approval is proof.

"Need me to walk you out?" Rico asks.

"I'll be fine. Enjoy the rest of your night." Tipping up on my toes so no one can hear me, I whisper, "Besides, at least one of us needs to enjoy the evening, and the blonde in the yellow dress hasn't left your line of sight."

"Oh, I'm aware." He grins.

I shake my head before giving him a quick kiss on the cheek, that he returns.

"Of course you are. See you tomorrow."

Before Mom can break free from the group's conversation, I dip away. The last thing I need is a final lecture before bed.

Cutting through the crowd, I smile politely at anyone who glances in my direction but don't hold any stare too long. The crowd is tipsy this late in the evening, and it's hard to deal with when I'm sober.

What I wouldn't give for one drink, especially since I hired a driver this evening to take me home. But there's no way I felt like hearing Mom lecture me about the calories in alcohol. So I stuck with water.

A woman brings me my coat, and I wrap it around my shoulders before stepping outside. It's a crisp night for September. Fall is in the air in Denver, and I breathe it in, appreciating the relief I feel in the season's changing.

"Early night, sweetheart?"

I spin around so fast, I almost topple over in my heels, but Rome's hands grip my arms to catch me. He's ditched his tie and has undone the first couple of buttons on his dress shirt, showing off a V of inked skin, once more making me wonder how far it goes.

His head tilts the slightest, with his trademark smirk brightening his dark eyes.

I pull back, and he releases me. "It's almost eleven."

Rome tucks his hands in his pockets. Even in a suit, his energy is relaxed and confident. He casually leans a shoulder against the brick wall of the building and looks down at me.

"Like I said, early."

"Some of us have things to do tomorrow." I cross my arms over my chest.

He smiles, amused at my defensive posture. "Doesn't mean we should waste tonight."

"Don't you have a date you should be worrying about?"

"Don't you?" He shoots back.

Date?

Then it hits me; Rico was technically my date. Although not the kind Rome was clearly on.

"He's a friend." I drop my arms and try my best to sound confident. The last thing I need is Rome thinking I'm jealous.

Rome's eyes skim my body before he meets my gaze again. "Same."

I laugh louder than I expect to at the comment.

"What?"

"A *friend*." I lift an eyebrow. "I'm sure she is."

Rome shrugs one shoulder but doesn't offer much more. I don't like what the nonchalant gesture does to me. Or anything else about him for that matter. I shouldn't care who the woman he's with is to him. It makes no difference.

It *needs* to make no difference.

"Come out with me," Rome says, narrowing his eyes in a challenge. "It's too early, and you're too young to not have a life."

"Is that an insult?"

"Only if you take it that way." Rome stands up straight and it adds to his height. "One night won't kill you, sweetheart. Let me show you what the world's like outside that pretty little tower they've got you locked away in."

It's dangerous.

It's a bad idea.

And yet, looking into Rome's eyes, I can't help the single nod I give him.

11

LILI

OF ALL THE PLACES Rome might take me in the middle of the night, I should have expected this. Because every time I think maybe he'll prove my assumptions about him wrong, all he does is prove them right.

"What?" He stops, grinning at the annoyance I'm failing to hide from my face.

I shake my head. "A strip club? Really?"

"We're broadening your horizons." He steps in close.

Holding my breath, I try to steady myself because his cologne is putting my brain into overdrive.

"I'm sure," I say, shaking my head. "You're just trying to get me to chicken out."

The smile that stretches his face is breathtaking and completely uninhibited.

It's also how I know what I said is right—he's trying to see if I'll crack. But if this is Rome's attempt at testing how far he can push me to my limits before I start pushing back, I'm inclined to prove to him that he can't phase me.

"Well, if you'd rather go home…" Rome trails off, looking me over.

I shake my head and step toward him. If he thinks he can back me into a corner and scare me away, I'll prove him wrong. While the world might think I'm a delicate dance princess, I don't want him to.

"Lead the way, Riff King." I tip my chin up, and he smiles.

The doors to the club open, and I know this is a bad idea—but that's everything about Rome. And for some reason, I can't seem to help myself. I want to feel the parts of his world that are forbidden. I want to test my boundaries in a way I've never been allowed to. I want to see if I can survive being demolished by the Riff King.

But as we step inside, I realize my bravery has set me too far out of my element. Because debauchery is his world, not mine.

As if Rome can sense my nerves, he reaches behind him and takes my hand, wrapping his fingers through mine. It's a small gesture but calming.

He leads the way into the club, and it's classier than it appeared from the outside. A long dark corridor that opens into a dimly-lit club. The walls are a blue so dark and deep it reminds me of the middle of an ocean, which is fitting because walking through here in my evening gown feels a little like I'm drowning in unfamiliar territory.

There are three stages, each occupied by a topless woman. They're curvy and gorgeous and feminine in a way I've never quite felt in my own skin. Men and women are scattered around the room, unable to tear their eyes off them. But surprisingly, Rome's focus is straight ahead as a bouncer leads us through the club to a hallway at the far side.

A few club patrons have their eyes on me as we walk past, and I'm reminded of just how revealing my dress is, cutting down to my naval and high up my thigh. Rome tugs my hand and pulls me closer to his side, almost as if he notices it as well. But he doesn't look at me or say anything, so it's probably my imagination.

His grip relaxes in the quiet of the hallway, and he only lets go once we reach a door at the far end, guiding me inside with his hand on my lower back. One touch sending heatwaves through me.

I should have said no. I should have gone home. I should have stayed far away.

What have I gotten myself into with him?

The room is dark, except for a dim light coming from a private stage with a single pole in the center. I've spent my life performing, but something about this room is different from anything I've watched or experienced. There's music playing, but I can barely hear it over my heartbeat pounding between my temples.

Rome leads me to the couch positioned against the back wall, taking my coat, and setting it aside before sitting down beside me. While I feel every nerve ending on edge and tense, he seems relaxed and in his element.

There's no doubt in my mind he's been here before. The bouncers knew him by name when we walked in, and he even nodded at the bartender as we passed. They put him in a nice room I get the impression is reserved for big spenders, and he's probably spent more time here than I want to know.

Rome rubs his palms over his thighs, and I realize how close we are, almost touching. The gap of space between us is almost more tempting than if it wasn't there at all.

"You hanging in there, sweetheart?" He looks over at me, but his expression is surprisingly placid.

I nod, forcing a smile, not really sure. But also wanting to prove to him that I'm not the sheltered, fragile creature he probably sees me as. Or maybe I'm trying to prove it to myself.

"Drinks." A waitress stops directly in front of us, and it's not a question because she's handing me a vodka martini and Rome a glass of whiskey.

Rome takes both and thanks her before handing me mine.

"When did you order these?"

Rome shrugs. "On the way over."

I reach for the martini glass. "What if I didn't like vodka?"

"But you do." Rome winks.

"But..."

"Stop thinking about it and relax for five seconds." Rome tips his head back and lets out a dark chuckle.

Once more I'm not sure if he's laughing at me or genuinely amused, and as much as I feel like I can read him sometimes, there are moments like this where it's impossible.

To hide my frustration, I bring my drink to my lips and take a sip that goes straight to my head. The vodka drowns out my thoughts, and as much as that should unsettle me, it's strangely relaxing. I set the glass on the table beside the couch and try to ignore the tension in my neck.

"So is this what you do with your free time when you're not touring? Sit around drinking and watching women take their clothes off?"

"Sometimes." Rome shrugs. "Why? Judging?"

He smirks as if challenging me with his question. Rome isn't the type of guy who hands over control, and his verbal sparring is just one of many ways he maintains power in any conversation.

Sitting up straight, I plant my hands in my lap and don't miss that he watches the slit of my dress slowly fall open to bare one leg. When his eyes flick back up to meet mine, I can't help but smile at how I'm able to draw his attention in a place filled with beautiful women.

"Just curious."

I'm not sure what about my statement confuses him, but his eyebrows knit, and his mouth pops open the slightest. But before he can say anything, the music kicks up in the room and movement on the stage draws our attention. A single beam of light glows over the pole, keeping the rest of the room cloaked in darkness, as a woman walks out in lace that is sheer enough that there's almost no use in her undressing.

She grabs onto the pole and does an initial spin to get her bearings, stopping long enough to look over her shoulder and wink at us before moving into her routine. Her red hair sweeps her pale skin, and she reminds me of a siren who calls out to sailors the moment before wrecking their ships. She kicks her legs overhead and wraps them around the pole, one straight out like an arrow as she spins.

And spins.

And spins.

Her movements are fluid, and for some reason I find myself thinking about what Pauline said as the woman twists around, landing only long enough to slip off her top to put her full breasts on display. She moves like her body is one with the pole, with the air, with her heartbeat. Seductive and sure, no hesitation. And I find myself jealous of the freedom I feel in her dance. Not because she's so beautiful that the man beside me hasn't taken his eyes off her, but because she embodies everything I've longed to feel my entire life.

My chest tightens with my racing heart. It's pounding so hard I feel the hammer of it under my ribs. Squeezing and thinning the air. My thoughts are fogged from vodka and sin.

Rome leans in and I'm hit with the spice of his cologne, setting me on edge. He brushes my hair off my shoulder, trailing his fingers along the path of skin as he does it, before whispering in my ear.

"Ready to run yet?"

I almost scream *yes*. Between the alcohol, the music, and this club, I can't think straight. But add in the feel of Rome's fingers on my skin and his breath tickling my neck, and something deep in my belly feels on the verge of snapping.

So I shake my head, swallowing hard.

I don't have to look at him to feel him smile. The small huff of a laugh crawls my skin, and I feel his excitement radiating. He's playing with me, seeing how far he can push, and for some unknown reason, I want to be his toy to mess with.

Rome snaps, and it's loud enough to make me jump, which he soothes by pulling my hair back and resting his arm over the back of the couch behind my shoulders.

The redhead stops spinning, planting her feet on the ground, and walking toward us. She's watching Rome, and I'm fully ready to ignore whatever kicks up inside me at the thought of her grinding all over him in front of me, but he tips his head, and she moves in my direction instead. Rome doesn't move his arm, or pull away, as the woman stops in front of me.

I turn to face him and realize just how close he is because it puts us almost mouth to mouth with me looking up at him. His eyes watch mine, skipping to my throat as I swallow, and to my chest as I feel my breath racing.

He lifts his hand and traces his fingers down the side of my face, tucking my hair behind my ear before continuing the path downward, along my neck and stopping in the center of my chest, right between my breasts. His touch is barely a graze, but it might as well light a path of fire along my skin.

"Let go, sweetheart." He smiles, but it feels serious. Almost as if Rome wants to watch me come apart for him just to play in the mess.

As he moves his hand, the stripper starts to dance over me. Her hands running along me, and her breasts brushing my chest as she bends forward, before turning around and gliding her body down mine. It's sexual in a way I've never felt, but I don't break my stare on Rome. I can't. Something about the way he watches—*he absorbs*.

I can't escape him.

The stripper arches her back against me as she takes my hand in hers, lifting it and planting it on Rome's thigh. Like we're all one, and she's reading what I need so deep I'm scared to unearth it. She trails my hand along his leg and my belly warms with every inch she moves it upward.

Rome swallows, and I don't know if I've ever felt more connected to someone because the tension written on his face is the same as the fire ripping through me. Every inch my hand moves along him, the pressure builds, and I want the freedom from the release.

My hand trails dangerously close to parts of him I don't let myself think about, when I realize she isn't stopping. I'm about to pull away, but Rome beats me to it. He plants his hand over the stripper's. And I'm thankful and disappointed at the same time.

I'm not sure I can handle where this is headed, even if my body wants it.

Rome ticks his head toward the stage, not taking his eyes off me, and I feel the weight of the woman's body leave mine, drawing out the coolness of the room as we're once more left alone on the couch.

It's only then I realize that even though she left, I haven't moved my hand. It's planted on Rome's leg, with his hand over mine, and I tighten my grip on instinct. Like at any point, he'll pull away and this moment will snap back into focus. I'm not ready for reality. I want Rome to drag me under and make me forget how heavy this world feels all the time.

From the corner of my eye, I notice the stripper is once more twisting around the pole, but neither of us is watching.

"Why did you stop her?" I ask, gripping his thigh tighter.

If this is a game of chicken, I'm not sure who is winning, only that it feels like we're both about to lose.

Rome reaches up and wraps his hand around my neck gently, pressing his thumb under my chin to lift my face up to him, and I know there's no hiding my racing heartbeat with his fingers on my pulse.

"Because if someone is going to make you come apart, it's going to be me, and me alone."

I'm struck by the possessiveness of his statement. He's the one who brought me to a strip club, but in this moment, all I feel is some unspoken need for him to claim me as his own.

His jaw ticks and I think he actually means it. I press my lips together and swallow, knowing he's reading the effect of his words with his hands. His fingers might be on my throat, but I feel him through my entire body.

"Is that what you want, Lili?" He tilts his head, analyzing my reactions. "Do you still want me to mess you up like you wanted at your house?"

"Is that what you'd do?"

"It's all I'm capable of."

There's a kind of pain in that statement that tells me he really believes it. And it should scare me, but it only makes me want to test his theory. I want to know once and for all if he's right—that once you get too close to a man like Rome Moreno, there's no going back.

"I'm not as breakable as you think, Rome." I swallow hard, facing off with him. "I'd like to see you try."

He grins and I feel it all the way between my legs. His eyes darken and his fingers tighten on my throat. And I want so badly for him to live up to his words. For him to have the kind of power that can change me forever, even if it means there's going to be no putting me back together again.

12

ROME

THE GIRL LIKES TO play with fire, I'll give her that.

I expected Lili to put an end to this before walking into the Velvet Room, but here she is with her hand on my leg so close to my cock I swear I feel her fingers grazing it. And even if I'm the one who put us in this situation, and I know it's a bad idea, I can't help but push for more.

And more.

Seeing her at the party tonight was some strange form of torture. She looked like a goddess in her green dress that cut low and high in all the right places. But then there was that douche on her arm, and for some reason, I was tempted to rip his eyes out for just looking at her.

If anyone is going to wreck Lili, it's going to be me. And I'm going to enjoy every pretty sound she makes while I do it.

She should have run by now. She should have taken the out instead of following me along my path to hell. But she didn't, and I want to make her pay for that decision.

Why is she so determined to prove to me she can handle it anyway?

She's better than me—than all of this. She belongs decorated at a party like the one we were at tonight. She deserves to be lavished and appreciated. She deserves all the things I'm not willing to give someone, even if I was capable.

And fuck if it doesn't make me curious why she's testing the waters.

I release my grip on her throat and she almost looks disappointed, telling me underneath the polished exterior there's a girl begging to get dirty. I slowly trail my hand down her throat to her chest and rest my palm where I had my fingers earlier, in the space between her breasts.

This dress should be illegal she looks so damn good in it. A scrap of fabric that cuts all the way down in the front and all the way up her leg, showing off enough to tempt, while hiding enough to drive me insane.

Lili's heart is racing in her chest, but it's in sync with my own.

"You wanna fall apart, sweetheart?"

She swallows, hesitating, before she slowly nods her head. One small movement on her part and everything I told myself I wouldn't do rushes through my brain.

"Come here." I tug her hand and guide her into my lap, so she's sitting with her back to my front.

It's dark on this side of the room, but it doesn't make us invisible, which I think Lili realizes as her eyes dart around, before focusing on the stage in front of her. The dancer is still going, but I honestly don't give a fuck. Even when I was staring at her earlier, she wasn't the vision playing in my head. From the corner of my eye,

I was focused on Lili and her strange interest in the situation I put her in. She wasn't uncomfortable like I expected—more like curious.

I want to know why.

I want to know what makes her tick.

I want to make her do it.

Lili adjusts in my lap and she no doubt feels me hard as steel beneath her ass. Her wiggling isn't helping, and I have to swallow a groan so I don't bend her over right here. Because even if she's testing her limits, I have a feeling that would push her a little too far.

Reaching up, I pull her hair off her shoulder to expose her slim neck to me. She smells exquisite.

Expensive.

Out of my fucking league.

With one hand wrapped in her silky strands, I plant the other one on her bare thigh, teasing the edge of the slit that's been taunting me all night. Her skin is warm and soft, and with my hand trailing upward, it feels like a lot longer than a month since I've felt the heat of another person's body.

Except I might as well be holding shards of glass in my hands because Lili feels like she's cutting through the barriers I've lived comfortably behind since I was old enough to discover you can't trust anyone but yourself.

And instead of setting her down and walking away, I want to hold tighter. I want to feel her deeper. I want to wrap my fingers around her throat until she understands how weak she makes me feel.

She follows me into the darkness I can't find my way out of. Her life is sunshine, yet she seeks out my shadows. Nothing scares her.

"Why are you watching me?" she asks, tipping her face in my direction, and I realize I am.

"Because you're beautiful."

Her eyebrows pinch like she's confused by my confession, but she doesn't ask me to elaborate. Instead, she sinks against me, not turning away. Watching me like earlier when the dancer was in her lap.

"Tell me something real, Rome."

"Real." I can't help but let out a half-hearted chuckle because this girl wants things she won't know what to do with.

Lili nods. "I want to know you."

"Why?"

"I don't know." The pain in her tone hits me in places deep.

I trail my hand further up her bare leg, moving my fingers inward, and watching how she parts her lips with her quickening breaths.

"You don't know what you're asking for," I warn her.

"You don't scare me."

"I should."

Lili's eyes narrow, and I feel her palm land over my hand, moving me further between her legs. So close I can feel the heat of her pussy as my finger brushes lace panties. Just enough that I feel her dampness, and it makes my dick ache between my legs.

"Everyone around me is fake." Lili pauses my hand, staring into my eyes. "They want me to be like that—like them. But not you."

"You're better off staying in the world they put you in." I lean in and brush my lips along hers barely, tasting the vodka on her breath and getting drunk on it.

Lili's grip on my hand tightens. "I'd rather see yours."

Wrapping her long hair around my fist, I tug on it, tilting her head so I can bring my mouth to her ear. "My world would eat you alive. I would eat you alive. Whatever you're looking for, I won't be the one to give it to you."

"Try me," she says with a dark smile.

"Want to know something real?" I can't help but chuckle. "How about this—Want to know why I haven't fucked you yet? Because all it would take is one time for me to get you out of my system. And even an asshole like me knows you're a girl who deserves more than that. I'm not a good guy. I don't stick around. I don't feel guilt, and I don't look back."

I release my grip on her hair and feel her body tense, either from my cruel statement or the fact that my fingers are digging into the soft flesh of her thigh. But she needs to know there's nothing good left in me and to stop looking for it. There's a reason I don't do relationships. I'm vile, poisonous to a girl like her.

Her eyes close as she relaxes her head against my shoulder. "You really believe that?"

"I know it."

She tips her face toward me once more, opening her eyes and digging her stare into my own. "I don't need you to love me, Rome. There's nothing left to love."

Lili closes her eyes again and lets out the sweetest exhale as she tips her forehead to me and relaxes.

Nothing left to love?

Maybe I've had her wrong this entire time. Because while holding her feels like trying to contain an exploding universe in my palms, she sees herself as a shell of a person. And maybe that's what draws us to each other when we both should know better. She's the calm in the center of my storm, and I'm a hurricane raging hard enough for her to finally feel something.

"I'm fucked up," I whisper, resting my chin on the top of her head.

She sighs. "I know."

But it doesn't make her pull away. Nothing seems to. My words, my world, my actions. She sees right through all of them and comes back for more.

"Touch me." She tilts her hips, putting the pressure of my hand directly on her pussy. "Get it out of both of our systems."

It's a sad statement. Because I think if we were different people with different histories and different lives, it would change the ending inevitably laid out before us.

Lili releases my hand and slides it down to my thigh, holding me on either side like she's handing herself over to me. It's not a smart move, but I can't help but be intoxicated by the pure innocence of it.

Drawing one of my hands up to her neck, I tip her chin up, so I can bury my nose in the sweet smell of her neck and feel her heart racing on my lips. I drag my fingers between her legs and put pressure on her pussy. She tries to lift her hips to meet me, but I hold her down, grinding her ass against my dick.

I feel like I'm going to rip free as her perfect ass cheeks rub against me. But I'm not going to let myself. I don't lose control for a woman, and I'm not about to hand that power over to her. The wrecking is mine alone tonight.

I slide her panties to the side and drag my thumb over her slickness. Fuck, she's hot and ready and begging for my touch.

"Open your eyes." I grip her jaw and force her gaze forward.

Her eyes go wide when they open, and she's met with the sight of the now fully nude woman dancing on the stage like she forgot we weren't alone.

"Should we...."

Her words cut off in a moan as I slip a finger into her. She's tight. Her pussy shivers as she adjusts to my finger, and I roll my thumb over her clit.

I'm a selfish lover because I don't give a fuck about the women I take to bed. But as I slide another finger into Lili and she loses her breath, I want to learn what makes every inch of her desperate.

"You like toying with the devil, sweetheart?" I whisper in her ear, slowing my thumb on her clit to torture her. "Good. Because angels like you are so much fun to mess up."

"Rome." My name is a beautiful moan it feels like she's chasing.

"Spread your legs wider."

She does, the slit to her dress falling open, and even if it's dark, we both know the dancer can see what we're doing from up on stage.

"Be a good girl and show her what I do to you." I curl my fingers inside Lili's pussy and her whole body shakes. "Show her what happens when you don't run like I warned you to. Let her watch you get all hot and needy."

"Yes." Lili's breaths quicken as my thumb moves over her.

She's soaking my hand and the feel of her quivering around my fingers is almost enough to make me come in my pants.

"That's it." I drag my teeth along her throat, wanting to taste every inch of her. "You've never been touched right, have you? You've never really been fucked? I'll fuck you up so bad there's no going back. You want to feel something? *Feel me.*"

I shove another finger inside her and there's barely room, which makes me wonder how tight she'll feel riding my cock. I'm tempted to find out right now, but I'm having too much fun making her come apart on me to stop.

Her nails dig into the sides of my thighs and her mouth falls open as she tightens around my hand.

"Beautiful," I whisper in her ear, and that's all it takes to send her over the edge.

Lili gasps as her head tips back, and her whole body is shaking on me. Her hips circle, riding out the waves on my hand, and it's the most gorgeous sight I've ever seen. Watching the pleasure flush her face. Her puffy lips parted and searching for air. Her eyes fluttering.

I watch her fall apart on me until she finds her breath and finally turns to face me.

"You were wrong," I tell her, pulling my hand out of her on an exhale. "There is something left in you, and I'm going to be the one to take it."

Lili's eyes widen as she watches me bring the fingers that were just inside her up. I suck on one of them and she tastes so good I'm tempted to bury my face between her legs.

"Open your mouth."

Hesitantly, she does. And I stick my fingers inside, playing with her tongue and forcing her to taste herself, to see if it'll make her understand what she does to me. Because even if I told her one time is all it would take to be over her, it feels like a lie in this moment.

I hold three fingers on her tongue and my thumb on her jaw, realizing how beautiful she is when she's flushed and relaxed.

"I'm going to break you," I say, tightening my grip.

Lili lifts her hand and grabs my wrist before closing her perfect lips over my fingers and sucking on them.

She pulls my hand out of her mouth and tips her chin up, bringing her mouth so close to mine she's brushing my lips. "Good."

13

LILI

TODAY'S REHEARSAL IS RUNNING twice as long as usual, but I've never felt more energized. As the final song ends, Rico tugs me to him, and my chest is heaving from exertion and energy.

"That was hot, Lili," Rico says, pulling back to smile at me. "You're on fire today. What's gotten into you?"

I pull back and hope he doesn't see me blush because it's not about *what* got into me, it's about *who*. Tattooed fingers and a black hole of a soul I'm free falling toward. It doesn't matter that I haven't seen or spoken to Rome since that night, I can still feel him in every part of me.

"Nothing." I brush Rico off. "Got some sleep last night, that's all."

"Sure thing." Rico winks, like he doesn't believe me at all. "Well, whatever it is, keep it up."

I'm not sure that's a good idea, but I nod before walking off the stage and grabbing my sweater. Rico is right about one thing: I felt every ounce of my performance today. There was no beat, no counting. I was liquid, I felt it. Time slowed and it was me and the air as I danced on stage.

It was almost as if someone took a key to my ribs and set my heart free. I've never felt more one with the music. Only, it's not so simple. Just because I've felt free ever since that night I spent with Rome, it doesn't make it a reality I can entertain.

While he's been on my mind for days, he probably forgot about me the second he shut my car door and I disappeared down the road. He probably even found some company back at the club he took me to. After all, he got me off but didn't let me return the favor.

Whenever I get close, he pulls away.

The stage empties, and I see Mom beeline for Pauline. The excitement from my performance is replaced with a familiar sick feeling in my gut. If I don't get out now, they'll drag me into whatever they're planning for my future, and I'm not prepared to deal with that right now.

Before they can pull me into their conversation, I disappear out the side door. I make my way to the bathroom and lock the door behind me, sinking down in front of the toilet and feeling myself spiraling.

The show.

Rome.

My mother.

I'm losing control and there's only one way I know how to get it back.

I stick my fingers down my throat and watch my soul leave me. It's a waste anyway. All of it. While what comes out looks like food and bile, it's unimpressive pieces of myself in the toilet swimming around.

I'd like to think Rome is right and there's still something in me worth searching for, but it's a lie. As proven by the contents in my stomach.

I'm nothing but ruin.

Ask any man I've dated. I was fragments when they found me, and they took trophies of the rest. I might be objectively pretty for a girl in my field, but there's nothing underneath worth looking at. Which has been fine up until now. I've been living out my dreams and using my soul to pay for them.

It never mattered until Rome grabbed me like a snow globe and shook me up. Forcing me to face what I can't have.

While I'm cold bones and emptiness, Rome is fire and scar tissue. Scalding to the touch and intent on burning the memory of him into me.

But we don't actually fit.

So why did he insist on waking me up? Planting flutters in my chest and tying me in knots.

When he put his hand up my dress, and I came apart, it was unlike anything I've ever felt. Not because of the club, the dancer watching us, or the circumstances. It was him. All shadows in my open space, creating figments I've long missed in my years of loneliness.

It was him reaching into places he doesn't belong.

I stare at my puke in the toilet bowl and wish things could be different. That I was more—and he was more—and we weren't simply two broken people on a mission to test the limits of the universe on each other.

I still remember the look in Rome's eyes as he held me when my orgasm faded. The sarcastic ease slipped away, and for a moment, we were lost in each other's darkness. Pain, shattered glass, and spilled ink.

And I wanted all of him.

The parts that made me fall apart and the parts that hurt. I wanted to swim in the sea where he drowns his secrets to discover what can make a man who feels so good think he's bad. I wanted to see if my imagination was lying as I played with the idea of him tearing me to shreds.

I sat in his lap and felt myself falling—until the moment snapped. So I did the only thing I could think to salvage myself, and I pulled away.

For a second, I thought I saw disappointment flash in his eyes at the move, but like always, Rome plastered on an unreadable smile and pretended he was fine. No matter what flickers of his true self I glimpse, he blinds me before I manage to get too close.

He's as good as I am at burying true feelings. But nothing has been the same since I walked away from him at the club that night. He hasn't left my mind, and I wish he would. I'm not capable of anything with him—or anyone.

As evidenced by my insides swimming around in the toilet.

I flush my feelings and stand, but my head immediately starts swimming. A rush that used to be frightening but now feels like control. Knowing I'm the only one with this power over my body when everyone else is always trying to take it.

Stepping out of the bathroom, I almost run into Mom, who is waiting for me in the hallway. I figured she would have left by now, but no such luck.

"Lili." She straightens the purse strap on her shoulder. "Before you go, we need to talk."

I tighten my ponytail. "Is this about the show?"

"Not exactly." Mom's lips press in a thin line, and I realize she's about to tell me something I'm not going to like. "Vaughn Davis is coming to town."

My stomach plummets at his name.

Vaughn Davis is worshipped in my social circle because he's got the kind of money that bleeds out of his pores. He's the type of man who takes anything and everything, using it until there's nothing left. And worst of all, he's my ex-boyfriend.

We were together for almost two years before I faced the truth about what kind of man he really is. And even if Mom hoped for a ring on my finger and a few babies in order to improve her social status, I knew what I had to do.

If only the breakup didn't deepen my rift with her in the process. She assumed I'd done something wrong. If only she knew the truth.

Vaughn Davis is a wolf in sheep's clothing. I'm lucky I got out with what I had left.

"You'll have dinner with him," Mom says, ignoring the fact that she knows I can't stand him.

"Dinner?" I frown.

"Don't," Mom snaps. "He's the owner of the company. This isn't the time for temper tantrums. If Vaughn Davis wants to meet with you, you'll go. And you'll behave."

Meet with me. What a loaded statement and she knows it. I've been keeping him at an arms-length distance for the year since we split, and if he wants to see me now, it's not for anything good.

"When?"

"Sunday." Mom smiles proudly at the fact that I've all but given up my fight. "Wear something nice."

She means something pretty and tight. God forbid I am not presentable for a rich man. Sometimes I wonder if Mom was always like this, or if she once had dreams of her own before it became all about mine.

"Actually, I'll have something delivered," Mom decides, pulling out her phone and typing away.

It's statements like that one that make me feel like a child. Like she thinks I'm incapable of such things as picking out my own clothes.

"Is that all?" I cross my arms over my chest.

Mom's eyes narrow, focusing on my face. She no doubt notices my colorless cheeks and the hollow flush from puking, but she doesn't say anything. Nodding instead, almost looking proud of me for slowly deteriorating.

"Get some sleep this weekend." She brushes past and walks away. "You look tired."

One final insult as she disappears.

At least I have an entire weekend to myself. Pauline is traveling to New York for the show she's choreographing after this one, so I have five whole days without someone else's schedule determining my every move. A freedom I'm basking in right now.

My phone pings, and I pull it out of my purse as a text lights up the screen.

I didn't expect to hear from him after our night at the strip club, but like the man he is, always catching me off guard, he can't seem to help himself.

Rome: Party at my house tonight, sweetheart. Worked me out of your system yet?

I wish.

He's in my veins, swimming around. He's the flicker sparking life through the butterflies in my chest. He's the apple dangling from the tree of life, tempting me. He's the headrush at the start of a downward spiral.

Rome is worse than a heartbreaker, he's out for souls. And mine seems more than willing to hand itself over.

With the burn of bile still fresh in my throat, and a familiar sourness in my gut, I tuck my phone away. I barely recognize myself anymore, and it scares me that somehow Rome does. He sees the broken girl I hide from everyone else and wants to play with her.

Rome's text falls somewhere between an offer and a threat. He knows he's got his hooks in and that I enjoy it.

Popping a mint, I make my way to my car and slowly weave out of the city. All the way to my house in the middle of nowhere. Where I know just beyond the trees is a man waiting to destroy me.

14

ROME

No response.

I unlock the screen again like the pathetic ass I am and check my messages, but there's nothing there I want to see. A hundred texts and none of them are from her.

Not sure what I expected but… something. Anything.

Women are usually clawing to get to me, but not Lili.

Even when I was knuckle-deep inside her with her pussy squeezing my fingers, she still felt unreachable. What's that all about?

This is why I don't step past the point of one night with a woman. I know what I'm good for—what I'm worth. No point thinking beyond it when I learned it at such a young age.

"You feel so good." Maxine moans and rolls off me.

She reaches for a joint on the nightstand and lights it up. The glow of the lighter turns her red hair orange.

"Here." She takes a drag and then holds it, handing the joint out to me.

I take it and let the smoke take me away. Besides music, there's nothing more relaxing than smoking and fucking. Especially when Dad's on a bender and hasn't been home in a few days.

"Feel better now?"

"You know it." *I grin at her.* "But I'd feel better if we went again."

Maxine swats at me as I try to reach for her. She's always too quick and one inch out of my grasp.

"I can't. My parents are going to flip if I'm not home by midnight."

She leans in and takes a hit of the joint straight from my hand before hopping off the bed and reaching for her jeans.

"Just stay. Who cares."

"Some of us have responsibilities." *Maxine buttons her pants and narrows her eyes.* "Besides, if they even knew where I was, they'd kill me."

"God forbid Miss Honor Roll gets fucked by trailer park trash, right?"

She frowns and pauses putting on her shirt, looking from me to my room. We both know I'm right, even if the truth is ugly. Her parents still think she's dating that douche from the basketball team who comes from the same kind of money and bullshit she does.

"Rome..." *Maxine climbs back onto my bed and crawls across it to me.* "Don't say shit like that. You know I like you."

"You like to fuck me," *I correct her.*

"Well yeah, but I also like you as a person." *She straddles my lap and plants her hands on my shoulders.* "Don't pre-

tend you aren't in it for the same reason. You were fucking Sarah just last week."

She's not lying. I was. Except I didn't like Sarah.

I'm not even sure if I like Maxine or if it's just that she's willing to come over, and I feel less alone in this dump of a house when she's here. But it doesn't matter. She's right.

"Come on, Rome." She swivels her hips in my lap.

A distraction.

I'm not smart, but it doesn't mean I'm an idiot either. For all the crap I get at school about using women, people don't realize it goes both ways.

"Fun," I say, planting my hands on her hips and wishing it meant I was actually holding a person and not just an idea I'll never fully realize.

"Exactly." She leans in and plants a barely-there kiss on my lips before hopping off me. "Tomorrow at eight?"

"Sure thing, babe," I say as she grabs her shit and barrels out the door, leaving me once more alone in my own personal hell.

I take a hit of the joint, but even that isn't enough to carry me away from my thoughts. Because she's right, if I'm honest with myself, I don't like her any more than she likes me.

She's here for the same reasons Sarah was—to fuck the bad boy and whisper to their cheerleader friends about it. And I'm here to get lost in anything that feels better than what my body's been conditioned to for my entire childhood.

So why can't I just accept that's all I have to offer? Not like there's anything good if they dug deeper down.

Use me, lose me. Doesn't matter. At least sex is something I'm good for.

"Expecting a call?" Merry nudges my shoulder.

Her eyes drop to my phone, and I realize I'm white-knuckling it.

"Nope." I shake my head and force a grin, trying to bury the fact that... She. Still. Hasn't. Responded.

What the fuck?

Merry narrows her dark eyes at me like she doesn't buy what I'm saying.

"Shouldn't you two be off somewhere fucking by now instead of sitting here obsessing about where I'm putting my dick?"

"First, gross." Merry sticks her tongue out in disgust. "I don't want to know what you do with your dick. At this point, I'm surprised it doesn't have its own passport it's so well-traveled."

"I'll take that as a compliment."

Merry rolls her eyes. "You would. And second, we already fucked in your guest room thirty minutes ago, so don't worry about us."

Noah's mouth falls open before he bursts out laughing. He's not surprised by Merry's blunt tongue by now, and apparently, her calling me out is hilarious to him.

"Touché." I wave my hand at her.

I appreciate a woman who owns her sexual needs, and Merry is definitely one of them. Not that I've ever been into her. Noah pissed on that proverbial tree the second she started working for the band, and he's my boy so I'd never do that to him.

"So, spill. Who's the girl?" Merry asks, leaning closer.

"There is no girl." I brush her off. "*Girls*—plural—always. Don't try to put your relationship shit on me."

"It's cute you think I can't tell you're lying." Merry smiles, sinking against Noah's chest. She wraps her arms around his neck, and he breathes her in.

What is with all the weird couple shit?

I look to Noah for some backing, but he's got his eyes on me like he also knows I'm full of crap.

I'm not.

It's nothing.

Lili is an itch that needs scratching. Once I finally grow some balls, I'll use her to break my celibacy streak and then throw my dick a "welcome back" party with a couple of strippers. Problem solved.

My phone lights up and my stomach jumps to my throat. But the feeling sinks when I look at the name on the screen.

Jude is calling again, not taking the hint that I'm really not in the mood to deal with the shit going on back in LA. I hit ignore and put my phone back in my pocket. Maybe if I stop staring at it for five seconds it'll do what I want it to.

The party is in full swing around us, and Noah and Merry fluctuate between making out with each other and talking with me. My house is filled with people and it's how I like it. At least, I used to. Tonight, it feels a little suffocating.

"Rome, baby." Some blonde chick with big bouncy tits and no bra plops herself in my lap.

I'm eighty percent sure I've fucked her, but who knows. Women are handsy with me, whether they've had my dick in them or not. Rockstar problems—or lack thereof.

Merry shakes her head at the girl, but I ignore her. Before Noah, Merry probably would have had her tongue down this chick's throat in no time. Screw the judgment.

"How are you, baby?" The blonde chick leans in close.

I hate it when women call me baby—or anything other than my name. It's hypocritical since I'm the king of nicknames, but whatever.

"Relaxing." I stretch my arms along the back of the couch, and she seizes the opportunity to sink against me.

She's hot and warm and something to sink into if I want to get my mind off the chick currently occupying every corner of my brain. And she's not looking at me like she wants me to love her, which makes her the perfect solution to my problems.

If only it sounded better than it does right now.

"Wanna roll?" She holds up a pill with a happy face on it and winks at me.

I usually cut the hard shit out when I'm not on tour, but I'm a piece of shit with no self-control, so I shrug and open my mouth.

She sticks the pill on my tongue and drags her finger out slowly, lingering on my bottom lip before letting it pop.

"Thanks, babe." I clench the pill between my teeth to show her before swallowing.

"On that note..." Noah stands up, lifting Merry off him, and she looks at me, disappointed.

I'm such an ass. Who pops Molly when their recovering addict friend is sitting right next to them?

Me. That's who.

Noah and Merry walk away before I can apologize for being a dick, but the blonde in my lap ignores the entire thing. She pops a pill in her own mouth and sits back with me.

I wait for it to kick in—or wait to disappear.

Either would be fine right now.

I can't handle the fact that Lili never texted me back about tonight.

It makes me want to get in my car and go hunt her down. I want to find her, prove to her that she can't escape me. I want to rip off her clothes and be in her skin.

If only the room wasn't filling with static and making it impossible to think.

The pill must be kicking in because I feel my brain expanding. A few chicks walk past and their skin is vibrating like the bass is loud enough to shake their hair follicles. Or is it mine? Something sticks in my brain, and I feel myself losing my connection with whatever tethers me to the earth.

Blonde Chick must feel it too because she's flickering like a streetlamp beside me. Or maybe she's a lightning bug.

Flick. Flick. Flick.

Her hand wraps around mine and she pulls me up.

The room might as well be magnetic because it's pulling me in all directions as Blonde Chick drags me through it. Sand sticking to the different people as I spread myself out with them. Energy spirals in a neon room.

Neon vomit.

Electric lights.

Buzzing people.

Why is that guy's neck twisting through the air?

Slowly or quickly, light is swallowed in darkness. Time doesn't exist when you live in my skin. Only I live here and it's a wormhole.

Blonde Chick's head is starting to glow as she guides me down the hallway. My arm becomes putty because I don't think my legs are moving, but my arm follows and stretches wherever she goes.

It reminds me of the Gumby episodes I used to watch as a kid. He was always stretching, never breaking. Even if breaking was all I ever did.

The blonde chick leads me into a room I should recognize because it's my house, but everything is blurry and neon. All I know is the room isn't mine. My house is built like a hotel because I built it for fucking and partying and all this... buzzing.

I blink and I'm sitting on the bed. Time in this wormhole is skipping, and the lightning bug chick is now topless in front of me. I think I've seen those tits before. And those eyes. They're so happy they make me want to forget I'm not.

She giggles as she moves down my legs and reaches for the button on my pants. Sliding the zipper down before brushing her blonde hair over her shoulder. Her tongue darts out, like she's hungry for my cock.

Her head glows, and I glow, and I burn at the sight. Because she's all light and I want darkness.

"Wait."

She pauses her hands on my jeans, so I know I did say it out loud. I grab her wrists and stop her, realizing even with her bouncy tits and wet tongue licking her lips, something is trying to crawl out of me and it's not good.

She's not right, none of this is.

She's all velvet, and I want thorns. I want barbs. I want dark eyes that cut me until I bleed.

I want Lili.

"Rome?"

I hear my name but the blonde chick's mouth isn't moving. She's half naked between my legs and I'm holding her wrists in my hands. But she's silent, tipping her head to the side.

Rome... I hear my name replay, and I realize it wasn't the blonde at all.

My gaze snaps to the doorway and I squint. "Lili?"

Maybe I've manifested her. These are some trippy drugs and I'm definitely seeing shit. But the longer I stare at her, the sharper her lines become. A shadow in the darkness with her galaxy hair and Saturn eyes swirling.

One look and she eats my entire soul in one bite.

What does it taste like?

I wonder if I ask her if she'll tell me.

Lili's gaze falls to the woman at my feet, and I follow.

Fuck, this looks bad. It is bad. Not sure why I care or if I should. Bad is what I do best.

"Sorry." It's Lili's voice again this time, but distant.

I watch her turn to leave, and I feel her tug that cord attached to my stomach. A lifeforce she's trying to snap, and it pulls me to her. I almost fall as I stand up and try to chase her down this rabbit hole she's jumping down.

My brain is twisting things.

I'm thinking in cursive but at least it's beautiful.

"Lili." I grab her arm and somehow catch the butterfly in my hand. Surprising myself when I don't break her wings off from the force of it. "Wait."

She spins around and her face is all eyes, looking at me with every emotion that exists.

She came. She actually came.

Not that she looks happy about it.

"You're here."

"I shouldn't be." She tries to pull away, but I don't let her because I caught the butterfly and that's hard enough to do once, much less twice. "Rome, please."

"That wasn't..." Fuck, what wasn't it?

It was.

Kind of.

I was stopping it.

I think?

"You don't have to explain yourself." She pulls away, and I feel myself falling into an endless oblivion.

My back hits a wall and thrusts me into another dimension where Lili stands with her hands on my cheeks and worry in her eyes.

People don't worry about me because I don't need them to. I've got thick skin and thicker emotions. I'm fucking molasses.

"Rome." Lili's eyes search my face, and I'm not sure how she's still here when she was just walking away. "What are you on?"

I think I nod, not that it's an answer. But I'm on something—like a roller coaster.

"Hey." She pulls me closer. "Come here."

Her hands wrap in mine, and we click together. I actually hear us—click.

LEGOs.

I wasn't allowed shit when I was a kid, and I always wanted them. And here she is.

Lili leads me to a room and shuts the door behind us. Looking around, I realize it's mine, and somehow, she knew. Or I told her?

Why is she here?

"You texted me."

Did she read my mind, or did I ask that out loud?

She guides me to the bed, and I lay down. The ceiling is a kaleidoscope of her face. Happy. Sad. Worried. In. Out. Distant. Near.

She places something cool on my forehead, but I'm not sure where it came from, only that it feels so good on my skin. *She* feels good on my skin.

I need her Saturn eyes more than I've ever needed anything.

I reach for Lili and pull her down onto the bed next to me, pressing my body against hers. I'll melt us together to be her whole. Only, she doesn't melt with me, staring at me instead, like she can't read my cursive thoughts.

"I'm a mess," I tell her.

Lili doesn't say anything. At least not with her mouth. Her eyes do a lot of talking. She leans back and props her head in her hand, facing me.

"Please stay."

Because I'm melting. I'm falling. I'm nothing.

She surprises me by nodding and not pulling away when I reach for her hand. One touch and she coats my whole body with every feeling.

She stares at me—in me. So long it's minutes or weeks. At some point, I'm sure I close my eyes. Or maybe they were shut all along, and I'm imagining her face as she holds my hand.

Fucking LEGOs.

15

Lili

I should have left.

Instead, I'm in Rome's bed, staring at him with less than a foot between us.

How do I keep falling down this well? Tossing myself in like a penny and wishing for things the water has no power of granting.

I stare into the abyss of the water, anyway, replaying last night in a loop. I went home, intending to sit on the couch and watch a movie. Finding myself changing and re-reading Rome's text over and over again. Until the words drew me to his house—a place I knew I didn't belong the moment I stepped inside.

People flooded every room, overflowing to the driveway like it was leaking chaos. It took ten minutes just to find him, and when I did, he was moments away from getting blown by some topless woman.

I should have run right then because nothing good comes from getting involved with a guy like Rome. But while I stood in the doorway waiting to be overcome with jealousy or anger, all I felt was disappointment.

That I thought this was more.

That I thought he cared.

When it comes to Rome, I should know better because he's always clear on his intentions. But while I spend my life able to see through every other situation, he makes my head foggy.

I should be smarter than to listen to the creeping shadows that bleed from his pores and through my skin. Because once more, he found a way to prove to me who he is—a wildcard. A man who does what he wants without caring who he steps on to get it.

And it hurt.

I should have left.

I should go now before he wakes up.

So why can't I stop staring?

Rome is sharp and painful, but it's his thorns that fascinate me. The dark parts that hurt and should scare me away make me want to hold tighter. Because then maybe I'd finally feel something that resembles life again.

The people I'm surrounded by are polished and careful and boring. Not Rome. He's impulsive, a raw nerve. He bursts at his seams while I'm strangled by my own. And somehow, he seems to be the only person who notices.

My gaze falls to his tattoos peeking out from every corner of his T-shirt. I want to feel the wrath of the demon on his forearm. I want to know the story of the wings on his neck. I want to be watched by the third eye on his throat. I want to trace him to see if he's as endless as he feels every time I'm around him. I want to taste the energy in his soul.

But before I get the chance, Rome rolls to his back and his eyes blink open. He takes a breath so deep it's like he's coming back to life. His face pinches with the pain of a man who looks like he's waking up to a world he no longer wants to be part of. Pain mixed with frustration—something he rarely shows through his carefree façade.

I wonder which nightmares haunt him more, the ones in his dreams or the memories in his head.

Rome blinks up at the ceiling, and I try to shift back because it occurs to me I'm lying really close to him. But my movement draws his attention, and his face snaps in my direction. His eyebrows furrow as he examines me in his bed.

"Good morning." I almost choke on it.

It feels small and big in the light of day, and I'm not sure how Rome makes everything feel so insignificant and overly important at the same time.

His eyebrows pinch. "You came?"

I'm not sure if he's saying it out of shock or because he forgot, but he's the one who invited me over.

"I did."

"And you stayed?" More confusion as his eyebrows pinch further.

I roll onto my side and prop my head up to face him. "You asked me to."

He doesn't seem to know what to do with that bit of information, so he rolls to his side, mirroring my position and tucking his palm under the side of his cheek to face me.

The action tugs his T-shirt up at his hips and puts his lean body on display, showing me a path I'd like to follow. Along with a peek of the twisted yin and yang tattoo on his hip.

"Why are you always running toward trouble, Lili?"

His words snap my attention back into focus, and I look up to see him smirking, likely because he just caught me checking out the lean muscles of his stomach.

I could try to deny it, but everything about Rome is gravity, pulling me toward him.

"I'm not. I guess it's just you." It's too honest, but I don't regret saying it. Rome uses women and drugs to feel high, and I use him.

The tick of amusement on his face falls with my confession, but I don't know why.

"Why do you do it?" I ask.

Rome's eyebrows furrow, and this might be the most serious I've ever seen him. "Do what?"

"Let go?" I sigh. "Last night you were so free—"

"They're called drugs, sweetheart." He smiles.

But I shake my head. "That's not what I mean. If I let my guard down, everything will fall apart, but the way you live life is so... untethered."

I'm not sure what else to call it. But it's how Rome feels, free of the strings that constantly tug at me.

Rome's smile fades as he scans my face, and I swear the air becomes palpable. Him, this close on the bed. Me, coming undone every moment I'm around him.

"My entire childhood was about maintaining control," Rome says. "It's what my father expected. One wrong move and..."

He lets his mind trail somewhere as his sentence cuts off. But the truth is there—on his face and in his voice. A past I guess still haunts him.

"My life was dictated to me for seventeen years, and that was enough."

"And your dad?"

"Is dead now." Rome's cold expression doesn't match his words.

"I'm sorry."

"I'm not," Rome huffs. "Unless you can count the fact that I wish I could have been the one to do it. Asshole finally got what he deserved."

"What's that?"

"Two bullets to the chest and a world that didn't miss him when he left it."

I've never seen this side of Rome. His carefree nature stripped down to a hard man who's hiding a lot of pain underneath.

"I'm guessing you had a complicated relationship?"

"If that's what you want to call it." His hand trails down his ribs like it hurts just thinking about it.

"Complicated or not doesn't mean it's not going to affect you."

"I'm fine." He rolls onto his back once more and closes his eyes, taking in a deep breath. It's enough that I wonder who I'm seeing in front of me, the man Rome is or the boy who was hurt in order to create him.

I roll onto my back because if I don't, I'll probably just keep staring. "I lost my dad last year."

Pausing, I wait for him to say something cordial or forced like most people do. But Rome is Rome, and he doesn't.

"We weren't close though. My family has always been more of a business than anything else. Hold up your obligations and you're rewarded. Don't and..." I trail off, not sure how to finish that statement. I've never actually been brave enough to disappoint my parents.

I turn my head to find Rome looking at me again. His dark eyes search for something deep in mine.

"And your mom?"

"She's protective," I say, not quite sure how to explain her to him. "I know she cares. I just don't think she's capable of showing it as a mother should."

Rome watches me. Absorbing every word.

How long has it been since someone has been this interested in something more than my body or my dancing?

"What about yours?" I try to divert the subject away from my messed-up family. "Are you and your mom close?"

He hasn't mentioned her, and I'm not sure how to take that.

Rome swallows hard and something dark flashes in his eyes. I've never seen eyes hold the depth his do. What I read as arrogance when I first met him, I now recognize as something more. A life lived—experience. It's stained glass he hides behind, yet in this moment, he offers me a glance through it.

"She died." Rome doesn't blink. But the words cut the air and make me flinch.

While normally I'd respond as I did with his father, I don't this time because his crisp tone stops me.

"She died giving birth to me," Rome says, letting out a breath it feels he's held a long time. "I've never told anyone that before."

"Anyone?"

He shakes his head only once, but it's enough for me to know he just trusted me with a piece of him. And even if I have so many questions, I keep them to myself. Rome isn't the type of person who opens up. But for some reason, he chose to pick this particular scab off and share it in this moment.

It's heavy. It's beautiful. It's going to haunt me.

Maybe he's not the man he tries to make me believe after all.

I reach for his hand on the bed between us, and he takes it as an invitation to pull me closer to him. He tugs me against his body, and I curl into his chest, burying myself in the distinct scent of fall. Leaves shedding and seasons changing. A sky full of colors that no camera can fully capture.

Rome buries his nose in my hair and breathes me in the way I do him. I wonder if I'm fresh air or fog. I wonder if he feels closer or farther. Because I feel all of it.

I pull back and dare to reach out and trace the scars and tattoos on his forearm. Like maybe I can feel the story out of them. Things he's hiding beneath the veiled comments he's made about his father.

Rome watches my fingers move over him, letting out a slow exhale as I trace the marks that look like cigarette burns. It takes everything in me not to ask him about them because if he wanted to share his pain with me, he would.

When I reach a jagged mark on his shoulder, he plants his hand over mine, stopping me.

"Did they hurt?" I look up at him, not clarifying if I'm talking about his scars or his tattoos because I'm honestly not sure what I want to know—just that it's everything.

Rome works his jaw, biting the inside corner of his lip. "Not more than anything else."

The amount of physical pain Rome's experienced is beyond that of most people.

"I've never even broken a bone."

Rome slides his palm up my arm, to my shoulder, brushing my hair back and tracing my unmarked skin with his fingertips. There's nothing for him to follow like there is on him. But with his eyes fixed on me, a part of me wonders what it is he's seeing.

"You've felt it all," I say. "And I'm just numb, in every way."

Except when you touch me.

But I don't dare say those words. They're too honest. They expose everything I'm not ready for. They slither into cracks I didn't realize were showing.

"There's a fine line between pain and numbness, Lili." Rome trails his hand back up until his fingers wrap around my throat gently.

His thumb rests on my pulse, making it impossible for me to hide from him.

"I'm numb in ways you'll never know." His thumb traces up over my chin, playing with my bottom lip. "At least, I thought I was."

Panic flashes in his eyes, and I wonder if deep down he can relate to how I feel around him—out of control and desperate.

And I can't help but meet his thumb with my tongue as he trails it over the crease of my mouth. I can't help but love the taste when he pushes it into my mouth, and I wrap my lips around it.

Everything about Rome is explicit and sexual. But it's the intimacy that consumes me.

How he drags his wet thumb from my mouth and runs it once more over my lips. How he hangs his head a breath away but doesn't reach for more. How he's total chaos, and somehow, in complete control.

A dichotomy.

A yin and yang like the tattoo on his stomach.

Pleasure and pain.

16

LILI

Rome's house is a labyrinth I could get lost in. While the main space is wide open with large windows that look out over the forest, the hallways seem endless. Bedrooms, bathrooms, rooms I'm not sure have a purpose. Every inch of it feeling like the man who designed it—unique.

The floors are polished concrete with large geometric rugs in the right places. Pictures scatter the walls, and they're all artistic shots of guitars, instruments, and concerts. On one wall in the living room is a shot of an audience, and the frame is made from guitar picks.

I stop in front of it and stare at the faraway faces, wondering if this is what it's like for Rome when he's up on stage. Thousands of people watching him, screaming for him, crying for him. An energy unlike anything I've experienced on stage.

And I wonder if he feels freedom in their devotion or the weight of expectations.

"You like that one?" Rome asks from the kitchen.

I look over my shoulder and find him across the space with his back to me. He's adding spices to whatever he's cooking, and it's such a normal thing it catches me off guard.

He turns to look at me and tips his chin to the image behind me.

"I do," I say, looking at the picture once more. "It's got a certain energy."

"It's a shot from our first tour." He walks over, stopping behind me and planting his hands on my shoulders. "The first tour we headlined, anyway. A photographer for some magazine took this shot and blew it up for me. One of those moments you don't want to forget, you know?"

I nod, knowing the feeling well. The first time you're on stage and all eyes are on you. It's unlike anything, a dream come true, and the pressure is terrifying.

"See that pick?" Rome points at a red one on the left side of the image. "That's mine from the show that night."

"I love it."

Looking up at him, his face is lit in a way it rarely is. Brightness that shines light into his dark eyes. Music is to Rome what dance was once to me—like the air he breathes—his lifeforce.

He looks down and his eyebrows pinch. "What?"

"Nothing." I shake my head, spinning in his arms, expecting him to let go, but he continues to hold onto me when we're face to face. "I just love hearing you talk about your music. It's inspiring."

"You're inspiring." He drags his hands down until one latches onto my own, and he lifts my arm up to spin me in a circle.

I can't help but laugh as I come to a stop in front of him, and he winks at me before releasing my hand.

"Back to breakfast before it burns." He steps away, still facing me as he points in my direction. "Now who's the distraction."

"Me?" I plant my hand on my chest. "Never."

He grins, shaking his head and walking back over to the stove. "Lies, sweetheart. Beautifully wicked lies."

My chest flutters, but I'm quickly distracted by the deep growls coming from my stomach as I follow him into the kitchen and am overwhelmed with the smell of food. I can't remember the last time I ate something that smelled nearly as decadent as this, and it makes me crave it more.

If Mom knew what I'm about to eat, she'd probably put me on an even worse diet. But I have no intention of telling her. Like all things with Rome, this feels like a secret between just the two of us.

I watch Rome mess with the food he's cooking, looking built for sin, with every painted inch of his back and chest on display. Everything about him is forbidden and indulgent.

"You weren't lying. You can cook." I drop into one of the chairs at his kitchen table, and he turns his head just enough to smirk at me over his shoulder.

His gaze travels to my legs, which are on full display in short shorts and black fishnets. My outfit is out of place in the light of day, but I wasn't expecting to still be here.

Dragging his stare back up my body, I feel the sun through the windows drawing out the blush on my cheeks. And I'm sure there's no hiding what his look does to me.

"Told you I could." He grins, turning back to the pan. "Results of limited options as a kid. It was either I learn how to cook or eat trash."

It's blunt like he is whenever he mentions his past. But it's also something I sense he doesn't share with many people, so every time he does, I'm thankful he trusts me enough to let me hear it.

"Well, I'm not complaining, seeing as I can barely fry an egg." I pick at my thumbnail. "The downside to having my meals prepped and delivered most of my life. Never had to learn my way around a kitchen."

It's rare I eat anything that isn't weighed, measured, and part of a specifically laid out plan. Food has always been for necessity, not enjoyment. Not that I admit that bit to him.

"No worries, I've got you." He winks.

A small, insignificant thing he probably throws around like compliments and nicknames, but I *feel* it. All the way in my bones. He shatters a shield I didn't realize I was holding. Those dark eyes take bites out of my carefully built barriers. Just like his tattooed hands make me lose all sense of control.

In Rome's presence, I'm lost, and I'm not sure I ever want to be found.

I shift in my seat, changing the subject before he notices what's running through my head. "Your house is almost spotless. You can barely tell there was a party last night."

A cleaning crew showed up first thing and ushered away anyone who was lingering before getting started. Which I get the impression is a regular thing.

"*Barely?*" Rome scoffs at the word, then smiles wide. "Guess I need to pay them more then."

I almost roll my eyes but catch myself, and Rome shakes his head.

"What?" I cross my arms over my chest.

"It's cute how you try to pretend you're never affected."

How is it I'm always so transparent to him?

"Cute?"

He shrugs a shoulder, going back to stirring the sausage in the pan.

I watch him move around the kitchen, grabbing things out of the refrigerator and cabinets, pouring me coffee. His face neutral, calm, relaxed. His muscles flexing with every movement. It's illicit, while also completely innocent, mirroring how being around him makes me feel.

Rome finishes cooking, sliding a plate in front of me. The food looks like it could be on the cover of a cooking magazine and smells to die for. Dropping into the chair across from me, he watches me pick up my fork and slide the food around my plate.

It might look incredible, but I'm also aware it's at least four times the amount of food I'm normally allowed to eat in one sitting. I can only imagine the butter, oil, and calories. Pushing it around, I try to focus on the vegetables and eggs, hoping he doesn't notice.

But when my eyes meet his, there's the faintest frown on his face as he watches me between his own bites.

"It's delicious," I say with a smile, trying to reassure him because it's not his fault I can't look at food without seeing numbers.

Besides, it really is amazing. The balance of spice, flavor, and heat is overwhelming in the best way.

"Really," I say, taking another bite. "This is incredible. You're so bad for me."

That at least makes him smile as he goes back to focusing on his own plate.

We eat in silence, but it doesn't take long before my stomach starts to ache. At least, I think it's my stomach. It might just be the idea of food filling me up, and knowing I can't allow it.

Setting down my fork, I push my plate away and lean back.

"Not going to eat more?" He leans back and kicks an ankle up on his opposite knee, planting his hands on the back of his head, watching me.

His question catches me off guard. In my line of work, food isn't something we talk about. There's an unspoken understanding that we're all starving for our dreams. And it's perfectly acceptable to watch people waste away physically and mentally in the process—even if it's also entirely fucked up.

But like Rome does with everything, he forces the question in front of me and makes me face the reality head on.

"Show prep. It's exhausting, but you have to do what you have to do, right?"

He nods, not looking amused, but not pushing the subject either. He unlaces his hands from the back of his head and leans forward.

Reaching his finger out, he plucks at my fishnets. "You want something more comfortable? Not that I'm complaining about the outfit because, fucking hell, you make my head spin. But it's just you and me."

I can't help the heat that rushes to my cheeks at his comment. "You're just trying to get me out of my clothes, aren't you?"

It's a joke.

Or wishful thinking?

"Caught me." He smiles, and it lights up his whole face. "Or maybe I really am a gentleman."

"Sure you are." I roll my eyes and can't hold back my laugh.

Rome shakes his head, looking younger in this light. Something about seeing him in his own element, just the two of us, has me more comfortable than I've been around him. He feels less like a projection and more like a person who wants me to see him beneath the layers. And it makes me want to dive deeper into him. To have it all.

We've shared a bed. He's had his fingers inside me. He's given me the best orgasm of my life. But that's it. And I can't help but want more. Even if there's a risk that the moment we do, we'll both snap out of this.

"Come on." Rome stands up and holds out his hand to me. "I'm sure I can find you something to change into."

I place my palm in his and his calloused fingers rub the back of my hand. Years of making music has imprinted on his skin, but he doesn't seem to mind these marks on his body like the others he buries in ink.

Sun shines through the large kitchen windows, and I see everything in broad daylight as I stand to face him. Even with tattoos covering Rome's neck to hands, there are markings buried beneath them. A healed gash on his side, burn marks on his arms, and random scars scattered throughout.

It hurts to look at them, which is a selfish thought. He's the one who endured their pain. But as much as I wish I could take it away, I'm well aware they make Rome who he is. Strength and survival. Shadows in his eyes and marks on his soul.

Experience, where I'm sheltered.

Rome guides me down the hall to his room and doesn't stop until we're standing at his closet door. He steps inside, and I wait for him to come back. When he does, he's holding a pair of grey sweatpants and a black Enemy Muse T-shirt.

"Branding me, huh?" I look from him to the shirt.

"Nah, if I wanted to brand you, I could think of more permanent ways." He steps close and my heart starts to race.

"You don't have to do this; I should get home soon anyway."

"Do you have rehearsal today?"

I shake my head.

"Plans?"

"No."

He shrugs. "Then stay. Chill."

It's a loaded offer, and we both know it. But he doesn't step back, and I don't either. Playing the same game neither of us has been willing to quit since the day we met.

"Unless you're scared that is." Rome winks, and I feel it like fingers crawling into me.

I answer him in action, taking the clothes from his hands and walking around him toward the bed. "As I said before—you don't scare me, Rome Moreno."

He watches me circle the room, swallowing hard as I pop the button on my shorts and drag them down my hips with my fishnets. Sitting back on his bed, I peel them off the rest of the way before slipping off my shirt.

While I'm often undressed in front of people in my profession, with Rome it's different. He makes me want more.

Just. One. Taste.

It would be enough, right?

Rome walks over and kneels directly in front of me at the foot of the bed. He takes the sweatpants and holds them for me to slip my feet into. I stand as he draws them up my legs, but he stays where he is. And something about me standing here while he kneels in front of me is the most erotic thing I've experienced.

I have no doubt Rome could show me things beyond what I can even imagine. A world I don't dare to dip my toe into. But right now, I want to.

Finally, he stands and helps me slip the T-shirt over my head. And I'm not sure why he's dressing me when he seems to enjoy doing the opposite more.

He rolls the sweats a few times to tighten them around my slim waist, while I make a knot of the T-shirt to crop it. I'm swimming in this outfit, but it feels good.

It feels like Rome.

He pauses with his hands on my hips, and we're so close I'm forced to look up. Reaching for his face, I dare to place my hand on his cheek.

"Tell me something real, Rome."

"What do you want to know?"

I bite down on my lower lip and his eyes follow. "What's the real reason you haven't tried to sleep with me? Are you really that afraid to work me out of your system?"

The longer we play this game, the more I realize it's no longer a game at all. I want him in ways I shouldn't, but I'm scared he's not feeling the same.

Rome's smile falls, and the air is thick. He reaches up and brushes my messy hair behind my ear. I've washed off my makeup, and there's nothing special about how I look right now, but his eyes on me make me feel like something exquisite.

"Maybe I'm worried about the opposite," he says with a vulnerability I'm not used to hearing from him. His hands trace down my hips, and then he holds both my hands in his. "LEGOs, and all."

I have no idea what that means, and he doesn't elaborate, so I just shake my head. "LEGOs," I repeat.

I'm about to step back, but he catches me so fast my body crashes into him as he claims my lips. Suddenly, fully, completely. One hand wraps into my hair while the other snakes around my lower back and holds me tightly to him.

He kisses me like he's after more than just one breath—he wants them all. And even if it's trouble, I want him to have them.

I part my lips, and his shadows find their way from his heart to my lungs. From my blood to my bones. He's chaos sneaking in with intentions of ripping me apart.

Rome drags both of his hands to my face, and I'm a raw nerve. I melt against his firm body as his hips press his hard dick against my stomach. I want him—I need him. No matter the price.

But just as his hands move down and he cups my ass, the doorbell cuts through the silence of the house and tears the moment in two.

I pull back, and Rome's eyebrows furrow before his eyes go wide.

"What day is it?"

"Saturday."

He runs his palm over his face and shakes his head. "The band is coming over. Noah's going to ink Adrian, and we were gonna chill. I totally forgot."

"Oh. I can go then." I try to pull back, but his grip on my waist tightens.

"Stay."

He wants me to stay again.

I don't stay for anyone; all I do is go.

I'm constantly on the move—my body, my life. I belong to dance, to the company, to my family. I belong to the world, not myself. I don't grow roots. Yet Rome makes me want to plant myself under his skin like I could be the ink he cherishes.

I should run now while I've still got the strength to leave. I should never look back.

But like I'm lost in this labyrinth of a house, I'm lost in him, and I don't want out.

17

ROME

Fuck the band.

I don't care if we've had these plans for a week. Or that I was the one who offered up my house when we decided on them. With Lili's petite body pressed against mine, her ass in my hands, and my tongue in her mouth, I really couldn't give two shits about any other obligation.

Her lips on mine made every other care vaporize.

She's a high and I'm intent on chasing her to the end of it.

Whatever sparked from her kiss was more than what I'm used to feeling. It wasn't just a means to an end. It was her lips on mine, her teeth dragging my lower lip, her moans vibrating in my mouth, and her soul shaking my bones.

I needed every bit of her kiss.

Every bit of her.

And I had her in my arms. Lightning in a bottle. The other side of purgatory right there in front of me.

Until the doorbell rang and tore my intentions to shit.

I knew asking the band to leave would just make them suspicious, so I was forced to go with my only other option and ask her to stay.

Knowing the band is going to ask questions. Knowing they'll think I'm treating Lili like my girlfriend when she isn't. Knowing I don't let women hang around the band for those exact reasons.

Except...

I don't fucking care.

"Our boy is growing up." Merry laughs as she and Eloise follow me into the kitchen to grab beers while Noah sets up to tattoo Adrian's arm.

"Boy? Try grown ass man," I shoot back.

Eloise knocks me in the shoulder. "Sure."

I need a drink if I'm going to be subjected to this crap when I'm still coming down from last night's high.

"Nice try, Rome." Merry laughs. "But I'm not buying whatever this shit is you're spewing. Last I saw you some blonde chick popped a pill in your mouth. But now here you are with a fancy dancer walking around in your clothes like this is *her* house..."

"Not just any fancy dancer," Eloise points out. "The one renting *my house*. The one you were supposed to stay far away from."

"Fuck off." I shake my head and take a drink of my beer. "We're hanging out, that's all."

"Mm-hmm," Merry hums. "*Hanging out*, Rome's favorite pastime."

"It's not like that."

I regret the words as soon as they're out because if they think I'm just fucking Lili, they won't dig too far into it.

Eloise's eyes widen, and she freezes with her water an inch from her mouth. "Wait, you aren't sleeping with her? Like seriously?"

"*Like seriously*," I mock, a little pissed off because if they hadn't shown up, I'd probably be in bed railing her right now.

Lili looked so good standing in my room in her itty-bitty black lace bra and panties. But she looked even better swimming in *my* clothes. Looking like she belonged in them. My restraint snapped, and even if I'd just dressed her, I was ready to strip her down again.

"Holy shit." Merry smiles, holding her beer out to Eloise. "Never thought I'd actually see the day."

Eloise taps her water glass against Merry's drink.

"Don't get any ideas. You're seeing nothing."

"Uh huh." Eloise shakes her head, grinning. "It's all over your face, Rome, whether you like it or not. First Sebastian, then Noah, then Adrian. The last bachelor standing is about to fall. I'm calling it."

"Don't compare me to those punks."

Both girls frown, but it's the truth. Their men are whipped for them and it's pathetic. I might like Lili because I'm not allowed to have her, but that's it.

"Let me get this right then." Eloise leans forward on the counter, holding her hand up to count on her fingers. "You're hanging out regularly," she points at one. "She slept in your bed last night," she points to another. "And now she's walking around in your clothes. But you're not having sex and it means nothing?"

"Exactly." Wow, that burned on the way out.

What the fuck?

"Sure thing, Rome." Merry hip-checks me as she passes by, and I follow them back into the living room.

Adrian is sitting in a recliner, and Noah is setting up his tattoo gear beside him. Apparently, now my house is not only party central but also a tattoo parlor.

Lili watches it all intently, asking Noah question after question about tattoos, equipment, and anything else that seems to pop into her head. Both Noah and Adrian are smiling, and I can't explain what it does to see her fitting in with my band like she is.

We're rock stars for fuck's sake.

She's a prissy dance princess.

We don't belong in the same room, much less the same world. So why do I want to paint my ribs with her smile so I don't ever forget it? Why do I feel instantly protective of her?

Like this morning, when she pushed away her breakfast when she was only a quarter of the way through. I couldn't help that my vision turned red toward all the people in her life who made her feel like she had to restrict to feel perfect.

I'd rather watch her indulge. With me—for me.

I want to open her up and fill her with all the things I get the impression she denies herself. I want to make her see the good and bad because I believe she's strong enough to survive it. And it's fucking selfish.

Merry and Eloise sink onto the couch with Sebastian and Cassie. Cassie whispers something to Merry, and they both look from Lili to me.

At least Cassie didn't also follow me into the kitchen. Because the full force of the three of them is too much. And for the first time ever, I'm thankful for Sebastian's death grip on her leg.

Cassie laughs, and Sebastian pulls her closer, kissing the top of her head.

In the past, I've only ever looked at the two of them wondering why they thought it was a good idea to be in an exclusive relationship. But right now, watching him hold her, something tightens in my stomach.

I don't see Sebastian being a pussy-whipped bitch all of a sudden. He seems at peace. He seems genuinely happy. And I want that for him, don't I?

I know firsthand what a mess Sebastian was before he met Cassie. Even if I thought it was total bullshit for him to fall so hard and fast for her. And even if I thought he was changing everything about himself just to be with her. I see it now. It wasn't that she changed him, it's that she saw the version of him even his friends didn't, and she helped him drag that side out.

Too bad I'm not Sebastian. My shit goes too deep for some chick to save me.

As if my body revolts at the thought, my gaze moves to Lili, and I realize she's watching me. Those eyes of hers are magnets drawing out the lead that weighs me down inside.

I sink down onto the empty couch opposite Sebastian and Cassie as Merry makes her way over to Noah's side. Noah is fully focused on the warped demon he's drawing on Adrian's forearm, but he pauses long enough to look up to Merry for a kiss.

I'm surrounded. It's pathetic.

So why do I stare at Lili hard enough to telepathically draw her pretty little self over to me?

Fucking magnetic.

She leaves Noah's side as I stretch my arms out across the back of the couch, and she practically glides toward me. I'd think she's an angel by the grace of her movements if I wasn't smart enough to know she's actually the phantom of all things out of my reach. The whisper of all things too good for me.

Lili is swimming in my T-shirt and sweats as she sinks down on the couch next to me, and I feel a few eyes in the room on us. But I can't take mine off the dark orbs drawing me in.

Every universe has a starting point. And while I thought I had already left mine far behind, one look in Lili's eyes makes me wonder if I haven't even seen the beginning of my own world yet.

"Your band's friendly." Lili smiles, sinking against the back of the couch with barely any space between us. Her hair brushes my arm, and I have to grip the cushions to not reach for her and finish what we started in my bedroom.

"Figured you'd like them." I shrug.

"Why's that?"

"I'm the asshole. If I haven't scared you off yet then they won't." I chuckle, realizing I'm not sure why I haven't scared her off yet.

I'm an idiot about most things but smart enough to know what she probably sees when she looks at me. I'm a man who runs through women, indulges in whatever I feel like spending the days drowning in. I'm a trainwreck.

I'd think she wants to fix me if she didn't seem so damn curious looking at me as-is.

Lili doesn't try to hide from my broken parts or pretend they don't exist. The more I show her, the more she wants to see. Wants to stare my demons in the eyes like she's not afraid to face them with me.

And it's fucking terrifying.

"Is that what you've been trying to do, Rome? Scare me away?"

"I shouldn't have to try so hard."

"But you will." It's not a question because she can already read me too well.

Her mouth is in a firm line, drawing out the sharp lines in her heart-shaped face. And with one sentence she reveals my truth. I'd rather scare her away than face what this is becoming because I don't give people power over me anymore.

A thought that eats away at my nerve endings when she's looking in my eyes like she sees everything I hate showing people.

I've never been more tempted to piece together someone just to break them into a million pieces.

"So what do you think?" I tip my chin to where Noah is tattooing Adrian, changing the subject.

Lili almost frowns, but catches herself, as she follows my gaze. "It's interesting. I didn't realize rock stars doubled as tattoo artists."

"Too much downtime when recording and riding on buses. We pick up weird hobbies."

"So then what's yours?"

I can't help the smirk that climbs my face. "That might be more than you can handle, sweetheart."

She bends her knee and twists to face me on the couch. "Try me."

This girl has no defense mechanisms. Always asking questions she won't like the answer to, and I can't seem to lie to her.

I tip my head back, leaning it against the couch but facing her, knowing a smart man would know when to keep his mouth shut or sugarcoat shit. But I'm not smart when it comes to her, and I can't help my desire to show her exactly who I am just to see how deep she's willing to get.

"I don't have specific hobbies, per se. When I'm horny, I fuck. When I'm bored, I party. When I'm lonely, I surround myself with people. The perks of not having an addictive personality. I indulge when I want to. I chill when I want to. I don't get hung up on things. All shit comes and goes eventually. I'm just here to enjoy the ride."

Lili's eyes narrow like she's trying to see through my statement, but all that lies there is truth. I don't get attached, which is why my fascination with her is so damn irritating.

"Sounds like you've got it all figured out," Lili says, but it doesn't sound like a compliment.

I reach over and trace my fingers on the back of her hand, drawing circles over her soft skin. Her breath remains even, but the faintest blush climbs her neck, and I'd like to drag my tongue over her just to get a taste of it.

I'm not a liar. I don't get addictions. I don't get attached. I don't obsess. Everything is temporary, from the people I surround myself with to the breath in my lungs.

Then I met Lili, and I can't get her out from under my skin.

"I thought I did."

Before I met Lili—I really thought I fucking did.

18

Lili

Rome walks the band out of his house while I wait for him on the couch.

Today didn't go anything like I expected it to. While I thought his band might be like many of the cold celebrities I've met in my line of work, they were warm, kind, and comfortable to be around. In their element, they're laid back and surprisingly friendly. The girls played a game of cards while the guys hung out and Noah tattooed.

They're nothing like the uptight world I'm used to.

Except now, as Rome files them out the door, the tension from earlier creeps back into the room because once more we're alone.

I should probably change back into my clothes and leave. I've been here all day. It's well past dinner, so I might be overstaying my welcome. But after the interruption this morning in Rome's room, I can't seem to drag myself away until I know for sure that's what he wants.

Rome's eyes meet mine when he walks back into the room, and the heavy weight in them is all consuming. He circles around the island in the kitchen, quietly watching me as he fills a glass with ice water, taking a long drink before coming to meet me on the couch.

I'm propped against one of the arms, facing him, and he sinks at my feet with an arm stretched along the back in my direction. He takes another drink, drawing ice into his mouth with it and clicking it over his teeth as it slowly melts.

He chews what's left, swallowing it down. "How long has it been since you've fucked someone?"

I'm caught off guard by his question and can't help pulling my knees to my chest as if it offers some kind of protection from his blunt delivery.

Rome smirks at my obvious reaction but doesn't take it back.

He's pushing again. Doing what he does best—seeing if he can get me to the point where I'll run.

"A little over a year," I answer honestly.

I'm sure to him it sounds like a lifetime, but sex is one area we're clearly different. My life is all about control and resisting urges, while his is pure indulgence.

I wait for some kind of reaction, but he doesn't flinch. His gaze holds mine and the intensity is almost unnerving.

"Why?" I ask when he doesn't say anything for too long.

Rome takes another drink of water, the ice once more clicking against his teeth. I'm tempted to take a drink myself and feel the coolness on my own tongue, but I don't move. I don't flinch as he chews another cube and rests the glass on his thigh.

"Just curious," he finally answers.

"How long's it been for you?"

I'm not sure I want to know the answer, but he's the one who started this conversation, and I can't help my own curiosity.

He smirks. "Thirty-three days."

"Someone's counting." I might know it's been a year for me, but that's a round number. I'm not checking off the days like he seems to be. "Is that some sort of record for you or something?"

He shrugs one shoulder, tipping the glass of water side to side, watching the ice move around. "Not one I've been working for or anything."

"You just do what you want."

While I resist and hold back, he devours, regardless of the consequences.

Rome nods once, his dark stare meeting mine. "Until I met you."

"What does that mean?"

Rome turns to face me, his arm still up on the couch. His jaw tenses, and I can't help but let my gaze drop to the third eye tattoo on his throat. The full force of him watching me.

"You complicate things."

"I'm not trying to." Not that I mind the way his confession sends my head spinning.

Swirling the ice around in the glass, he keeps his focus on me. "You're too good for all this shit. And if I was a good guy, it would make me let you go. But all it seems to do is make me want to fuck you up more."

His eyes narrow, and I'm about to open my mouth to argue, but he ticks his head, assessing me and stopping my thoughts in their tracks.

"If you were smart, you'd have taken my warning and run when you had the chance." He bites his lip.

"So, you're saying I no longer have a chance?"

The corner of Rome's mouth curls up, and I feel my insides liquify. "I don't know. Do you?"

I swallow hard but can't answer because it would either be too revealing or a lie.

"Tell me, when's the last time you did something *you* wanted, Lili? For yourself, no one else."

"This morning."

If I'd have been smart, I would have left, but instead, I got tangled in this web. Rome threaded my mind like the ink laces his skin—everywhere. Embedded.

Rome drops his hand from the back of the couch to my knee, tracing circles over it, and on instinct, I feel myself opening in all the ways I shouldn't.

"I don't lose control with people," Rome says, his eyes on my leg and his fingers tracing it. "And that's all you make me want to do."

This might be about sex. This might be about more. I don't care because underneath, the answer to either of those things is a need I've never had fulfilled. Tipping my legs open a little further, I watch as he drags his hand from my knee to the inside of my thigh, gripping tightly, like if he doesn't hold on, he's going to fall apart.

"You shouldn't do that, Lili," he warns.

"Are you telling me you're already calling chicken?" I challenge, hoping he isn't.

We're standing on the train tracks, and it's headed straight for us. Headlights closing the distance. Air leaving my lungs. Bracing for impact.

I'm not sure why Rome's been holding back, but all it does is make me want to be the temptation that breaks him. And I want him to be the hammer that shatters the glass around me because I'm curious if I can survive.

"One chance, sweetheart." Rome smirks, one hand holding my thigh as the other one grips the glass. Beads of water drip over his skin. "Because if you don't run now, I might not let you."

I lean forward, which opens my legs further, bringing my face right in front of his. "Do your worst."

The dark that drinks his eyes seeps through me. Amusement, challenge, ferocity flood his gaze. One shift and I'm reacquainted with the man I first met on the sidewalk. The one who wasn't holding back. The one who would eat me alive and enjoy every moment of my destruction.

"Can't say I didn't warn you." Rome leans back against the couch with a wicked smirk on his face. "Take off your clothes, Lili."

Five words, and I see the train's headlights again. I feel it moments away from crashing into me. I feel the moment like a palpable thing playing out in Rome's eyes as he waits to see if I'm going to run or meet him. And I want more than anything to soak in his chaos and prove myself.

I stand up, sweeping my hair to one side of my shoulder, feeling his eyes on me more intently than they've ever been. I reach for the hem of his band's T-shirt first, stripping it off in one movement, appreciating how Rome's gaze trails my bare skin. He doesn't so much as flinch as he watches me toss it to the side.

I spin until my back is to him, wrapping my hair over my shoulder to expose my back, and I reach for the clasp on my bra, unhooking it and slipping it off one shoulder. Rome's gaze is fixed on every movement, every piece of clothing coming off. And I want so badly to be on display for him. For the sight of me to be the cause of his racing heart.

Maybe it's the performer in me, or maybe it's whatever his eyes are doing to the blood in my veins, but as I toss the bra to the side and swish my hair over my back once again, I can't take my eyes off him.

Teasing, just so I can drown in his reaction.

There's no doubt in my mind this man can possess me without so much as a touch, and I want all of it.

Reaching for the band of the sweatpants, I hook my thumbs in, catching my thong with it, and bending at the hips as I strip them all the way down my legs. Pausing when I'm fully bent in front of him, knowing my ass and pussy are on full display and loving the power it gives me over a man who makes women beg.

Straightening back up, I step out of the sweats, and I'm fully naked, standing in front of him.

I turn with all my vulnerability, knowing he's going to do what he wants, and anxious for it.

Rome's gaze travels the full length of my body. No secrets, no holdbacks, no reservations. He claims me with one snap of his gaze.

"You should have run, sweetheart." He takes another drink of his water before leaning forward and setting it on the table behind me.

In one swift movement, he grips my ass and tugs me toward him, so I have no choice but to fall forward, gripping the couch over his shoulder. But his hands hold my hips at his face, and without warning, he dives his mouth to my pussy. Only, instead of feeling the heat of his tongue like I expect, I'm met with a cool chill that sends a shiver through the full length of my body.

"Rome." I grip his shoulders.

He rolls the ice in his mouth over me. The alternating sensations of his tongue mixed with the frozen cubes throw my body into chaos. He grips my hips and twists us, tossing me back down onto the couch, before once more diving between my legs. It's more than I can take.

His tongue rolls the ice over my clit before he slides it down and drives it inside me with a coolness that somehow burns hot. For all the credit Rome gets for what he can do with his fingers, the man works his mouth like he's out to ruin me.

I dig my fingers into his scalp, trying to hold on—or maybe I'm trying to let go. I'm falling apart around him. Becoming the pieces he warned me he'd shatter me into.

Rome's tongue goes wild as the ice melts between my legs, soaking the couch and his face as he works my clit like he's pissed at the fact that he can't maintain composure around me anymore. And I want to be the release for his rage. I want to feel the full wrath of him losing control.

His fingers grip onto my ass, and he holds me against his tongue and thrashes it. Relentlessly flicking over my clit and then driving inside me until I scream so loud it's silent. And I fall apart just as he warned me I would. I shed every last bit of sanity as I dig my fingernails into his scalp. I'm left as nothing more than a mess beneath him, frantic and panting.

When I stop shaking, he finally lifts, kneeling between my legs and wiping his mouth with the back of his hand, grinning like he's proud of himself. As he should be because I think I saw actual stars as I left my body.

Reaching down for the button on his pants, he smirks at me through hooded eyes. "I could get drunk on the taste of your insanity on my tongue."

"Is that what I taste like?"

Rome reaches into his pants and strokes himself.

I see the same bulge I felt when I was sitting on him at the club, making me swallow at the nervous energy that rushes through me. He unzips his pants so slowly it feels like slow motion.

"Insanity. Chaos. It's you coming apart. I think I'd like to do it again." He tugs his pants down, freeing his large cock. And that's when I catch sight of a bar running through the thick head, making me wonder if I'm really up for this challenge. "Except this time when I ruin you, I think I'll do it with my dick."

19

Lili

Rome strokes his pierced dick, forcing a bead to drip from the tip. The sight alone makes me feel like I'm going to pass out.

It might be that I'm still coming down from the rush of my climax, but sounds are fuzzy in my ears and my head spins at the sight of him. He kneels over me with his dick in his hand, stroking it, watching me. He's still clothed besides his unbuttoned pants, and I see his tattoos travel even further down.

"Scared yet, sweetheart?" Rome asks, smirking at me, taunting me to see if I'll call chicken on this whole thing and run for the hills.

What he doesn't realize is I'm too far in for that to happen. Knee-deep with a man who is a sinkhole. Carefully standing here, knowing at any moment the ground beneath my feet is bound to cave.

I want to fall.

I want to break apart.

I want to be pieces for him.

I sit up and climb up to my knees, facing him. For some reason, it makes his smile drop, confusion pinching his face. I reach for the hem of his T-shirt, and he releases himself long enough for me to pull it up and over his head, revealing every inch of him.

His chest is a map of his past, etched in secrets and pain. And as I run my fingers over his skin and down his stomach, I want to fall into the history of a man who has traveled so many paths, I fear he no longer recognizes his own.

I move both hands downward until I'm wrapping one around his dick and feeling the full size of him. He swallows hard, watching me. My other hand traces the scar on his waist, feeling the ridges of something that must have hurt more than anything I've experienced, even if I don't know the story.

But while I explore the feel of him hard and hungry in my hands, my eyes don't leave his.

"I'm terrified." It's almost a whisper.

It's honest.

I'm exposed.

He's too much for me, and I'm too much for him. Scars bleeding all over each other the closer we get. Dreams we each chased, that somehow also shattered us into unrecognizable pieces. Two people searching for whatever exists on the other side of giving up everything for the one thing we had to have.

Rome wraps a hand over mine and forces me to squeeze his dick harder, while his other one finds my jaw.

"Fuck." He tips my mouth up so his hangs directly over me. In his eyes I find lust and need, but also pain, and I'm desperate to know where it's stemming from. "You shouldn't let me do this."

But it's not an out because he leans down and catches my mouth with his. His teeth sink into my lower lip and there's no opportunity to ask why, or question if he's right. We're a train colliding at top speed, and I feel the full force strike me.

His grip tightens on my jaw, and it edges on painful as he matches the pressure with his hand on his dick. It must hurt him, but I get the feeling that's what Rome wants. He lives for the things that remind him he's alive. He chases pain like he chases pleasure. Everything with him hurts and feels good. It heals and it breaks.

He lets go long enough to strip off his pants and offer me the full sight of him, solid lean muscle covered in tattoo ink. A work of art I can't stop staring at.

Sitting on the couch again, he pulls me onto his lap and I'm straddling him. His dick is almost unbearably large as I grind against it. The piercing at the top rubbing against my clit each time I roll my hips. He's not even inside me yet, and I feel like I'm going to black out from the feel of him.

"You like it?" He plays with my hair as I move my hips.

"Mm-hmm," I hum, drowning in the sensation. "Is it going to hurt?"

The question might make me sound inexperienced, but I've never been with a man like Rome, much less one with metal running through the head of his dick.

Rome grips my sides and guides my hips over him until the feel of the piercing on my clit once more sends my eyes rolling in the back of my head.

"I know all about pain, sweetheart." He does the motion again, and I feel the tension building. "Trust me when I say this is for your pleasure."

He reaches for the table next to the couch and opens a drawer, pulling out a condom. I'm not sure how I feel about the fact that he probably has them tucked in every corner of his house, but him pressing his hips up to grind his dick against me has me forgetting everything.

Lifting my hips, he carefully rolls the condom over his dick, and I have to raise further so he can position himself beneath me.

This is going to hurt, there's no doubt about it. His thickness alone looks like he might rip me open. But Rome is Rome, and without giving me a chance to think about it, he shoves my hips down over him, and I'm impaled by the intensity of all things him.

My scream is drowned out by his mouth on mine, and like he senses my need to adjust, he slowly helps me circle my hips while he traces my lips with his tongue.

Even relaxed from him going down on me, it's hard to adjust to his size. I have to breathe deep and focus on the sensations of his hands on my skin and his teeth on my lips. God, he feels good. I keep circling, twisting, like a dance, and I'm losing myself in the motion.

Rome holds my face with both his hands as I ride him slowly, not breaking the kiss, as if he's feeding on my moans. His fingers dig into my neck, and I'm lightheaded from the pressure, but he doesn't let up.

I start to ride him faster, chasing the pleasure mixed with the pain. Chasing him down the dark alley and hoping this is enough for me to find my way out the other side again.

"That's it, baby." He bites my bottom lip so hard I swear I almost bleed. "Take me."

He moves his hands down my chest, pausing on my breasts and tugging my nipples between his thumbs and fingers, making me scream from the incredible pain of it. Releasing them, he moves all the way to my hips, holding me hovering a few inches over him so he can lift his hips and drive up to meet me.

His heels dig in as he thrusts harder. A merciless claiming as the piercing at the head of his dick hits a secret spot deep inside. All other thoughts and feelings drown out as he slams into me over and over again, relentlessly hitting a place that makes me fall off the edge of the universe.

I have to grip my fingers onto his shoulders, and I'm digging my nails in hard enough to draw blood. But it doesn't make him flinch or pull away. Instead, his face lights up with a wicked grin.

He lifts me up and throws me onto my back, stretching my leg up by my head as he climbs on top of me and thrusts in again. He reaches a hand up to his shoulder, and when he hovers it between us, I see the blood my nails drew from his skin.

Smirking, he rubs his hand up my leg, and it smears the blood over my skin as he wraps his fingers around my ankle.

"You want to hurt me?" Rome smiles, leaning in to bite the tender skin at the base of my neck. "You're not ready to play those games."

He grips my ankle tighter and holds it up over my head, forcing my legs into the splits as he thrusts in harder, stretching my flexibility to the limits. His eyes watch as his dick moves in and out of me, and it's so erotic seeing my body stretch around him.

"Fuck, Lili," he grunts, and I feel his body trying to meet me where I'm at. "You're so fucking tight for me. This sweet pussy is going to strangle my dick."

His words, mixed with his piercing hitting me so deep inside I didn't know the spot existed, is all it takes to send me over the edge. Rome holds me wide open as I come apart for him. And as my climax hits and my insides get sensitive and tender, all he does is fuck me harder.

He fucks me like he wants to destroy me for anyone else.

And he does, as his body collides with mine and our eyes lock gazes. I see past the rock star. I see past the scars. I see past the persona.

And all that's left is Rome. A man who chases life with such fullness he resurrected the dead parts within me.

His jaw clenches, and I bring my hands to his face—to hold him or this moment, I'm not sure. I want to frame it and keep him when this passes, and when I leave this city. I want to remember that even though there was nothing left but dead soil inside me, someone had the power to grow something better with their sunlight.

Rome's speed slows as he dips his lips down for a kiss. And even though the hard thrusts have eased, there's more intensity to it. He crawls inside me and burrows himself. He hands me a part of him. His thrusts get uneven, and he clenches as he spills inside me before collapsing.

But his lips don't leave my own.

We live in this secret as long as we stay like this. A moment that doesn't need to end. With no room for air and no space for regret.

His fingers release my ankle, and I bend my leg, sitting it over his shoulder as he holds me.

I'm paralyzed with fear all of a sudden. It rushes through me, the same way my need for him flooded my system. Because I don't want to let go. I don't want to feel anything other than what he brings out in me.

Rome breaks the kiss and lifts up, hovering over me, and I trace the tattooed wings on his throat with my fingers as he does. His expression is tight, and I can't tell if it's him already shutting down because it's still so difficult for me to read him.

"So..." I let out a breath that sounds almost like a chuckle, even if deep down I don't feel the lightheartedness of it. "Am I finally out of your system?"

Why I'm asking him this while he's still inside me is baffling, but I can't help myself. I need to know if I'm in his veins too, swimming through his blood.

He traces a finger along my hairline, tugging stray hairs off my face, and looking me over while I memorize this expression and hope the darkness in his eyes doesn't do what he said it would.

"Am I out of yours?" he asks in return, instead of offering me an answer, which hurts a little when I need his truth.

But, I brought this on myself.

"I don't think so."

"Good," he says, brushing his lips against my mouth. "Because you're like fucking fuel in mine."

One sentence, and even though I know he's going to incinerate it, I hand what's left of my soul over to Rome Moreno.

20

ROME

You can hear a song a hundred times and think nothing of it. It could be background noise. But all it takes is hearing it once at the right moment for it to strike a chord and make an impact.

One time when the sounds hit differently, and the lyrics give purpose to something in your chest. And in that moment, you don't just listen, you feel it. So deep that years later the same song holds the power to drag you back in time.

Sex is like music to me. Always has been. It's an expression, a release, a changing of energy. It's a way to pass the time or get familiar with a different side of yourself and someone else.

I've sampled every genre, appreciated a spectrum of sounds and lyrics. All bright colors and good feelings.

But then there was one.

A beat, unlike anything I'd heard before. A song with new lyrics, and a tempo all its own. Soft and controlled with an undercurrent of wild energy.

Lili fills my silence with her heartbeat. She's neon lights painting a dark room. Moans and sharp inhales and chaos. I could listen to her beautiful sounds all night.

Fucking perfection.

"You done yet?" Lili tries to peek down at her ribs.

I hold my hand so she can't see what I'm doing. "Not yet."

She laughs in an octave that shocks my system. The sound is melodic. Haunting the most broken parts of my bones.

I trace the Sharpie up her rib and continue working on my design, trying to ignore the fact that even if I told her I'd be over her the second I came inside her, I'm nowhere near feeling that way yet.

"Your skin was made to be inked." I draw another line, loving how the dark marker stands out on her skin.

"I don't think my dance company would agree."

"Fuck them."

She laughs again, and I want to keep saying things that force that sound from her lips.

"You don't need ink anyway." I shrug.

"Says the guy covered in tattoos?"

"You're already perfect as is. Unblemished."

She peeks over her shoulder at me, narrowing her gaze through her dark eyelashes. "What does that make you then?"

"The messiest piece of art you'll ever meet." I try to avoid her stare because that shit does something to me.

From the corner of my eye, I spot her lips curling into a smile and it's beautiful, just like every expression she offers. She tries so hard to bury her reactions that they feel like a mission accomplished when I spot one.

I snap the cap on the Sharpie and plant a kiss on her smooth shoulder before backing away so she can roll onto her back. She's naked in my bed, covered from the waist down with her dark hair fanning across the white pillows.

I love how comfortable she is in her own skin. Even if she tries to give the impression she's closed off, around me she lets me see her fully without hesitation. When we kiss, when we fuck—she's stripped wide open.

Lili gazes up at me with innocent eyes, and she looks too good exposed like this. I have to break her gaze before it crawls too deep inside me.

She moves her arm and glances down at my drawing on her skin. I couldn't help myself. I get primal with this girl, and I need to mark her in every way I can think of.

"A lily," she says, tracing her fingers over the flower I drew on her skin. "Why's it bleeding?"

Her eyebrows pinch as she scans the drops of blood falling from the petals. Bright red Sharpie ink against the stark black drawing on her skin. It's twisted how pretty the sight of it is.

"Your life spills out of you." Lifting my hand, I follow her fingers over the drawn-on petals. "How you dance, how you look, how you move. You give yourself away in everything you do."

Her lips turn into the slightest frown. "I'm not sure I have anything left."

"Because you're always giving it to everyone else."

"It's draining."

I run my hand up her chest and plant it between her small, perfect breasts. "I'd like to drain you."

A smirk climbs her cheek. "I'm sure you would."

It's an odd feeling. I should be over her by now. I'm a shitty guy who lives up to my rock star reputation. I leave girls after I screw them on a daily basis, and that's what I should have done with Lili as well. But whatever mess I'm making in this pool of regret is so much worse.

"What's this mean?" Lili brushes her fingers over the tattoo on my throat.

"The all-seeing eye?"

She nods. It's no secret she's curious about it, seeing as it's the one tattoo on me she's always staring at. She watches it like I watch her. Like it sees everything.

"It's a reminder that people can only ever really take what you give them."

"I don't get it."

"It's a piece from my past."

Lili glides her fingers over my throat, and it makes me swallow thickly. "It watches me."

"You're worth watching."

Her gaze snaps to mine, and I'm lost in the darkness of her eyes. How she stares directly at what should scare her. How she makes me want to believe there's still the resemblance of a person inside me.

"I like it." She lets her hand drop to the bed, and my skin instantly misses her touch.

"I know."

I smirk when my comment forces an eyeroll out of her.

"Your ego knows no bounds, Rome Moreno." She shakes her head.

"Yeah?" I grin. "Well, I'll take an ego over a bleeding heart any day."

"Don't underestimate the power of the heart." Lili tips her chin up proudly.

But I smirk. "I don't believe in following your heart."

"Why not?"

"It's blind and reckless. You can't trust it."

"So, you're logical then?"

"Nah, can't trust your brain either, you'll rationalize every decision to death." Not that I'm one to be rational. Perks of having money and fame. It's acceptable to be a total self-centered dick.

"So, what then?" Lili asks. "If you can't trust your heart or your head, what do you follow?"

"Your gut." I drift my hand down her stomach and plant my palm flat on the center of it. "Good or bad, your gut always knows."

Lili runs her fingers along my arm, her gaze following the path she's making on my skin before her eyelashes flick and her stare focuses back on mine. "And what is your gut telling you right now, Rome?"

"That I'm fucked," I say way too honestly.

But it doesn't scare her or make her pull away. Instead, she sits up and leans over, kissing a bare patch on my stomach. One of the few spots of skin I've still yet to get tatted. And I feel her lips imprint on my skin like ink.

Even when she pulls away, I see it—I *feel* it on me.

"Technically..." She kisses a path up my chest. "I'm the one who's thoroughly fucked at the moment."

Something about a bad word coming from her sweet little mouth makes me laugh, and I can't help but grab the sides of her face. "Not thoroughly enough."

But just as I'm about to catch her lips in a kiss, her phone buzzes from the nightstand. I let go of her, and she rolls over to grab it, frowning at whatever is on the screen.

"What's wrong?"

"Nothing." She shakes her head, but I don't buy it.

It buzzes again.

"Are you going to answer it?"

"You don't mind?"

I can't help but laugh. "So polite, sweetheart. I like it. But answer the phone."

She rolls her eyes and lays back, answering, and even though it's mumbled, I distinctly hear a man's voice on the other end. I shouldn't care. Jealousy is for whipped punks.

"Hi, Vaughn."

Vaughn.

I already fucking hate him.

"It's fine. I'm not in the middle of anything."

I quirk an eyebrow, not sure why that statement gets under my skin. I'm the one who told her to take the call. But something about how she casually said it makes me want to break her phone.

Instead, I settle for distraction, stripping the sheet off her in one pull.

Her eyes go wide as I sit up and look at her, but she doesn't try to hide from me. She allows herself to be on full display and hands herself over, watching me as I hop off the bed and grab a condom from the nightstand.

I toss it onto the bed beside her, already noticing her chest rising and falling with quickening breaths.

She's beautiful splayed out on my bed. I'm hard at the sight of her, and it's nearly painful as I kneel between her legs and peel her knees apart, seeing her own excitement. Spreading her legs wider, anticipation flashes in her eyes. It's intoxicating.

She's a performer like me in more ways than she realizes. She likes being watched, and even if she doesn't say it in words, her body reacts when my eyes are on her.

I pump my aching cock in my hand, and her gaze dips down to it. She barely pays attention to the voice on the other end of the phone as I pull a bead of cum from my dick and let it drip onto her pussy. Fuck, it's hot. I want to fill her up and watch it slowly drip out, which is not something I've ever done with a chick.

It's official, I've lost my mind for this girl.

Leaning closer, I glide the tip of my cock through her wetness and watch how it makes her whole body shiver, before smacking her pussy with it. I have to slap a hand over her mouth to silence the gasp that comes out.

"Quiet, sweetheart," I whisper, tipping my chin to her phone.

I remove my hand, and she bites her lip. "Sorry, I'm here... yes... I just... something came up, so I was distracted."

Damn right she was.

Her gaze drops once more to my dick in my hand.

"Tonight, yes, I'll be there," she says, even if she sounds distant as I rub my piercing over her clit. "Eight sounds good. See you then."

She hangs up and tosses the phone with a moan. "Rome, you torture me."

"What's tonight?" I ask, ignoring her comment.

She opens her mouth to answer, but I sink two fingers into her at the same time, so her words come out in mumbles. Her back arches and her eyes roll back. She's so tight it's almost painful to be inside her, but at the same time, I'm obsessed with the feeling of it.

"Tonight, Lili. What's going on?" I ask again, curling my fingers inside her and making her squirm.

"Tonight…" she pants. "I have a date… well… I mean—"

"A what?" I pull my hand away, realizing something in my head might have just snapped.

She senses it too because she lifts her head to look at me. "It's not like that. He's an old friend. It's just dinner."

"Mmhmm." I look her over, reaching for the condom.

"Rome…"

Whatever look I have on my face must mirror what's raging around in my chest because Lili looks nervous.

"It's not like what, exactly?" I ask, rolling the condom on slowly. "It's not you spending the day with me dick-deep in you and then going out with an ex? That's what he is, isn't he, Lili?"

"Well, yes. But it's not like that."

"It's fine, sweetheart, want to know why?" I lean over her and grip the hair at the back of her head, pulling hard enough that it forces her chest to arch. I lean in and latch onto the flesh of one of her breasts, biting hard. It'll probably leave a mark but I'm a little unhinged, so I don't give a fuck. "Because he can't do to you what I can."

"He can't," she moans as I sink my teeth in again.

"But just in case..." I lick all the way up her chest, her neck, her face. "Let me remind you."

I thrust inside her in one brutal move. It knocks the air from her chest, and I breathe the life of it in. But I don't stop or slow down, instead, I slam into her so hard I'm sure it's hurting both of us in the best possible way.

I sink back to my knees and grab her ankles, wrapping one hand around them and bringing them to one side of my head so she's extra tight. And I fuck her with every bit of rage I'm feeling inside. For her making me like her, for her getting in my head. For her sliding under my skin and making a home for herself in the ink.

I fuck her like I hate her, and need her, and can't get enough of her. I fuck her like it's the last thing I'm going to do before I walk through the gates of hell.

Maybe I'll fuck her until we both disintegrate and then no one else can have either of us. Because as she looks into my eyes and her climax hits, she pulls my own out of me—along with everything else.

21

LILI

I HATE THIS DRESS. It's sheer and skintight. And even if it reaches the floor, it dips low in the back and shows off every inch of my spine. Mom knew what she was doing when she picked it out. I'm on display like the trophy she sees me as.

I hate this place. The food is overpriced and underwhelming. It's not worth the calories I'm going to have to work off later.

Worst of all, I hate this man sitting across from me. Ordering my food for me like I'm a child incapable of doing it myself. Basking in the fact that the waitress is batting her eyelashes at him.

It's not her fault she doesn't know what hides beneath his polished exterior. To her, he's all emerald eyes, strong features, dark hair, and chiseled perfection. If only his sharp smile was the extent of the pain he's capable of causing.

The waitress walks away, but not before glancing back at Vaughn over her shoulder. I remember when that used to offend me, now I wish he would find interest in her and leave me alone.

"I've missed Denver," Vaughn says, circling his red wine in his glass before taking a pretentious sip.

It makes me miss the way Rome drinks booze, like he's trying to drown his demons with it because at least that feels real. While everything about Vaughn is measured and perfect—a mask he wears well.

"It's nice," I agree, taking a sip of my own wine.

I don't need the calories, but something has to take the edge off this dinner.

Vaughn sets his glass down and fixes his gaze on me. "You've certainly been enjoying yourself."

The playfulness he had with the waitress has been replaced by a cold stare and condescending tone. Both of which I wish I wasn't so familiar with.

Holding my wine glass in my hand as a barrier, I shrug, trying to avoid his gaze. "The city has a lot to offer."

I know he's not talking about the city. There's a wrecking ball in his gaze waiting to decimate me with whatever his reason is for dragging me out on this dinner. I brace one hand over my stomach and wait. Hearing the haunting sounds of a proverbial chain clinking a cement ball into place.

"I know you've been spending time with a certain guitarist." Vaughn's statement is calm and to the point, but it knocks through me. And I see this meal for what it is.

Jealousy. Control. Humiliation.

Somehow he caught wind of the fact that I've been spotted with Rome, and he isn't happy.

Since ending things a year ago, I haven't dated, and because of it, Vaughn has left me alone. But all it took was one whisper of me possibly moving on for him to show up and upend any progress I've made since things with him ended.

It doesn't matter to Vaughn if Rome isn't my boyfriend. It's that something is happening at all. Because apparently, he's the only one allowed to throw his body around.

"I don't know what you're talking about." I take another sip of my wine and feel my endorphins already swimming in it.

What I wouldn't give to escape this table and fall into Rome's bed right now, so he could help me work out whatever's stirring inside me. It might be wrong, and he might not fit into my world, but escaping with him—playing this game of chicken and seeing how far we can handle it—makes me feel *alive*.

"Word gets around, Lili." His expression falls in disappointment, and it reminds me of my mother.

"He's a friend," I lie.

Vaughn swirls the red wine in his glass, around and around. Letting it breathe in a way that feels impossible for me right now. The red liquid swirls in circles with my head. His eyes never leaving mine.

To anyone else, his stare might be captivating, but I'm haunted by it. By the reality of knowing who he really is, and how he made me his puppet.

I didn't always see him this way. There was a time before I realized I was simply a girl handed over to him by her parents because he owned the dance company, and his status made us all look good. Before he used me up for what he thought he was owed out of our arrangement.

There was a time when I actually thought I loved him. Even with him repeatedly cheating on me, putting me down, and controlling my every move. I thought he was worth it.

Love is messed up like that. It gets in your head and plants ideas, offering just enough sunlight to grow them.

This is why I don't mess with love anymore.

"Is that what this is about?" I ask, before he pounces at the chance to ream me for whatever he deems fit.

"I understand we've been on a bit of a break, so I'm willing to let it slide." Vaughn takes another drink, finishing the glass with a large swig. It's improper in a restaurant as classy as this, so regardless of what he says, I know he's upset.

"A break?" Calling our very public breakup *a break* makes me want to burst out laughing. "You left me for your assistant."

"Rebecca and I are old friends." Vaughn leans forward, giving me the full force of his disappointed gaze. "You were twenty-one and needed some time to grow up before we could properly move forward."

"And you needed time to screw half the women on your staff?" I cock an eyebrow.

"Don't be ridiculous," he scoffs. "Jealousy isn't an attractive quality."

It takes everything inside me not to reach across the table and smack the smug look off his face. I dig my fingernails into the flesh of my palms and remind myself causing a scene will only result in worse problems.

"We've both clearly had our fun." His teeth are gritted as he says it, as if he expected to be the only one who was allowed to move on from us, and he's not happy to see me doing the same. "But it's time we start thinking about the future."

I search for my spine under the pile of bones this man left. "There is no future for us."

"You don't mean that," he says, shortly. Like he's the only one with the power to decide what I mean and what I don't.

The waitress circles to refill his glass of wine, and he leans back, pausing the conversation. She can't take her eyes off him, and the wink he shoots her as she walks away is a reminder of everything I've always gotten from this man.

Disrespect.

"I'm willing to forgive your disgusting little discretions." He grips the stem of his wine glass and starts swirling the wine around again. "But this isn't up for discussion."

I open my mouth, but he holds up a finger, smirking, stopping me. Like I'm the child he and my mother have always treated me as.

"Before you throw a tantrum, let me remind you of something, Lili. You're impressionable, always have been. You're young and your musician boyfriend probably loves those innocent little stars in your eyes. He's having fun playing with you because he knows there's no future in it. And he's not the kind of guy who wants a future, as evidenced by his reputation. You think I'm bad? He'll get tired soon enough and throw you out like the trash he discards on a daily basis."

"And if he doesn't?" Even in my head, my argument falters because I walked into this knowing exactly who Rome is. He's scarred—damaged. He doesn't believe in love any more than I do. This isn't permanent.

"He will." Vaughn taps his fingers on the table, watching me. "I'm sure you're enjoying this little bit of rebellion, but tell me, how well does he really know you? Does he know who you're at dinner with? Does he know I'm the only other man you've been with?" He pins me with his gaze, waiting for me to respond, but I don't. "Does he know that before you were his whore, I was the one who taught you how to properly fuck a man?"

Vaughn is angry. He's using profanities in the middle of the most expensive restaurant in the city. And even if he's quiet and no one can hear us, I see his rage coming through his statement. He might have screwed a harem of women while we were together, but when it came to me, he was possessive. I wasn't allowed to breathe without him knowing about it.

Sitting here across from him, I once again feel him tightening the chains, taking my air away.

"That's what I thought." Vaughn smiles, but it's not relaxed or friendly. "Don't fight this, Lili. You know what I can do to you—to your career."

I swallow hard. Vaughn is well aware of his money and power, and how to use it to make me do what he commands.

I want to argue. I want to scream. But I know how Vaughn works, he's begging me to fight him, and I'm not going to give him that, no matter how helpless I'm starting to feel.

Luckily, the food shows up and gives us both something else to focus on, not that I'm hungry anymore.

One man leaves me feeling empty, and the other makes me ravenous for more.

We eat in silence, apart from Vaughn's flirty banter with the waitress. He watches me from across the table, daring me to challenge him. Daring me to fight back so he can put me in my place.

I don't. Instead, opting to push my food around while I try to ignore whatever seeds of doubt Vaughn has watered in my head.

When we finish our meal, Vaughn sticks to my side and walks me out of the restaurant, likely feeling he won whatever battle he waged tonight. Maybe he did because as much as I'd like to tell him to go screw himself, he holds more power over me and my career than my mother ever did.

He pauses as my car comes to a stop for me outside the restaurant, and I feel uneasy from the cool night. The paparazzi buzz around, watching him as he holds the door open. He might not have Rome's fame, but he has a sickening amount of money and beds enough heiresses that they care about who he is.

"Think about what I said, Lili." He looks down at me, knowing I won't react when I'm surrounded by all these people. "Have your fun if that's what you need to do. But once this show is over, you'll be leaving Denver, and it won't be with him."

"You don't get to decide that."

He smirks. *Evil. Devilish.* "But I do."

I try to see something in his eyes past the void of the man I once thought he was. I try to escape his stare like a sinkhole that's sucking me downward. I try to breathe with what little life he's left in my lungs.

It feels like no use.

I try to slip by him and put this whole evening in the past. If I don't leave now, I'm not sure what will become of what little this man left.

My parents are controlling, my dance company is demeaning, but Vaughn Davis surpasses them all.

But as I step toward the car door, his hand on my arm stops me from getting in. And before I can process what's happening, he grabs my chin and plants his mouth on mine, to the excitement of what feels like a hundred cameras around us.

He holds my chin painfully tight so I can't break away, and his kiss tastes sour. He's poison flooding my veins. And when he's had enough, he breaks away.

"See you soon." He grins, holding my face an inch from his before letting me go in an effort to remind me I'm nothing without him.

I climb into the car, but even as the door closes and it drives away, I know I'm sinking.

Sand all around.

Earth pulling me down.

And there's no getting out.

22

ROME

Fuck 'em and leave 'em.

The mantra I live by.

Something I've had zero issues with in my twenty-eight years on this earth. That is, until Lili went on a date with her ex-boyfriend five minutes after I fucked her and proceeded to ghost me for the past three days.

I really shouldn't give a fuck. I should be dick-deep in another chick after breaking my stupid celibacy streak. So why is it that all I can do is think about her?

How she opened me up and took a walk around inside my chest. How she messed me up with her footprints and left.

I look at my phone again—at the picture that was sent to me from an unknown number—Lili with some guy's mouth on hers. But all I see is red.

I know who it is; I've spent an unhealthy number of hours looking into this asshole, Vaughn Davis, planning the many ways I can rip him to pieces.

When Lili said she was going to dinner with an ex-boyfriend, she left out the part about how she dated him for two years. Or that he was a total piece of shit to her, as evidenced by the fact that in that time he was caught with multiple women.

Guy fucks anything that walks, apparently.

Something I can relate to.

But here's the difference—I don't commit to a woman and make her think she's the only one. For all the crap people give me about the number of women I've been with, at least I'm not pretending to be something I'm not.

Being a fuckboy and a cheating dirtbag are different.

I turn off my phone screen and try not to break it. Instead, lifting my joint to my lips and taking in a deep inhale, trying to chill the fuck out. A girl has never gotten under my skin before, and I really don't like it.

"You like her," Sebastian says from the other side of the couch, where he's watching me with a smug look on his face.

Adrian is at the control panel with his back to us, but I still catch his chuckle at Sebastian's comment.

"She was a good lay," I say, plastering on the grin everyone prefers I wear. "That's it."

Sebastian shakes his head and laughs. "Keep telling yourself that, Rome. But I'm not an idiot."

"Debatable."

He tosses his pen at me.

"Seriously, you're not fooling anyone." Sebastian stretches his legs out, letting his gaze move to the band working on a song in the booth. "Since when do you let chicks hang out with the band? And don't even get me started with how many times I've seen you check your phone today."

"Tell chicks to stop texting me pictures of their tits, and I'll set my phone down." I lean back, even though it's total bullshit.

Sebastian shakes his head. "Cut the crap. We're your friends. You know you're allowed to talk to us, right?"

Easier said than done. I'm used to being on twenty-four seven, even around them. People don't come past these walls I've built. Something Adrian and Sebastian are well aware of.

"I'm good," I assure him.

The band in the sound booth finishes their song, and Adrian cuts the microphone before spinning around in his chair. With them both facing me, I feel like I'm suddenly sitting in front of the firing squad. Stares pinned on me, and a bullet loaded in the chamber. Part of me wishes they'd just pull the trigger and put me out of my misery.

"Lili's cool, alright. I like hanging out with her. But we're just friends." I try to play it off. "Haven't even seen her in a couple days. She's been busy."

"With her ex?" Adrian crosses his arms over his chest. "Eloise told me."

I'm not sure what annoys me more, the fact that Adrian makes it sound like Lili's been hanging out with her ex more than the one night I'm aware of or the fact that Eloise is keeping tabs on the situation.

This is exactly why I should have never joined this codependent second family.

"She can do what she wants." I shrug. "Or *who* she wants."

God. That. Fucking. Hurts.

Only because I liked how it felt being inside her, right?

"Since when are she and Eloise friends anyway?" I ask, not able to help myself.

I blame the guys in the band for whatever is wrong with me lately. Their relationships are turning me into a pussy when I should be out chasing it.

"They had a girl's day," Adrian says.

Wonderful, they've initiated her into their group like traitors.

"Seriously though, Rome." Adrian's expression is tense. "If you need to talk to us, we're here for you."

"I know, and I appreciate it. But I'm not like you guys. Sure, Lili's cool and all. But it's not like she's sticking around here. And neither am I. We'll be on the move again eventually. I'm not turning her into my girlfriend or some shit. Don't worry about me."

Sebastian and Adrian share a glance that reads more than I want them to, but they keep their mouths shut.

The door to the recording booth opens and Gage, the lead singer for Manic Idols, steps out.

"We done for the day?" he asks Adrian.

Adrian nods.

"But hold up a quick second," Sebastian says, standing and walking over to him. "Let's chat about the chorus before you take off."

Sebastian follows Gage into the recording booth, and I feel like I'm watching my friend growing up in front of me. It's been slow over the past couple years as Sebastian stopped messing around and got his shit together. But looking at him now, it's clear.

The guy who used to smoke shit and chase skirts with me now cares more about bettering his life and career. The kid who convinced us to start a band has become this dude who decided we needed to take the next step with our own label.

When did we turn into adults?

Adrian's phone rings, and a smile paints his face when he looks at the screen. He presses the button to answer. "Hey, babe."

It's no surprise they're all wondering who's going to take me off the market. The entire band has hearts in their eyes, and I'm surrounded by them.

But that's the problem. Even if I was the type of guy who wanted something more serious, I don't attract the type of women who do. Evidenced by the girls just after my dick and fame.

Which I guess is better than Lili—out of my league and completely unattainable.

Not that I'm within reach either.

"Rome?" a sweet voice stops beside the couch, and I look up to see Izzy, the guitar player from the band smiling at me.

She's pretty, talented, and has a perfect pair of tits that almost spill out of her itty-bitty tank top. I probably would have tried to fuck her already if she wasn't part of a band we're signing. At least, that's the reason I tell myself I'm not trying. Deep down, I'm just not interested.

"What's up?"

She crosses her arms over her chest, pushing her tits up even more, but the sight doesn't stir anything.

"I was wondering if I could pick your brain." Izzy smiles, and I realize I'm being a total dick sitting here thinking about her body. I'm supposed to be a mentor to them, but all I've been doing lately is overanalyzing and drowning in my own problems.

"Sure thing."

Her eyes move to where Gage is singing with Sebastian in the sound booth. "Somewhere more quiet?"

I nod, standing up, and she follows me up the staircase to Adrian's main floor. Walking down the hallway, I stop at an open guest room and dip inside.

"Thanks. I'm struggling with the second chorus." She props herself on the edge of the bed as I shut the door and lean against it. "Something doesn't feel like it's translating like the rest of the song is."

"Let's hear it." I cross my arms over my chest.

Izzy holds her guitar and starts stroking the strings, starting at the beginning of the song the band was just playing downstairs. Her fingers move effortlessly because she has natural talent. And it's hard to tear my gaze away.

I've seen plenty of performers over the years. Playing guitar is a skill that can be taught, but those who have a quality like Izzy are rare. Her ability to play is captivating.

Songs bleed from her fingertips. She hasn't yet been beaten down by an industry trying to squeeze her for perfection. There's a raw quality that isn't polished, but it's her. It's a sound that can't be bottled. Something I used to appreciate in myself, but over time, I lost it.

It's easy to fade away in this industry. Enough fame and money will do that to a person. And although I've always stayed true to myself as much as I could, I always knew going mainstream would mean losing a little bit of the music along the way.

It's a feeling shared by the rest of the band and one of the reasons we started our own label.

But it's never been as apparent as when I hear Izzy play. Because she's not watered down. She's *real*. And the sounds she thinks aren't translating are just an edge that's not heard much anymore—raw need.

She's thinking when she needs to be feeling.

As I watch Izzy play, it all becomes clear. I started the label with the band because I'd follow them to hell and back, but also for the music. I wanted to remember what I got into this business for.

I'm tired of an industry washing out artists like her and the rest of her band. I want to be someone who lifts them up. At its core, music is truth. Music is purity. Even for those of us tainted in the pits of our soul.

With music, there is no judgement, only acceptance.

Izzy finishes the chorus, slapping her hand over the strings to pause them as her eyes look at me for guidance.

"It's a bit messy at the end—"

"It's not," I cut her off. "Don't change a thing."

Her eyebrows knit.

"Izzy, why did you get into music?" I walk over to her and plant a hand on one of the posts of the bed.

She looks confused, but it doesn't stop her from answering. "I guess I just had to. Ever since I was little, it was a part of me."

I can't help the smile that climbs my face. I love her innocence—her fresh eyes in an industry that's going to try and rot her from the inside out. She's what rock and roll needs more of.

"Exactly, it's a part of you. And that means sometimes it's going to be messy and imperfect, but you need to embrace it. Could you ramp it up at the end? Sure. But I like that it sounds a little broken. So, it's up to you."

She smiles, sweeping her white-blonde hair off her face. "You like it?"

I nod. "Don't let anyone tell you any different. Gage might be the face of the band, but you're the feeling."

She tips her head back and laughs, probably thinking I'm joking. I'm not.

When people think about music, the lead singer is always who comes to mind first, but what they don't realize is that lyrics are bare without the life the beat draws from them.

Not that I don't one hundred percent commend Sebastian for being the face of all our shit. He's got his own weight on his shoulders. But I just don't believe in underestimating the rest of the band because of it. Something I've appreciated that he's never done.

"Thanks, Rome." She smiles, pulling her guitar off her shoulder and holding it at her side. "Well, I should get going before the guys forget I'm here and ditch me."

"They wouldn't."

It probably sounds like I'm hitting on her, but really, it's that I've seen how they all look at her—the way we look at Eloise. And I know they won't let her fall through the cracks.

Another reason I knew they were worth signing.

"Whatever you say." She smiles, brushing past me. "Thanks for everything, Rome."

She swings the door open and almost runs into a tiny body moving through the hall as she steps out of the room. She barely has time to swerve before they collide.

"Sorry." Izzy steps to the side and walks away.

But I'm not watching her. My focus is locked on the black hole of a girl standing there in a cropped white T-shirt and high-waisted acid-washed jeans. And so many emotions come to the surface all at once. Excitement, annoyance, rage. I want to fuck Lili and slam the door in her face all at once.

But before I get the chance to do either of those things, she swallows hard, and her eyes turn once more to Izzy disappearing down the hall behind her.

"I didn't know you were here, sorry. I was dropping something off." She looks at me one final time before she walks away.

She walks away.

Like she hasn't just ignored me for three days and now gets to be pissed I was in a room with some chick.

Fuck. That. Shit.

23

Lili

I lied.

I knew Rome was going to be at Adrian and Eloise's house when I stopped by. Eloise told me as much when she warned me it might be noisy with Rome and Sebastian working on a demo with a band. And even if I've been avoiding him, I couldn't help forcing an accidental run-in.

I should have called and faced him after my dinner with Vaughn, and part of me is still unsure why I didn't.

Because you're a coward.

After all, what was I supposed to say?

One night was all it took for Vaughn to make me feel like a fraction of the girl Rome's been spending time with. And as much as I want to be near him—to feel him again—I don't want him to become collateral damage in whatever game Vaughn thinks he's playing.

I've felt Vaughn's people watching me since that night, waiting to see what I'll do, and the last thing I want is to bring more heat to Rome. Especially considering I'll be leaving Denver soon. It's not fair for me to mess up

Rome's life just to distract myself from the reality of my constricting world.

But then he walked out of a bedroom with a beautiful woman, and even if I know better than to let it affect me, it hit me deep in my chest.

"Lili, what the fuck?" Rome's voice is firm as he follows me down the hallway.

Why is he chasing when he should run?

Why does he try with me when he swears he never does with anyone?

Why am I the one woman who caught his attention?

And why do I love it?

"I need to go." I don't turn or stop as I head toward the front door.

When I reach it, I swing it open and am met with pouring rain. It's fitting, given the landslide inside me, breaking loose every feeling I no longer thought myself capable of having. And I have no choice but to step out into it if I want any chance of escape.

I'm immediately soaked, and I don't care. I need to run—from Rome, from these feelings, from the unwanted magnetic force that pulls me in the moment he's around me.

But he doesn't let me, following me into the storm and once more proving he doesn't care how messy things get. He follows what he wants in any given moment.

As I reach my car, Rome's hand grabs my arm, and he spins me around, pinning me against it.

"Lili, wait."

I'm not sure what's more desperate—his gaze, his voice, or this feeling inside me, begging me to listen.

"Rome—"

"Stop." He barely finishes the word before his lips are on mine, and I don't think I've ever felt more needed in a kiss.

His lean body presses against me, and I feel every part of my armor disarm itself for him. His tongue tangles with mine. Teeth and breaths and sanity fighting in a space neither of us belongs. We're too different, and our worlds would spit the other one out.

But one kiss—one whisper—and the three days we've spent apart become nothing, because he imprinted himself on my body and it only comes alive for him now. For a man I can't have, who won't stay, who can't love. And stupidly, I wish for it all.

I ignore self-preservation and cave at his touch.

Rain spills between us, and I'm drinking the sky as much as I'm drinking him. Maybe Rome is the sky, out of reach and echoing with thunder. He hurts like lightning and soothes like rain.

Rome grips my throat and pushes me back, breaking our kiss. Water runs in rivers over his face, but even the blur of the storm can't hide the pain in them because I feel every bit of darkness that consumes him.

"Get in the fucking car, Lili." He opens the passenger side door before taking the keys from my hands, walking around to the driver's side, and getting in.

The moment we're both inside, the chill of the rain cuts through my skin. The sound of it hammering on the roof of the car is a drumbeat against the silence between us, and I can't hide my panting breaths no matter how hard I try.

Rome starts the car and heads down the driveway.

"Should we talk about this?"

Rome's eyes cut in my direction. "Do you want to?"

He knows it's a challenge. Neither of us actually wants to break this trance we get in around each other. I keep my mouth shut and look out the window instead, not saying a word as he turns in the direction of his house.

The lion's den.

A place he knows he's in control. A place I've stopped myself from going a hundred times over the past three days.

It doesn't take long to get there when he's barreling down the road. We're at Adrian and Eloise's house—I blink—we're at Rome's.

When he stops the car, he gets out and slams the door behind him, disappearing into the downpour. I almost think he left me sitting here until my door swings open, and I see him standing in the rain with a hand stretched out to me.

Taking it feels like a promise I'm in no position to make, but I can't help it, planting my palm in his.

He keeps me close as he guides me to his house, and we soak the entryway with puddles the moment we step inside. Much like being in the car, the silence of the house is unnerving. Even if the echoes of rain outside try to fill it.

Rome laces his fingers through mine and guides me into the house, through the living room, where my eyes trail to those two stripper poles standing like a statement in the center. A warning for what this is and isn't. An answer to the question I keep asking myself, even though I know we won't find any permanence. And although I don't mind the poles for the reasons I probably should, right now they feel like a reminder of the limits he places on what he's willing to give.

The house is dark in the middle of the afternoon due to the stormy sky. And I follow Rome into that darkness. Down the hallway I know leads to his bedroom when I should have been headed home. I follow him down this rabbit hole and wait to get lost in Wonderland with him.

"We're getting water everywhere." I'm not sure if I'm actually worried about ruining his house or if it's nervous energy, but he chuckles at my comment.

"Not the worst these walls have ever seen."

I have no doubt about that. The question is, do I want to be a part of it? Do I want to weave myself into the memory of what these walls remember when I'll be long gone in a few weeks?

When we reach his room, he walks over to a wall and flicks a button, which opens a panel and reveals a fireplace I didn't know was there. He pauses in front of it, the edge of his face lit by the glow of the flames. He reaches for the hem of his shirt and strips it off his body, throwing it to the ground beside him.

The flickering glow makes every cut of muscle on his torso more prominent. It draws out the demonic faces of the devils on his skin. It urges me to escape, but all I do is find myself closing in on him.

"I don't fuck around with chicks in relationships," Rome says, with an edge of hurt in his voice. "Are you seeing him?"

I shake my head, finally choking out a, "No," when he doesn't turn to look at me.

His gaze narrows, and finally, he looks in my direction. "You sure?"

"You saw the photo?"

Rome doesn't so much as nod but looks back to the fire, swallowing hard.

I wonder how dangerous a statement would have to be on his tongue for him to swallow it. Rome doesn't hold back, but standing in front of me in the heat of the flames, I feel him resisting.

"I didn't want him to kiss me," I say, even if it sounds mildly pathetic.

"Does he do that a lot—things you don't want him to?" Rome's stare finds me again, and it's darker this time.

I nod. "Always."

It's painful. It's true. It's how he destroyed me.

I take another step toward Rome. "Did you sleep with the blonde?"

I'm not sure I'm ready for the answer, but I need it.

"No." Rome looks almost disgusted by my question, but I don't know why.

"I didn't mean to hurt you." I take another, more cautious, step.

"Who says you did?"

His statement makes me pause, a foot away from him, knowing it's his defenses coming up, but still not liking it. Rome is like me in a lot of ways, intent on never letting anyone in. But I saw it in the rain—in his eyes. I felt the truth he's resisting.

"I disappeared for three days."

Finally, Rome turns to face me, and I have to crane my neck back to look up at him. The same dark eyes I've fallen for every time I've looked into them are clouded in something I can't pinpoint.

"Do you make a habit of that?"

"It's how my life is."

Rome nods, his eyes raking me over. I wonder if he's trying to gauge whether I'll run again. Or maybe he'll be the one to do it this time. The thought alone makes me take another step closer.

"But you make me wish that wasn't the case." It's almost a whisper, buried in the crackles from the fire.

"Those are dangerous words to say to a man like me."

"Maybe," I agree. "But no more dangerous than the things you're *not* saying."

People don't call Rome out on his shit. He uses the fact that he keeps people at a distance as a shield of protection. But even if he tries to hide behind his demons and his ink, he made the mistake of letting me in.

Rome reaches up and brushes my wet hair off the side of my face, sweeping his fingers down my jaw and neck, before pausing with his palm on my chest. "Does your heart already belong to another man, Lili?"

It beats against my ribs, and I wonder if he feels it making music for him. I shake my head slowly. "No."

"Good." Rome's eyes are locked on mine, but his hand doesn't move. "Because I've felt all kinds of pain. Enough for it to make me numb."

"I know."

"You'd think it'd be a relief to feel nothing."

You'd think it would, but we both know it's not.

"But you—" His hand moves up again, and he wraps it around my throat in a way that only feels comforting with him. Because I want this man to hold my life in his hands and make it worth living. "You hurt like hell."

His grip tightens, but I don't flinch. I stare into his eyes and hold my ground.

"So do you."

Rome's touch sears, his eyes burn, his presence incinerates.

He leans down until he's an inch from my face, the dark smirk I love once more making an appearance in the corner of his full lips. "Good."

With one word, he closes the distance and sinks his mouth to me. He takes my air, my life, my heart. His ink might as well crawl from his skin and seep into my own. Because I'll never escape him.

He tastes like cinnamon and smells like apples. Fall coming, leaves changing, the air shifting.

Breaking the kiss, Rome looks at me with something wicked in his eyes. "You're perfect, and it makes me want to make a mess of you."

I tip my chin up, facing off with him. "You make me want to let you."

The corner of Rome's lip ticks at the challenge. "Are you on the pill, sweetheart?"

I nod, knowing there's only one reason he'd ask me that question.

"Do you trust me?"

I shouldn't. I *really* shouldn't when he's looking at me like he wants to slice me open and drag his fingers through anything that looks pure. But I can't help it, so I tell him the truth. "Yes. Why? Are we playing another game of chicken?"

Rome shakes his head with such darkness in his gaze I swear it quickens my heartbeat in my chest. "No, sweetheart, we aren't playing a game of chicken. If you want me to stop this time, you better start begging me for mercy."

24

LILI

Rome trails the pad of his thumb over my bottom lip, toying with it. He slides his thumb into my mouth and over my tongue, before dragging it back out. His gaze transfixed as he smears my mouth.

"Do you enjoy feeling dirty?" he asks, running his wet thumb over my lips, back and forth.

"Only for you."

His stare flicks to mine, and there's a satisfied haze clouding his vision that feels a lot like appreciation. I might as well be a drug he's inserting directly into his veins because he reacts to me like he's high off the feeling.

And I want to help him feel it. I want him to dirty me up for everyone else because there's no coming back from him.

"I could make a mess of this mouth," he drags his thumb over my lower lip once more. "Or this face. You make me want to do the most fucked up things."

Not taking my gaze off him, I reach for the bottom of my now see-through wet shirt and pull it overhead, which forces his hands away in the process. Unbuttoning my baggy acid-washed jeans, I strip them off as well. He watches me strip down to a white lace bra and panty set, not blinking once. Almost as if he's afraid he'll miss something.

Slowly, I sink to my knees in front of him.

There's no more running. No more hiding. It didn't do me any good anyway because all roads led straight back to Rome.

I kneel and look up at him, offering everything I can to the most destructive, inked man I've ever met. And I dare him to pretend he doesn't feel the same.

"Show me."

Two words that come out in a near whisper from my fear of them. Because I would like to tell myself this is just sex. That the tingle in my belly is nothing more than a reaction to Rome standing over me. But as I look up at him and willingly hand over control, I know it's not to chase a climax. It's *more*.

I sit back on my heels and pretend I still have a choice in what happens here. I pretend I can choose him and that he would choose me in return. I make believe in my mind that this wouldn't destroy both of our futures, and there's no expiration date on these games we're playing.

Every part of me wishes for things I can't have.

Rome reaches out for the sides of my face, raking my wet hair away from it, looking like he wants to have me and hurt me. Love me and leave me.

"Hands behind your back."

I do as I'm told, handing over control to him. Excited at the prospect of what degrading way he'll make me pay for willingly submitting to him.

His hands leave my face, and he undoes his pants, tugging them down in the front, just enough to release his hard cock, while still standing there like he's in complete control. He wraps one hand around his dick and pumps the length of it slowly. A bead drips from the tip, and I feel my head get light at the sight of it.

"Open your mouth."

His gaze is focused as I follow his commands, and I realize I'm not the only one drunk on this moment. The sight of me kneeling before him has him breathing harder, and I'm empowered by the fact that I have the ability to do that to him.

I've never felt overtly sexy in my skin, but Rome makes me feel like I'm everything worth looking at.

With his free hand, Rome grips the back of my head and tilts it so I'm forced to look up at him. It's hard and hurts a little. Walking the fine line between punishment and pleasure.

"Tongue out."

He watches me do it, bending at the waist to lean his face down to me. And he licks my tongue. It's the most strangely erotic thing I've ever felt.

"Beautiful." He stands at his full height and replaces the spot he warmed my tongue with the head of his dick.

The piercing smears around what is already leaking out of the tip.

"Now be a good girl and breathe through your nose." A final command before he thrusts himself in.

His piercing hits the back of my throat, and I have to fight not to gag. Both his hands lace in the back of my head, and he fucks my face like he fucks my body, without mercy. Tears stream from my eyes as he thrusts into me punishingly, again and again. But I don't try to stop him; I don't move my hands. I lace them behind my back and wish I could be touching myself instead. Because the sensation of Rome's dick stretching my mouth to its limit is making me achingly wet.

"You look perfect taking my cock down your throat, sweetheart," he groans, before pulling the back of my hair to tug my mouth off him. "But I have better plans than coming in your mouth tonight. So get on the bed."

He steps back with a tight fist around his dick. The sight knocks me off balance, and I stand up on shaky legs.

Walking over to the bed, I sit on the edge of it, feeling his eyes on me the whole way. There's a warning in his gaze, and I know he plans on destroying me. But while I should be scared, I welcome the ruin.

I watch him cross the room, going to his dresser and grabbing something off it, before stripping himself naked and walking over to me.

Fully undressed, he still has so much power. Strength in his gaze, sureness in his movements. Maybe it's his ink, devilish and taunting. Or maybe it's his presence.

Owning me.

He stops in front of me. "On the bed."

I press my hands behind me and do as he says, scooting back until I reach the headboard. Only then does he move, climbing between my legs and resting on his knees. His hand flicks, and I realize he's holding a switchblade.

"Scared yet?" He grins, lowering the knife to the flesh of my thigh and running the flat edge along my skin.

I shake my head, even if I'm not sure that's the truth.

He cocks an eyebrow and runs the cool blade of the knife up my thigh, slowly moving to the edge of my panties. He slips it under the band of my underwear, and in one smooth motion, he cuts through the lace and rips them off me.

"Those were expensive," I say, not that I really care right now.

"And pretty," he agrees. "But you don't need to cover this pussy around me, so they were also unnecessary."

Rome cups me and drives two fingers in. The sudden sensation of him hitting all the places I ache sends my brain into a tailspin. I throw my head back as he fingers me slowly, just enough to tease.

The flat edge of the blade is back on my skin, at my stomach, moving upward. I have to fight not to move so I'm not sliced by it. Something Rome makes more difficult as he presses the heel of his hand against my clit and drives his fingers in deeper.

"Fuck," I exhale, as the blade grazes over my ribs.

"I like it when I can make your prissy mouth say dirty things."

Rome smiles and it floods my heart because it's not wicked or punishing, it's genuine. He's pleased with me—with us. And I want to please him.

Regardless of what he tells himself, I did hurt him by disappearing. But with each touch—each confession—it heals a portion of the pain.

The blade slips under the band of my bra, and I have to hold my breath so it doesn't cut me. But it's only there a second before he cuts that off my body, too. And before I can complain, he curls his fingers inside me and makes me see stars.

He folds the blade back inward before tossing it to the nightstand. At the same time, he pulls his hand out of me, and I groan at the loss of him.

"Don't worry, baby." He smiles. "I'm going to fill your pussy with something better."

Rome takes my sliced bra from my body and slowly wraps the strap of it around one of my wrists.

"What are you doing?"

"You like to run, sweetheart." He grabs my other wrist and brings it in to wrap the strap around it as well. "You like to disappear on me. And we aren't going to be having any of that tonight."

Dragging my bound hands over my head, he slowly ties them to a slat of wood on the headboard. When he pulls back to look at me, I try to tug, but all it does is tighten the grip of the straps around my wrist.

"You can fight all you want, but you're not getting away." His eyes roam my exposed body before him.

"Did the infamous Riff King just admit he wants to keep me?"

His eyes narrow, and he bites at the corner of his lip as he slowly moves his gaze back up to mine. "Guess we'll have to see."

It's dangerous for me to want his answer to be a yes. We both know all roads lead to me eventually walking away and him going back to his rock and roll world that has no room for a dance princess. But I can't help but cling to this moment and wish for time to slow so I don't have to let go of it.

In Rome's bed, tied to his headboard, the feeling of his dick still fresh in the back of my throat. I want him to have me—to keep me. Just like he wants to be the one to tarnish what he views as perfection. I want to be the woman with the power to decimate the heart of Rome Moreno.

Proof there are no winners in this loser's game.

Rome grabs his dick and pumps it in his fist, his gaze focused on my spread legs and exposed pussy. He rubs the head of it against me, and the piercing flicks back and forth over my clit.

"I've never fucked someone bare," he says, dragging the head through my wetness and nudging at my entrance.

I'm breathing so hard I might be hyperventilating.

"I can't be the man to own your heart, Lili." He looks at me, and I think I spot sadness in his gaze. "But I need you anyway."

"You have me."

My heart, my soul, my body. Little does he know he already has all of it.

I lift my hips, dragging myself along the head of his dick. "Get lost with me."

With one hand, he positions himself again, planting the other firmly on my chest, holding me down. He nudges in once, twice, before thrusting fully inside. It's so hard and brutal, it kicks the air from my lungs to my throat. I see nothing but darkness for a split second.

There's nothing between us, and I feel every bit of him inside me. He moves and his piercing rubs against places that feel like magic.

"Fuck," he says, still barely moving. "Your pussy feels so good."

I open my eyes to see him bracing himself with one hand on my thigh and one on my chest. His eyes are locked where our bodies connect.

"You almost made me black out," I tell him.

He looks up at me and smiles at my statement. "Almost?"

Rome leans in, bracing his hands on either side of me to bring us face to face. I tip my chin up to brush my lips over his.

"Almost," I repeat.

"Well then..." He starts to move. His hips might be waves the way he rolls them. He's yet to pick up pace, but already, I feel myself building from the feeling of him fully inside me. "Let's see if we can't make that happen."

He starts thrusting into me harder. His lips claim mine, and I wrap my legs around him. Without the use of my hands, I'm at his mercy. I open my mouth, and he dips his tongue in, so I suck on it, wanting all of him—in every way.

I can barely hold myself together as he goes faster and harder. It hurts so good I feel like I'm being lit on fire. Rome kisses me along my jaw and down my neck, before kissing a path back again. His hips roll, and he hits the back of me with his piercing at the same time as his teeth sink into my lower lip.

And that's it. I see darkness. Stars. A universe. I become fragments swimming around. And as I tighten around him, I feel his warmth spill into me. Rome buries his face in the crook of my neck and fucks me through his release.

And I couldn't be more excited or scared. Because Rome wants to destroy me, and I want to let him.

25

ROME

THE COFFEE MUG IS *broken.*

I'm staring down the barrel of a gun, and it's all I can think about. The coffee mug with the all-seeing eye etched into it is in pieces.

To anyone else, it might seem like an insignificant thing to think about at a time like this. But it's all I can focus on—the shards of an object. So breakable, easy to lose, and temporary.

But this was hers.

I only have one picture left of her, and in it, she was holding that mug. She had both hands wrapped around it and the rim hid her smile. But I saw it in her eyes. She was happy.

Only now, this mug that buried Mom's smile is in shards on the floor.

The only physical evidence I'm not one hundred percent my father is shattered on the floor, erasing all proof I'm anything better beneath the chaos.

"Where is he?"

The dude in the ski mask presses the barrel of the gun against my temple, and I'm tempted to tell him to just pull the trigger and get it over with.

"I don't know," I say instead.

Self-preservation is a funny thing like that. You might think you're tough as shit, but at the wrong end of a gun, you're still likely to give 'em a little if it means not having to eat a bullet.

"How old are you, kid?"

"Fifteen."

Guy in the ski mask chuckles, but I'm not sure what's so funny. "Come on, kid. Tell me where he is, and I don't have to do this."

"I'm good."

After all, Dad finding out I ratted him out will only result in worse. At least this guy might actually kill me and save me from the torture of my father.

He winds his arm back and smacks me across the side of the head with the butt of the gun, and I go toppling. I'm faintly aware of the fact that it should hurt as my vision flickers, but I feel nothing.

There's no pain when you've spent your life surrounded by asshole drug dealers coming to collect on Dad's debts. Or when you've been raised by my father and treated like a punching bag every time he gets high or pissed off.

Which is most of the time.

He says it's my fault he needs the drugs, so I deserve it.

After all, I killed her, and he had to numb the pain of the fact that my soul entering the world was the result of the devil taking hers away. She died for me, and he'd make me regret it.

The dealer kicks me in the stomach, but it's almost welcome at this point because at least he's not degrading me. If it was Dad, he'd have a lot to say about how I'm a worthless piece of shit who disgusts him.

Nothing cuts deeper than emotional torment.

"When he comes back, tell him this was a warning." The guy in the ski mask points the gun at me. "Seven days to get me my money."

He walks away, leaving me on the floor. I roll onto my back and look up at the ceiling.

If that guy thought beating up Roy Moreno's son would get him to do what they said, they're going to learn fast they need a different tactic. Dad doesn't have money to pay them, hence the dump we're living in. And he's more concerned about himself than anything that could happen to me.

I turn my head to look at the shattered coffee mug on the floor once again. It feels a little like my hope lying there in pieces. I was dumb enough to think someday I'll escape this. I was dumb enough to think I might be good like her.

Dad was right.

I'm nothing but bad... for myself and everyone around me.

I startle awake and instinctively reach for my throat. To the third eye that sits there. A reminder to Dad, myself, and the world that people can only take from me what I decide to give them.

I won't go as easy as the coffee mug years ago. They'd have to look me in the eye, slit my throat, and drain my life in the process.

It takes a moment for me to catch my bearings. Breathing deep, I wait for my nightmare to settle, so I can swallow it back down. Only then do I remember what day it is and where I am.

Reaching across the bed, I find it empty.

Lili must have climbed out of bed at some point during the night. I'm tempted to tie the girl down just to keep her from constantly running. But just as I'm knee-deep in ideas for how I could fuck the fight out of her to make her stay, noise from somewhere in my house draws my attention.

She's still here.

I sit up and feel her in the air. I feel her in my bones. The girl is downright dangerous.

Slipping on sweats, I make my way toward the music playing in my living room. And when I turn the corner, I freeze at the sight of her.

She's dancing in an open space in front of the glass doors that lead to the backyard. Morning sunshine coats her in a warm glow, and she looks almost angelic. She's wearing one of my T-shirts, tied in a knot at the front because it's too big, along with a pair of my boxers.

Something about the sight of her in my clothes feels like she's in my skin. And I don't know what I like more, that she's wearing them or that she helped herself to them without me offering because she felt comfortable.

It doesn't take a genius to know her seemingly perfect life is glass, one tap away from breaking. She's careful about every movement. But around me, she feels safe to move freely. To take what she wants without apology. No restraints, unless I'm tying her to my bed.

The music stops, but Lili continues to dance, almost as if she's still hearing the song in her head. She moves like she's feeling a beat in her bloodstream. Muscle memory as she hits her marks and glides across the room.

She bends back as her arms swim over her head and her leg sweeps up and around. Skipping, floating. She's practically weightless with her movements. And it's more than the fact that the girl is petite because it's clear her dance takes all her strength and flexibility. But she glides like the movements aren't just movements.

She is them.

Her other leg swings up in a wide arc that forces her into the splits at the top before she plants both feet on the ground. She tips her chin to the side and glances over her shoulder at me.

"Enjoying the show?"

"Lose the top and I'll enjoy it more."

She rolls her eyes but smiles at the same time. And I wonder if she sees through the joke as easily as it feels like she can. Because I don't need her naked and pleasing me for me to want to be around her. I just need *her*—her presence—in my house and in my life. I need her like I never thought I was capable of needing anyone. Because she makes me feel like I can let my guard down and be the guy I forgot existed years ago.

Lili walks over to me and wraps her arms around my shoulders. She's been working hard, and her skin is glowing with the slightest sheen of sweat. Her passion for dance leaking from her pores is the sexiest thing I've ever seen.

She lifts up onto her toes, kissing me, and it's casual and nonchalant. Like a habit we do every day. I'm not sure what to make of it.

"Are you trying to get me to strip for you, Rome Moreno?" Her eyes dart to the two poles in the middle of the room

"I mean…" I trail off, grinning. "I wouldn't complain if you did."

"I'm sure you wouldn't." She's still smiling, but there's a pause behind it, and a pinch forms between her eyebrows.

"What was that thought?" I brush her hair aside.

"You saw that?"

I nod, watching her expression shift as she probably decides if she wants to tell me or not.

"I shouldn't say it."

I tip her chin up so she's facing me directly. "Say it anyway."

"I was just thinking I'm going to miss this."

"The stripper poles?" I joke.

Lili frowns. "You."

"Already thinking about disappearing again, huh?" I brush my thumb over her bottom lip. "I thought we went over your punishment for that last night. But if you need me to remind you…"

I'm not good at facing conversations like this head-on, so I can't help but turn it sexual just to avoid the fact that her statement has me feeling like I'm drowning.

"You know what I'm saying."

Lili blushes, and I wonder if she just replayed last night in her head like I did. Because it was mind-altering. Wicked in a way that didn't feel cheap. Intense in a way that carved a piece of me out.

She took it, unapologetically.

I want her to keep it.

"My show is only two weeks away," Lili continues, when I wish she wouldn't. "I'll be leaving after that. To the next city—or country. And I'm sure you'll be on tour again soon enough."

I want to tell her I don't care, it's all the same and it changes nothing. I want to tell her to make this as painful as she wants because I can take it, unlike anyone she's ever met. I want to hand her the knife and let her do the damage.

But the reality is, she's already a figment of my imagination in my arms. Something I manifested in my darkness.

Every tour lately, I've been sinking, watching myself become less and less a person. And then there was Lili, seeing the parts of me that weren't my celebrity. Feeling the parts of me that hurt to touch.

But she did.

Except, I can't hold on when it's unfair to her. There's no staying for either of us. No room in each other's lives, no places we fit. It doesn't matter how good it feels or if she's the first person to make me want something more since I was a kid. I'll have to let her go.

So, I give her what she needs right now, even if it hurts—no strings. There are enough people in her life pulling them. She doesn't need another. If what she needs is escape or a temporary reason for existing, I'll be it.

"Then let's not think about it. We'll enjoy the next couple of weeks while we've got them."

It won't be enough. I've never wanted more than a night with anyone, but with her, I can't help but want all of them.

"Okay." She smiles, but it doesn't reach her eyes.

Somewhere deep, I think she might be feeling the same void from my response that I do. But if so, she doesn't say anything.

I lean down to kiss her, and her stomach growls the moment I do.

"Already hungry for more, sweetheart?" I tease.

"For food." She pushes my chest playfully.

"All right. I'll make you some breakfast." This girl makes me want to give her everything, and it's the strangest feeling.

"Actually, I should go home and grab one of my meals. I've been so far off my schedule and there are only two weeks until my show."

I don't like how she's clearly hungry more than she'll admit, or how she restricts. I don't like that the people in her life seem to feed into it—force it even. She might not realize it's a problem, but I know obsession when I see it. And the way she pushes food around and counts her calories has already been on my radar.

It's just not my place to say anything—yet.

Or ever?

Who fucking knows.

Two weeks isn't long enough.

"No," I say, shaking my head. "I'm making you breakfast. And if you argue I'll tie you down and feed it to you myself. You know I will."

She rolls her eyes but bites her lip, considering my statement. Finally, she smiles, and I like that of all the people she surrounds herself with, I'm the one who can make her do that. The one who can make her indulge her own desires. The one who gives her what she really needs—and also what she wants.

"Fine, but just breakfast."

I plant a quick kiss on her lips before dragging her bottom lip between my teeth. With a final tug, I pull back and smack her ass before walking to the kitchen.

"Sure, just breakfast," I say, but I don't mean it. Because I want more and more and more. I like her too damn much, and even if I've never been one to hold onto things, I'm tempted to keep her.

26

ROME

IT'S BEEN TOO LONG since I've held a guitar in my hands. The strings rub my fingers raw with how soft they've gotten in a matter of months. We've barely been playing an hour, but my fingers already hurt. And it's all worth it to be rocking out with the band again.

While our off time is usually spent recording or prepping for our next move, this down time has been different. Instead of making my own music, I've been helping others create theirs. And even if it's been fulfilling, I almost forgot how good it feels to lose myself once more in my own.

I close my eyes so I can see the music the way I feel it. Bright sounds with dark undertones running through them. A crescendo of something that used to remind me of pain, but now hints at peace. It used to sound like midnight and now there's a moon brightening the evening sky.

Life where none should exist in a universe this big. No gravity or air to contain it. Endless.

I'm no poet. Never a lyricist. But as my fingers vibrate with the strings, I almost hear a whisper of something echoing deep for a girl I can't get out of my head.

My life experiences taught me love is bullshit. Inevitably, all people leave or break your heart. So why did Lili have to creep her way into my house and my music? And what is this feeling she draws out of me?

Is it love to want to consume her?

To want to drain her?

To want to have her?

Or is it love that I know better than to do any of those things because eventually, I'll be letting her go? Because taking even an ounce of her would leave less of her for herself, and that idea kills me more than the thought of never seeing her again.

The song fades out and my thoughts of her ink black hair and endless galaxy skin vanishes.

I open my eyes and Sebastian is grinning. "Fuck that felt good."

It really did. I didn't realize how much I missed playing these past few weeks. But with my fingers aching and the music still humming in my ears, it's clear. And from Noah and Eloise's smiles, they feel the same.

It's moments like this that I appreciate playing for no other reason than to just fuck around with the band. Having fun with music without the added pressure of a label's expectations. No weight of fame, no outside opinions. Last tour going up in flames might have been a secret blessing.

I never thought I'd be a musician who would need a break. But for the first time in years of touring, I'm not missing it right now.

"You get to play this weekend, right?" Sebastian asks, turning to me.

I nod. "Yeah, Izzy had something come up with her family, so I'm stepping in at the Manic Idols show."

"Jealous." Noah tips his head back and groans, looking like he's missing the stage as much as I am.

I might not be anxious to head back out on tour, but I can't wait to feel my feet on a stage again, even if it's with another band. Besides, it's a small gig at an otherwise unknown venue. People will actually be there for the music.

"Who else is fucking starving?" Noah asks, standing up to stretch his legs.

He sets his drumsticks down and heads toward the kitchen with Sebastian on his tail.

"Be right there," Eloise says, crouched over her guitar case.

Sebastian and Noah disappear, and I walk over to Eloise. "Hey, got a sec?"

She looks up at me as she shuts her guitar case. "Of course. Something on your mind?"

In her eyes, I already see the wheels in her head turning, trying to figure out what I could possibly want to talk about. It's weird for me because I don't talk, I deflect. But this shit inside me is so loud I've got to get it out. And Eloise feels like the easiest person to talk to about it.

"Yeah, I guess." I sink down to the ground and take a seat facing her.

She sinks back and crosses her legs, waiting for me to speak.

"How did you get past it?" I ask, feeling like a punk for having to, but also because I've been really fucking lost lately.

I might have convinced myself I'm tough and nothing gets to me, but being around Lili makes one thing clear—I'm not as over the shit from my past as I thought I was.

"The rape?" She's so blunt, I almost flinch.

I nod. Although Eloise's rape and the abuse I experienced as a child are two very different things, trauma is trauma. And while I never thought I was still affected, lately, I feel it like wires holding me back.

"I don't know that I did," she says, frowning. "I mean, yes, I went through the steps. Therapy, opening up to the band, all that. But it doesn't erase that it happened. I just learned how to gain strength from it."

"I thought I had," I admit. "When he died, I thought I was finally done with him. That what he did didn't break me so nothing would have the power to."

"And now you're questioning that?" Her eyebrows pinch. "Why?"

I rub my palms over my face, raking my nails into the curls on my head. "I fucked her."

"Lili?"

"Yeah." I lean back on my hands. "But it wasn't..."

It wasn't what?

Just a release, something I've done a thousand times, purely physical.

"It was different," I settle on.

Eloise smiles, but it's genuine and not teasing. "You like her."

"I don't know how I feel about her."

Eloise sits there, pulling her knees up so she can wrap her arms around them. She rests her chin on the peak and looks at me.

"It's hard to let people in when you've experienced the things you have. I get that," Eloise says, looking at me. "They don't have to be the one who hurt you for it to still be difficult to trust them. The fear of pain exists either way, spreading until it infects everything if you let it."

"You let Adrian in."

She smiles at the mention of his name, and it makes me happy that's the reaction he draws out of her. "It took time and healing, something you're capable of, too. You're not ruined, Rome. There's so much good in you—care in you. Look at how you were with me when everything happened. You've got a huge heart when you let people see it. Sometimes you just have to be willing to get hurt."

"Pain doesn't scare me."

"That's physical pain, Rome." She narrows her eyes. "I'm talking about your heart."

I shake my head and open my mouth to tell her to fuck off because I don't care about that organ, but she holds up a hand, stopping me.

"Tell me something," she says. "Where does it hurt? If you're being honest with yourself, when you're with Lili, what's the pain that stops you?"

Some place in my ribs, that's where. Not that I say it out loud.

"Exactly." Eloise looks at me with a smirk like she's reading my mind. "I've known you since you were a dumb teenager getting into trouble with my brother. And whether you want to admit it or not, you aren't that kid anymore. It's okay to finally face that you're growing up. And if Lili is the one who makes you want to do it, then I'm thankful for her."

Not as thankful as I am, and I'm not even sure for what yet.

"I'm in so fucking deep, El. And it's no good." I rub my hands over my arms, but there's no warmth like what Lili's touch brings me.

For years I've covered myself in ink, drowned myself in booze, surrounded myself with women. All it took was Lili to surpass every other source of pleasure. One touch of Lili's hands didn't dull the pain but erased it. And experiencing Lili's drive and strength makes me wonder what the fuck I've been doing wasting my life with anything else.

She's in my blood.

"The deep end isn't always a bad thing." Eloise smiles. "Sometimes it's the only way through."

She hops up and holds out her hand, but I climb up without taking it and pull her in for a hug instead.

"Thanks, El," I say, realizing I'm officially being a pussy talking about my feelings but not giving a shit.

"You know I'm here for you." Eloise pulls back and holds my arms. "Now let her be here for you, too."

I nod, swallowing hard as she turns to leave the room. Because I've got two weeks left with Lili, and the hourglass is already draining. On one end is heaven and the other is hell, but for the first time in my life, I'm content in the middle.

Purgatory.

27

Lili

Marijuana smoke permeates every inch of air in the room. If I don't get a contact high, I'll be surprised.

Making my way through the crowd, I'm overwhelmed by how different this scene is from the places I'm used to. It's buzzing, full of life. Euphoric. Everyone's enjoying themselves as they wait for a band to take the stage.

I'm not sure if I'm overdressed or underdressed as I make my way through the horde of people. Either way, I'm out of place in my little black dress with my hair in a ponytail and barely any makeup. The exact opposite of all the studs and leather. Everyone in here is sharp in all the ways I'm soft.

I scan the crowd for Rome but don't see him, so he's probably prepping already. He's filling in with another band and invited me to come to see him play, which has my stomach in excited knots.

Looking at the stage, it's still empty, and I'm thankful. Rehearsal ran long, and I was starting to think I'd miss the show.

Someone bumps me and jolts me to the mass of people I'm standing in. This scene is untamed, so I make my way to the bar for a drink, hoping it will help me relax.

I cling to the bar top when I reach it, thankful it's quieter over here by the wall, and I wait for the bartender to notice me. It's crowded with women flashing smiles and cleavage left and right, so he's distracted at the other end.

Everything about this place is wild debauchery, while I come from a world parading under the pretense of chastity and perfection.

A yin to yang.

Pleasure and pain.

I'm about to give up on getting a drink and go find a place in the crowd to stand, when I feel the warmth of a body press close behind me.

"Hey, sweetheart." Rome's voice cuts through the noisy crowd, and it sends a path of goosebumps over my skin.

He grabs onto my ponytail and pulls, forcing my neck to crane back until I'm looking up at him standing behind me.

"I like this." He wraps his hand in my long hair again and pulls harder, which forces my back to arch against him, but he doesn't let go. Rome lowers his mouth to mine. "Think we'll have to play with it later."

He leans down and kisses me, still holding me in place with my hair. His dick presses against my ass through our clothes, and I feel him all over me. The room might be full, but everyone else ceases to exist. With Rome holding me in place, in a world I clearly don't belong, he's the one keeping me here. Dragging me under, and I can't help but let him.

His tongue slips into my mouth, and I'm in so far over my head I know two weeks won't be enough. The question is, what will?

Rome releases me from the kiss and loosens his grip on my ponytail.

"You made it." He smiles with the kind of relief that feels so genuine my heart breaks for both of us.

"Rehearsal ended up only running a few minutes over." I spin in his arms and face him, but he doesn't let me go, instead dropping his hands to my hips.

It's casual, like he doesn't think about the fact that he's standing here holding me like I'm his girlfriend when anyone could see him. And although I know he's not shy about being physically affectionate with women, there's something about his tight grip that feels possessive instead of sexual.

I shouldn't be here—with him or in this bar—but I can't leave either.

"Besides..." I wrap my hands around him and step closer, folding into whatever is happening instead of separating myself. "Couldn't miss a live appearance of the Riff King in action. I hear it's something women lose panties over. Must be special."

Rome grins so wide it stretches his entire face, and I absolutely love it. He leans down and grazes his teeth over my earlobe.

"It's so fucking sexy when you call me that."

"You and your ego."

"Nah." He shakes his head, pulling back. "It's just *you*."

I'm not sure how to take his statement, because any way I do is dangerous, so I play it off with a giggle that's so unlike me, only Rome Moreno could bring it out.

"Charming as always," I tease. "When do you go on?"

He looks over his shoulder at the stage, where movement is happening. "Soon."

When he turns back to me, his eyes move over my shoulder, and he holds up one hand with two fingers. I look to see a bartender pouring shots before sliding them over the bar top to Rome. Apparently, all it takes to get a drink in this place is to be a rock star.

Rome hands me one of the shots.

"To your show." I hold it up between us.

He bites his lower lip, looking me over, before our gazes once more connect. "To you being here."

He clinks his glass with mine before downing it. I do the same, but I feel it burn through my stomach, through my flesh, through my heart. I feel it burn me from the inside out because the man staring at me makes me raw and vulnerable.

Setting the shot glass on the bar behind me, I try to take a step back to find the air I can't seem to around him. He doesn't notice, or maybe just lets me, stepping back himself and placing his glass on the bar as well.

His stare cuts to the left, and he shakes his head before dipping his face near my ear. "Sorry about this in advance."

I pull back to look at him, but before I can ask what he's talking about, we're surrounded by people. Eloise, Adrian, Sebastian, and Cassie surround us.

"Who let you in here?" Rome says, taking a step toward them.

He slaps a hand on Adrian's shoulder before Sebastian pulls him in for a one-armed hug. Over Rome's shoulder, Sebastian's eyes are on me like they were the day I met him at Rome's house. I can tell he's protective of the members of the band, and I'm not sure what he's deciding as he looks me over, but he seems apprehensive.

"Hey, Lili." He nods at me as he and Rome pull apart.

Rome steps back, and I expect him to play nonchalant about who I am to him, like we did when we hung out with his band at his house, but he surprises me by throwing an arm around me and pulling me to his side.

But as quickly as he does, Cassie pops up beside Sebastian and reaches for my hand to pull me into a hug. I'm not used to warm greetings in the cold world of dance, but it makes me feel welcome in a way I don't usually, and I appreciate it.

"You made it." She steps back and smiles at me.

Her hair is up with the pink ends falling around her messy bun, making it look more bubblegum than blonde.

"Barely. Long day," I say as she steps back, and Sebastian tugs her to him. "But I'm glad I did."

"Well, I'm glad you did too." Cassie looks up at Sebastian. "On that note, we're going to grab drinks and find a spot by the stage before the set starts. You coming, El?"

Eloise nods, but Sebastian frowns at Cassie. He doesn't seem thrilled about letting her leave his side. Cassie must notice as well because she pops up on her toes to give him a kiss that distracts him.

Rome brushes my ponytail off my shoulder and leans down to my ear. "Have fun with the ladies, sweetheart. Because tonight, you're all mine."

He grips my chin between his thumb and index finger, turning my face to his so he can take me in a kiss. There's no apology in the possession of it. He parts my lips and claims my mouth with his tongue like we aren't standing in a circle of his friends. It's inappropriate and stirs the tension between my legs. And while I know Rome is sexual and not afraid of public displays of affection, it feels like something else as he melts into this moment with me.

When he finally lets go and steps back, I'm tempted to wrap my arms around him and say that I'm not done yet, but Cassie tugs my hand, and I disappear with her and Eloise to the other end of the bar.

We slide into a spot that a group of women just vacated, and Eloise props her elbows up on the bar to lean over and catch the bartender's attention. As with Rome, she has no trouble getting it, and she orders us all drinks. The shot is still swimming in my head, so I'm not sure more liquor is a good idea, but I don't argue and decide to live in the moment.

Once Eloise places her order, she spins around and leans her back against the bar to face me, mirroring Cassie, who hasn't taken her eyes off me.

Standing here in this bar, I realize Cassie's like me in that she's a stark contrast to this scene. All bubblegum pink and smiles. If I thought I was out of place, she's more so, but she doesn't seem uncomfortable about it.

"So, you and Rome?" Cassie smiles, and there's a definite question in the way she says it.

I rub my hands over my arms, not sure how to respond. It's not that I don't feel like there is a *Rome and me*, but I just don't know how to define us. We're not in a relationship. We're not going anywhere past my time in Denver. We're temporary, and that twists a knife somewhere in my gut.

"We're having fun." After all, it's true. "He's a good guy."

Eloise smiles brighter at the statement. "I love that he lets you see that about him."

Me too, I almost say. But I hold it in because I'm worried it would tell them too much. That I see it. That he lets me in. That I'm falling, and I want to grab him and take him over the cliff with me.

"We bring it out in each other." It's probably too honest, but I can't help it.

I haven't had female friendships in as long as I can remember, and it feels good how the girls in Rome's group invite me in like one of their own. There's no judgment, just kindness.

"That you do." Eloise nods, sharing a glance with Cassie.

I think they're going to keep asking questions, but they smirk at each other and then seem to shift gears.

"So, how's practice going?" Cassie asks. "You've got a big performance coming up soon, right?"

I nod. "Yeah, I'm performing in the show at Eden at the end of the month."

"Sounds incredible."

"It's a lot of work, but I love it." I shrug. "Then I'm off to who knows where. The company is working out my next move."

Them, my mom, and Vaughn. My stomach turns at the words unsaid. The people pulling strings, not offering me the scissors to cut them. I might be enjoying the small amount of freedom meeting Rome and being in Denver has allowed me, but soon enough it will end. It'll fade with any memory I try to hold onto, and I'll be numb again.

I'm not sure what the expression on my face looks like, but the smiles on Cassie's and Eloise's faces both shift into something unreadable. And even if they don't know me well, I wonder if they also feel the air leaving the room. My life becoming a figment of what could have been if I'd made different decisions.

The strike of a cymbal cuts the tension and my eyes dart to the stage, where I see the band getting ready.

"You said you'd be by the stage," Sebastian says, coming through the crowd with Adrian and latching onto Cassie.

"We hadn't made it there yet." She grins, turning her body into him.

The way they look at each other is palpable. Happiness, hope, light—whatever they have is something I've never thought myself capable of, but they make me want it.

Looking over at Adrian and Eloise, it's more subtle. They're holding hands, and he's whispering something in her ear. They aren't as outwardly affectionate as the other members of the band. Still, when he pulls back and their eyes connect, I swear the air crackles.

For the first time in my life, I want something more than the numbness that comes with zero attachments. My eyes move to Rome at the thought. He's on stage setting up—dark focus in his eyes and tattoo armor covering his flesh. I want to be the person he lets inside it.

A group of girls is forming in the crowd near him. He's easily the most famous person up on stage, and the crowd takes notice. But when he looks up, he scans the room as if he's looking for something in particular, and when his eyes find me and pause, I swear we both feel the permanence that shouldn't exist.

28

Lili

We're right up front, at the base of the stage, with a full view of the band performing. And for the first time, I get the full effect of what I've read about—the Riff King in action.

Rome Moreno.

Music spills out of him as his fingers dance over the guitar strings. He tips his head back and closes his eyes, but the third eye on his throat still watches the room of people, proving no one is capable of escape. He wants to see them beg for him—to ache for him. And I do. We all do.

Up there, Rome is relaxed in a way I've never seen him, not even after sex. Like the stage is his home, and it's the only place he feels comfortable letting his guard down completely. He moves his body with the music. His lean muscles flexing under the weight of the song. The demons on his flesh taunt the audience.

Women claw at his feet, crowding the edge of the stage with their eyes begging him to look at them. He's a god in his element. A man at peace—something I didn't think possible for him. And he makes everyone in the room want a piece of a man already carved to Swiss cheese through memories alone.

The song slows, and Rome backs off the heavy notes, smiling out at the audience. I don't know this band, but they're good. They have chemistry, even with Rome, who doesn't usually play with them.

Beside me, Cassie is caged in Sebastian's arms and swaying to the music. Adrian and Eloise are on the other side of them. And I wish I had the warmth of Rome's arms around my waist like they were earlier, but it would mean I'd miss seeing him like this.

I think I might love seeing this side of him.

All sides of him.

The inked enigma that messes up my clean slate.

The man who let me behind the curtain.

"You don't think I can land Rome?" Some girl's voice cuts through the crowd behind me, drawing my attention.

I don't dare look back at her, even if I'm now acutely aware of her conversation. Instead, keeping my gaze fixed on him.

"You and every girl in here are thinking it," someone, I'm assuming is her friend, says.

"Well, I'm *doing* it—him, more specifically."

They both laugh, and it makes my stomach ache.

"I hear he's better with his hands in bed than he is on stage."

"I heard he's pierced."

I should not be listening to this. I don't want to hear this. I should shut it out or shut them up. Why does this man make me feel violent?

"Fuck, maybe I should try to go home with him."

"I called him first."

I'm tempted to turn around and tell them I actually called him first, like some immature teenager. But the music kicks up again and drowns them out.

"Don't listen to them."

I turn to see Cassie leaning in. Sebastian's arms have loosened enough that she's edged her way closer to me.

"It's hard, I know." She rolls her eyes, gazing up at Sebastian before looking back at me. "Trust me, I *know*."

"It's fine," I lie. "It's not like I'm his girlfriend."

Cassie's eyes narrow, looking from me to the stage, then back again. "I've been where you are. Falling for these guys is like falling into the sun without armor. And people always want a piece of them; that's not going to change. But trust me when I say they're good guys, and when they love, they love hard. And Rome... I've never seen him with a girl like he is with you. I've never seen him *look* at a girl like he looks at you."

"How's that?" I purse my lips, trying to hold in my unease.

But Cassie doesn't answer me with words. Instead, she looks back to the stage, and my gaze follows hers until it lands on him. Rome's playing like his hands move without him having to even think about it.

In a sea of faces, he's looking straight at me. The smallest smirk tilts his lips, and he winks before turning away to drown in the song again with the rest of the band. Except even when he's not looking, I feel that wink fluttering inside me, wreaking havoc in a room filled with glass.

I feel myself shattering.

"Like that," Cassie says, drawing my attention back to her. "Rome doesn't care about them, never has. But he seems to care about you, and that says a lot."

She curls back into Sebastian's arms, and even if he's kept his eyes averted, I'm sure he heard our conversation because he smirks and bends down to kiss her on the top of the head.

I'm not sure what scares me more, the fact that Cassie might be right or the fact that it doesn't matter. Because it doesn't change anything. I'm leaving soon, and these girls fighting over him will get their chance with him the moment I'm gone.

◆

The band is drawing the attention of the room. Sebastian and Eloise might not have been up on stage with Rome, but once people realized most of the band was here, they flocked in droves.

People are pulling band photos out of nowhere to get them signed. And I'm amazed at the kind of attention that comes with being in a rock band because it's unlike anything I've experienced.

There's one woman talking to Eloise and crying, and I'm not sure how she handles it as well as she does. She's patting the woman on the arm and listening with what appears to be a genuine look of interest.

Cassie hangs back with me at a standing table off to the side of the bar while the band signs autographs. She doesn't seem phased by it, bopping her head to the music playing and enjoying her drink. I guess when you have the lead singer of Enemy Muse's attention, no matter where you are in the room, it's hard to mind. Sebastian might be signing some girl's Enemy Muse picture right now, but his eyes follow Cassie wherever she goes.

"Do you get used to it?" I ask her.

"After a while, I guess you do." She sets her drink on the table in front of us and shrugs. "The first tour was rough. But by the second, I learned how to acclimate. You must understand how that is though; you're always on the move, and I'm sure you've got fans."

"Yes and no," I say. "My shows aren't like this. It's *quieter*."

Cassie laughs. "Rock 'n roll."

I can't help but smile. Although Rome and I are both no stranger to fame in our own unique ways, his life is nothing like mine. While I'm surrounded by pretentious men in suits, Rome is currently surrounded by miniskirts, fishnets, and tops missing parts in the front and back that otherwise hold them together.

Some girl with jet black hair and an insanely curvy body presses up against his side and whispers something in his ear. Her fingers wrap around his arm, and I have to look away to avoid the sinking feeling I've been fighting against all night.

I'm not someone who gets jealous. Vaughn fucked his way through our social circle a couple of times when we were together. But the thought of Rome touching another woman the way he touches me draws out a foreign unease.

My reactions to all things Rome are deep—visceral.

How does he do it?

Daring to glance in his direction once more, another beautiful woman is sliding her hands over his chest. I tell myself the tightening in my own isn't me being possessive. It's just me being practical since I let him have sex with me without a condom. But the further down her fingers move, I know it's a lie.

My lungs squeeze and the walls around me shrink.

I spin around and break my gaze on Rome. "It's getting late."

Cassie frowns, looking down at my half-finished drink, before glancing back at the band. "You okay?"

I force a smile and nod. "Of course. I had a lot of fun, but I'm tired."

Lie.

"And I need to be up early."

Another lie.

Not that it matters when the smoke in the bar fills my lungs and the people all around me make me claustrophobic.

"Okay, well, it was nice seeing you again." She pulls me in for a hug. "We should definitely catch up before you leave Denver."

I press my lips in a firm line and nod. She's sweet and welcoming like Eloise, and if I was staying, I could see us being friends. But in reality, I've already got one foot out the door of this town.

"Are you gonna tell Rome?" she asks as I start to pull away.

"Tell Rome what?"

I jump at the sound of his voice coming from behind me. His hand slips around my waist so quickly, my body's hauled against his. A small gesture with the power to immediately settle the chaos raging in my chest.

I look up and my eyes connect with his. Darkness so deep light is incapable of escape. He's endless in a way that I could read every inch of him and still only scratch the surface.

His hand wraps around my jaw. "Tell me what?"

How is it one touch can set my entire body on fire? How is it one look and I belong to him?

"I was going to head home." I swallow hard, not sure why that statement makes me so nervous when it didn't a moment ago.

"Tired?" His eyebrows pinch, and I think he might actually be worried about me.

"It's just... a lot."

The eyes on this man are a lie detector. His touch black magic from the demons on his shoulders. Everything about him draws out my truths.

Rome scans my face, before he loosens his grip on my jaw. "Let's go, then."

"Rome." My mouth falls open. "I'm fine, we can hang out later. Enjoy your show—your night."

His hand slides to the base of my throat, where my heartbeat races. His other one firmly holding my body against him. "Sweetheart, you've given me two weeks with you. If you're leaving, I'm leaving. End of fucking story. Don't bother arguing about it."

Then he lets go, and I feel my breath rush back in. I look at Cassie who's watching us with a knowing smile on her face. While I was focused on Rome, Sebastian, Eloise, and Adrian rejoined the group.

"You hungry?" Rome asks, and I think he's talking to the group, but when I look up at him, he's looking at me.

I shake my head, even if my stomach growls at the thought of food. I headed straight here after rehearsal, and it's been hours since I've had anything.

"Did you eat dinner?"

When I don't respond right away, he frowns. "Exactly."

I'm about to argue that it's already one in the morning, so dinner doesn't matter at this point, but his hand laces with mine, and I'm distracted by our fingers tangling as he secures me to his side.

"We're grabbing burgers. Anyone else hungry?"

"Fuck yeah, I'm starving," Sebastian says, and the rest of them nod in agreement.

Burgers are off limits. Too much grease and too many calories. It's been years since I've had one, and Mom would have a heart attack if she knew I was considering it.

But as Rome leads me out of the bar, ignoring anyone who tries to stop him, nothing else matters—not even food.

He makes me absolutely insatiable.

I watch the faces as we pass, eyes looking from one band member to the next, and I'm reminded of what Cassie said to me earlier about falling into the sun. She's right. Because being with Rome is sunshine in the vastness of a dark universe. Warming me in the pits of my soul, but sure to burn me.

29

ROME

LILI IN A LITTLE black dress last night was something else. Hair in a ponytail like she was taunting me to pull it. Under any other circumstances, I'd have dragged her home to fuck her instead of taking her out for food. But that's the thing about this girl... I want to do more than just get inside her.

I want to take care of her.

Seeing her buzzing from the alcohol, nervous from the scene, and looking so fucking small and breakable as she stood there, I needed to wrap myself around her and fix whatever's broken. While she was fixated on the women surrounding me after the show, I was focused on her.

I hoped she saw they meant nothing. That this is my life, standing there while they take a piece. But I watched Lili as she drifted into her mind and out of reach with her thoughts.

Sometimes I feel like she's a ghost—a figment of my imagination. I feel like if I stare too long and hard, she'll vanish. Like she's always had one foot out the door, and it leaves a portion of her heart transparent.

I want to carve open both our chests and see how much either of us has left. I want to find out if two broken halves can actually make a whole. The math when it comes to love is all fucked up. I'm fractions and she's colors. No matter how hard I try, I can't add the two.

Her fingers dig into my stomach as she wraps her arms tighter around me, and I wish she'd claw all the way through. Instead, she loosens the moment the bike makes the turn and we're on a straight shot of road again.

Maybe if I keep driving, I can keep her.

I'll take us both far from whatever worlds we think we can't escape. Because I already sense her leaving. Even if we have ten days left, the sand is slipping through the hourglass. And like her, it goes straight through my fingers every time I try to catch it.

Finally, spotting the turnoff I've been looking for, I slow the bike, loving how it makes her body melt against my back. She feels so good holding on.

Not so much when she's letting go.

Pulling off to the side of the road, I cut the engine and hold out my hand so she can climb off my bike. She peels the giant helmet from her head, and her black hair is messy and full of static as she tries to press it flat again.

I shouldn't love making a mess of her as much as I do, but I can't help it.

"Where are we?" Lili hands me the helmet.

"The forest."

She narrows her eyes at my snide remark. "Thanks, Mr. Obvious. What are we doing way out here?"

I shake my head and grab the bag off the back of my bike, throwing it over my shoulder before taking her hand. "You'll see."

The girl cannot stand a surprise. It's clear she's used to living on a schedule because she always has to know where we're going, what we're doing, who will be there, and what we're eating.

Too bad her need for routine only makes it that much more fun for me to tear it all up.

Lili slides her fingers through mine and clings tight as I lead her down the path.

Noah told me about this place. It's only a short hike, but at the end of the trail is a nice little meadow. I don't really give a shit about nature, but it sounded like something Lili would like. And I'm such a punk when it comes to the opportunity to make her smile.

We walk in silence most of the way, and it takes about fifteen minutes. I can't remember the last time I've sat in my own head that long and not been fucked up on something. But in the silence of the forest, I realize it's not actually quiet at all. Birds, animals, even the sunbeams seem to be making noise.

Something in the universe is out there trying to talk to me.

Making a final turn on the path, the trees start to thin, and we're met with a large open space. It's pretty, I'll give Noah that, but I still don't really get it.

What I do like is seeing Lili's eyes widen at the sight. Her gaze moves from the open space up to the sky above. With her head tipped back, elongating her neck, she closes her eyes. She takes in a deep breath, and I wonder what it's like to feel a breath like that. An inhale that draws life in.

"It's beautiful out here." She opens her eyes and looks up at me.

"That it is." But I'm not looking at the forest.

I'm looking at her.

She's bundled in a pale green sweater on this cool fall day. Her jeans hug her legs, and everything about her looks perfect and comfortable. Once more, she's pulled her hair up into a ponytail. But unlike at the bar last night, it's messy and loose, leaving a few strands falling around her face.

Without makeup, her lips are still deep red, and I wonder if it's fair for her to be this alluring in such a fucked-up universe. Pretty, gentle things don't usually stand a chance. But that's what she is, everything beautiful that comes from pain. The spot where lightning struck sand, and instead of decimating her, she formed into a lovely pillar of glass.

Something everyone wants a piece of. Including me.

"You're staring at me." Lili cracks a smile. Soft, gentle, barely there. Innocence leaking from her cool exterior.

"I am."

There's no point arguing. I don't care about the grass, the flowers, or the leaves. She's the only beauty worth looking at out here.

I'm a pussy-whipped punk. It's official.

"Come on." I grab her hand and lead her further into the open space until we reach a flat patch of earth.

Opening the bag I've had slung over my shoulder, I pull out a blanket and lay it down so we can sit. Then I dig into the bottom for some food.

"You packed a picnic?" Her eyebrows pinch.

I shrug. "It's just a little food."

"It's a picnic." She laughs, but her eyes are bright and excited. "Who are you and what have you done with Rome?"

"I think the correct question is..." I lean in and wrap my hand around the back of her neck, bringing my lips a fraction away from hers. "What have *you* done with Rome?"

We're so close, our lips brush when she smiles. Our teeth almost clink when I lean in. Her breath is my air, and I need it like my own fucking heartbeat.

Lili tips her chin up and kisses me, sliding her hand onto my thigh as she does. Her sweet lips plant themselves on mine, and I lose all thought. Birds dance in the trees and it feels a little like the fairytales I never bothered myself with.

If that's the case, Lili's the princess in the tower, and I'm the villain who isn't allowed to keep her. Who definitely isn't allowed to taste her.

But she tastes like *mine*.

When she pulls back, her fingers curl on my leg like she's trying to hold on the same way I am, and we blink at each other for a minute, absorbing whatever this is. If only it didn't all feel fleeting as she shifts her body and turns her focus to the meadow around us.

I distract myself from my trailing thoughts by reaching for a bag of fruit. I grab a piece of cantaloupe and can't help but feed it to her. She hesitates for only a moment before wrapping her lips around my fingers to take it.

Fuck, she's hot.

But more than that, I love feeding her. Caring for her. Giving her things she's been deprived of. I want her to have it all.

"I didn't take you for a man of nature," she says, swallowing her bite and leaning back on her hands to look up at the sky.

"Probably because I'm not." I pop a grape in my mouth. "Noah told me about this place. Apparently, he and Merry come out here sometimes. Sounded like something you'd like."

"Me?"

I nod, and it seems to catch her off guard because her face pinches in confusion.

"That's really sweet of you." She sounds almost sad about it.

I'm not sure anyone has called me sweet before. I don't do things because other people will enjoy them. I please myself, first and foremost. Lili breaks all my rules.

"Come here." I lay down and stretch my arm out.

She lays down beside me and curls into the crook of my arm. She feels like she belongs there as we look up at the bright blue sky. There are only a few clouds, slowly changing shape as we stare at them.

"Elephant," Lili says, pointing up to a cloud with a long swivel sticking out the side of it.

I tilt my head slightly. "If you say so."

"I do." She laughs. "Besides, elephants are good luck, so maybe that's a good thing."

"Are they?" I brush her arm with my fingertips and feel her shiver through her sweater. The sweetest little shake that runs all the way through her.

"They are. An elephant is a symbol of good things because they stop all bad from passing them." She lets out a heavy sigh, and I wonder if it's because we both know an elephant in the sky isn't enough to stop the bad things coming to both of us.

The wind agrees, slowly changing the elephant's shape, erasing the hope of anything but pain.

I watch the cloud change. The trunk breaking off, the back arching further, the lines of it thinning out. And I swear I see it become a black cat in front of me, crossing my path in warning.

Lili rolls to her side and props her head up with her hand. "Do you think it's good luck or bad luck that I met you?"

"Depends how you look at it, I guess."

"How do you look at it?"

She's always throwing my own questions back at me, and I love how she's curious about the things most people don't give a shit about when it comes to me.

"Well..." I grab her hips and pull her up and on top of me so she's straddling my hips.

She tips her head back and laughs so loud it spreads out in the air around us. But like her, there's no chasing it, and I have to accept the silence as it vanishes.

"I don't look at me meeting you as luck, since I don't believe in it." I brush a strand of her hair away from her face. "There's no such thing as cosmic fate or chance. Sometimes good things happen, sometimes bad things. Sometimes coincidences. But it's not a higher power pulling strings. It just is."

"I can't decide if that's realistic or depressing." She frowns.

"Both, probably." I rub my hands up and down her thighs. "I'm glad you ran into me though."

She smirks and shakes her head. "Literally."

"*Literally*," I repeat, and she does a cute little eye roll at me mocking her. "You reminded me I'd lost it."

She leans in, folding her arms and propping herself on my chest so we're almost nose to nose. "What had you lost, Rome Moreno?"

"Existence."

"Isn't that all we do?"

"Technically, yes, we all exist." I brush my nose against hers. "But having, wanting, needing to get a taste of life again—I lost the part that makes things mean something."

"And I make you want a taste?" She narrows her eyes.

I love the little challenges she issues when she doesn't even realize it.

Grabbing her ass, I roll, flipping her until she's beneath me, out of breath in surprise. Her legs tighten around my hips, and even with clothes on, I feel connected.

"A taste of you would never be enough, sweetheart." I trail a line of kisses from her jaw to her neck, down to her collarbone. "You're the drug my body's been craving, and I can't get enough."

Kissing a path up the center of her throat to her chin, to her lips, I take her. I claim her with a kiss while the earth wraps us in the wind. She moans around my tongue as her arms cling to me.

Above us, I feel the clouds changing with the weather. Figures shifting because it's all temporary. But I hold her like we aren't because I'm not ready to pull away and see the different thing we're becoming if I can't have it.

30

ROME

She smells like fall. The outside air clings to her skin as we make our way inside my house, like it isn't ready to let go of her. Lili smiles at me over her shoulder and something inside me breaks.

"Drink?" I watch her walk into the living room as I make my way to the fully stocked bar in the kitchen.

My house is wide open, and I've never appreciated it more than in this moment when I can watch her circle. She strips off her sweater, leaving her in jeans and a simple cropped black tank top that shows off her toned stomach.

Lili is the definition of beauty and grace, and I'm in awe of her.

"Yes, please." She watches me cross the room.

I grab a bottle of vodka and start making her something sweet, mostly because I want to taste it on her lips. I want to get drunk on her mouth filled with vodka and cherries.

She continues into the living room, her eyes moving to the stripper poles in the middle of it. I wish I could read her mind to find out what she's thinking. It was clear when she first saw them they made her uncomfortable, but since then, she hasn't paid them much attention.

Except right now, she's walking up to one of them and brushing her fingertips over the pole in interest. So I can't help but ask, "Do they bother you?"

I've never cared, which was the point of installing them. They were a dare for women to tell me they were offended because it didn't matter. My house, my enjoyment. I've always been a bit of a voyeur when it comes to watching a woman dance, so fuck other people's opinions. But Lili's thoughts are different, and I want to hear them.

Lili wraps her hand around the pole and looks at me. "At first, maybe. At the very least, they painted an interesting view in my head of you."

Something about that statement hurts, even if it's accurate. I'm a fuckboy, an asshole, and so many other labels I shouldn't be proud of.

"But I think I get you more now," Lili says, slowly walking around the pole, holding onto it as she does. "You've got a lot of defenses, and you're smart at how you plant them, like with these. Making sure no one thinks they can get close."

She pauses with her back to me, looking over her shoulder and smiling.

"Am I right?"

I pour her drink and can't help but smirk. "You know you are."

That makes her let out a sweet laugh as she starts walking around the pole again, this time leaning away slightly so some of her bodyweight is on her arm, and she knows she has my full attention.

"They scared me at first," she says, going in circles that hypnotize me. "They're bold like you, and I'm…"

She trails off, not finishing her thought.

Picking up both our glasses, I walk over to the couch and take a seat, setting hers down and taking a big drink of mine.

"You're perfect." I set my drink beside hers.

She smiles, even if she doesn't look at me. And I watch the slightest blush climb from her chest to her neck.

"You know…" She leans a little more, so she's really using the pole for support as she slowly moves around it now. "Just because I'm not a stripper, doesn't mean I can't work a pole."

Fuck, this woman knows how to tease me. "I have no doubt about that, sweetheart."

Lili pauses in front of the pole and turns her back to it, grabbing it behind her, and I'm tempted to tie her to it so she can't ever get away.

"You make me someone else," she says with a solemn expression.

"Is that so?" I stretch my arms out on the couch and bite my lip in thought, not sure if it's good or bad, but also not really caring. "Well, you make me someone better."

It's the truth and a little fucking terrifying. Lili makes me want to be someone I wasn't raised to be. She makes me want to give a shit.

"Maybe you already were good, Rome. And you just forgot."

I tick my head to the side. "A good man wouldn't be thinking the kinds of things I do about you, sweetheart."

The corner of her lip curls up slightly. "What kinds of things?"

The little minx loves when I take control in the bedroom, and it might be the fucked-up result of the fact that she's never controlled a thing in her life, but in my arms, I don't mind it.

"Well, right now, I'm picturing you upside down and spread wide open," I say, noticing her blush become more prominent. "Does that offend you?"

She shakes her head very slowly.

"Then take off your pants, Lili."

Her muscles relax at my command, and I love it. She doesn't so much as pause before reaching for the button on her jeans and slowly dragging them down over her hips, kicking them off. Her black lace underwear is so tiny it barely covers her perfect pussy, and I can't help but grab my erection through my pants at the sight of her. Her eyes follow the movement.

"Do you want to show me how you can work a pole?"

She was the one who started this little tease, and I have no problem pushing her to her limits.

Lili nods, and I love the fact that she wants to please me, even if I don't understand it. I don't deserve it. But this girl—who tastes like pears and wine and shit I shouldn't be allowed to sample—hands me all of her.

I stretch my arms out along the back of the couch and try to ignore my cock aching to be inside her as she slowly reaches overhead. Her hands slide up her body, the sides of her chest, and into her hair, until she pulls out the ponytail and lets her hair fall around her shoulders. She brushes it away as she reaches up and grabs the pole above her head.

Her hips tick side to side as she grips the pole and slowly starts to lower, keeping her knees pressed tightly, teasing me with a hint of the view I'm desperate for. When her ass hits her heels, she twists around and straightens her legs, with her hands still low on the pole so she's bent over, and her perfect heart-shaped ass is on display.

Lili's gracefulness shouldn't surprise me since I've seen her dance before, but the power and fluidity in her movements have me speechless. She stands up and grabs onto the pole, jumping up to twist a leg around it as she starts to spin.

"You've done this before?" I ask her, feeling ready to rip the eyes out of anyone who's seen her like this, even if it's hypocritical.

Her spin slows, and she grips her thighs to the pole, bending her back almost unnaturally, because the girl is really fucking flexible.

"No. Just for you."

She plants one foot on the ground as her spinning comes to a stop, and her eyes are on me as she bends her other knee and slowly kicks her leg higher and higher, pulling it until she's doing the splits against the pole.

Her flexibility is enough to make me almost come in my pants.

"I've never been jealous of a pole before," I say, looking at her legs stretched open along it. "But I think that just changed."

Bringing my hand to my face, I scratch my jaw and let my eyes roam unapologetically over her.

"Come here, sweetheart." I curl my finger, motioning her toward me. "And lose the top while you're at it."

She drops her leg and starts walking toward me—an angel, a gazelle, weightless. She moves like the air is water and she's swimming through it.

Slowly, she reaches for the bottom hem of her tank and peels it overhead, revealing her hard nipples and no bra covering them.

I love her tits. Small and natural and perfect and hers. I love her confidence. I love the way she licks her lips when she sees me staring.

Lili stops in front of me in her scrap of black underwear, and she's absolutely flawless.

"Do you enjoy teasing me?" I ask, lifting a hand up to run it over her flat stomach, slowly trailing down, until it's just a finger, skimming over her panties and teasing her pussy.

She bites her lip, holding in a moan. "Maybe."

I slip my finger through the front of her panties from one side, all the way to the other, and pull her toward me, which makes the lace dig into her pussy. She gasps, and I want to do it again just to make her repeat the sound.

Tugging again, I make sure it rubs just right to hit her clit, and I can see the glisten of her getting wet from the friction.

"Two can play that game, you know?" I tug again, and her hips try to ride the sensation of her underwear rubbing against her.

I let go and she moans in disappointment, frowning at me.

"Don't worry, sweetheart. I'm going to fill you up so good; you'll forget you were ever mad at me."

She swallows hard as I reach down to strip my pants off, leaving them at my ankles and pulling her to straddle my lap. Lili wraps her arms around my shoulders, and I'm tempted to flip us around and fuck her from behind, so I don't have to look into her big brown eyes. Because as much as I enjoy the sight of her pleasure, it almost destroyed me last time.

But I'm selfish.

I'm stupid.

I have to have all of her.

"You wet from the thought of me fucking you with nothing between us?"

Lili's nails dig into the back of my neck. "I don't ever want there to be anything between us."

She seems almost scared of her statement. Scared to let go, scared to hold on. And honestly, I'm scared to hear it. But her hips grind, and I feel the excitement in the fear of it.

I grab my dick and slap it against her pussy, pulling her lace panties to the side. "Then sit on my dick and make me come, sweetheart."

Lili bites her lip, turning it a deeper shade of red as she lifts her hips. I position myself at her entrance, and she's so wet I'm already almost sliding inside her.

She's the first person I've fucked bare and continuing to do so is probably the dumbest shit I've ever done. But I don't give a shit as she impales herself on my dick, and it forces the air from her chest.

Her arms tighten around my shoulders, and she buries her face in the side of my neck.

"Rome," she whispers.

Why do I love hearing my name in that half-breath from her lips? A space midway between pleasure and pain. Because if she feels a fraction of how tight she is around my cock, it must hurt her too. But I don't care, I want all of it. I want to please her, to hurt her, to ruin her.

Because that's what she's doing to me.

"You feel so good, baby. I've got you." My hands dig into her hips.

She pulls back and grabs the sides of my face, looking so deep into my eyes I think she embeds herself in my brain. Her hips start to move, and I can see every sensation she's feeling. But she doesn't pick up the pace. She rides me slowly, and I let her.

She feels like the bridge between heaven and hell, but I can't decide in which direction I'm going.

Her thumbs graze my lips before she leans in for a kiss. And with my dick so far inside her I feel like I'm coming out the other side, she circles. She swivels. Our tongues dance like she did around the pole while her hips ride me like she can't get enough.

She moves until she starts to shake, and the pain of her pussy tightening around me brings me to the ledge. She moves until I do what I said, I fill her with all that's left of me. My release, my soul, my heart—and I didn't think that fucker existed anymore.

31

LILI

The tape measure is pulled tight around my waist, and on instinct, I hold my breath. I wait for the seamstress to release it and scribble a number down in her little notebook like somehow it holds the power to measure my worth.

While I'm with Rome, I want to be free of these chains, but the moment he's gone, they strangle me. I balance every bit of indulgence with starvation, and I feel myself slipping.

I can't remember a time in my life when I wasn't dieting, it's a habit that might as well be a part of me, and even if I'm exhausted and want to break free from these patterns, my mind is as trained as my body.

The seamstress releases the tape from my waist, and I breathe a sigh of relief. I watch her scribble down the numbers, and they haven't changed. If only they could measure how I'm disappearing in other ways.

Every day closer to my performance chips me away. The part that's falling for the man I'll never have starts to rot, and I feel the cavity in my chest growing. If I thought my lack of calories would waste me away, it's nothing compared to holes in myself no one else can see forming.

Rico gasps beside me, and it's so abrupt my stomach jumps up my throat.

"Thank you." He hangs up his phone call and slaps his phone down on the dressing room table.

"Good news?"

He turns to face me, grinning wide as he rakes his dark hair out of his face. "Only if you consider a lead in Lemmon Rue's next production good news."

Crossing his arms over his chest, he pretends to be nonchalant, but his eyes are glowing. After all, Lemmon Rue productions are the pinnacle of modern dance.

"That's incredible. I didn't know you were even considering Paris."

Rico props himself against the dressing room table and watches the seamstress take my final measurements.

"I'm never *not* considering Paris, Lili." He tips his chin down and looks at me like I've lost my mind for suggesting it.

The seamstress steps back, collecting her notebook and tape, and I grab my shirt off the back of a chair. It's freezing in here, and I wish they cared about the dancers enough to even consider turning up the heat when we do our fittings.

"Well, congratulations. That's incredible."

"What about you?" Rico ticks his head to the side. "Where are you headed after this?"

"No idea." I shrug. "You'd have to ask my mother."

"Or Vaughn." He pins me with his stare.

My stomach sinks at the mention of his name. Since the night at the restaurant, Vaughn has been staying extra close. He shows up at rehearsal unprompted and keeps an eye on me.

I have no doubt he's well aware I'm still seeing Rome, but he hasn't tried to do anything about it beyond his initial threats. Which is somehow even more unnerving.

Like I'm his, and I'm only offered this choice because he allows it for now.

"Why do you let them control you?" Rico frowns. "Come with me to Paris. I'm sure Lemmon would die to have Lili Chen grace her stage."

"I can't."

Rico's expression tightens. "They don't own you."

"They might as well."

"Lili." Rico pushes off the counter and walks over to me. "You've been so different here in Denver. I've never seen you like this. Free—actually enjoying yourself for once. And don't even try to lie to me and tell me it's the show because I know it's not. It's because you're choosing yourself for once and actually living."

"It doesn't change anything in the long run."

"It could."

I wish. But Vaughn would destroy my career before he'd watch me do what makes me happy, and I worry Mom might let him.

"What does Rome think?"

My eyebrows knit and my throat tightens at the thought of him.

"Don't even try to deny it." Rico shakes his head. "I see him picking you up from practice. You're fucking him."

"So then why does it matter what he thinks if that's all it is?"

"Is it?" He lifts an eyebrow. "Is that all he is, Lili?"

I bite my tongue because we both know the truth. Rome is the slice of energy in my otherwise dull day. He's the splash of color on my blank page.

I shake my head.

"Exactly." Rico smiles. "This is the happiest I've seen you in years and the best I've seen you dance. He's good for you, and you deserve it."

He's good in the worst ways because I know Rico is right, but it doesn't make him and I any more possible. We're having our fun, but Rome is even less likely to settle down in one spot than I am. And even if it hurts to think about it, I know him. The moment he finds someone else who catches his attention, he'll move on.

"I wish that was enough."

Two knocks come at the door before it swings open. Rico's eyes dart over my shoulder, and his smile immediately falls.

I turn to see Mom walking into the room as the air is sucked out of it.

"On that note." Rico walks up to me and holds my forearm, leaning close and giving me a hard look. "It can be enough if you let it. You're stronger than you think, Lili."

He squeezes my arms, and even after letting go, I still feel him.

Rico is the closest friend I've had since I started dancing. We've crossed paths in shows a number of times over the years, and since we were the opposite sex, there was never the competitive edge I felt from the other dancers.

While many of them looked at me like they were hoping I'd roll an ankle so they could take my spot, Rico stood beside me. He believed in me. He's been there when I've been tired and bruised and defeated. Something his eyes remind me of as they remain locked on mine.

"See you tomorrow." He leans in and kisses me on the cheek before brushing past Mom.

She walks in, not so much as looking at him as she circles me and takes the spot where he was standing in front of the mirror.

"How was the fitting?" Her fingers clutch the strap of her purse.

"Good." I nod.

In the mirror I see my reflection beside her. And for the first time in as far back as I remember, I see a hint of myself in her. Because there's something in her eyes I'm not sure I've ever seen before—a hint of sadness?

"Do you want to go to Paris?" Mom asks with a pinch between her eyebrows that's unlike her.

I grab my jeans off the back of the chair and slip them on. "You heard that?"

"Some of it."

I'm not sure what confuses me more, that Mom is asking or that she seems genuinely interested in my answer, when she never is. Mom has never asked me what I want to do next. She arranges, and I show up. But here she is with the strangest look in her eyes. One that makes me think she's actually curious.

"I don't know. I haven't thought about it."

It's a lie. I've considered every option on the table for what my life could be after this performance. The problem is, each scenario I try on feels wrong because there's only one thing that feels right.

You can't have him.

"Well, it's an option. Vaughn was hoping for something out of the country next, anyway. Spread your wings a little." Mom rolls her shoulders back.

I have to fight to not roll my eyes because I'm sure he is. But not for the reasons Mom might think. I have no doubt in my mind he wants me as far away from Rome the moment this show is over.

"Speaking of Vaughn..." Mom pauses, looking me over once more, and that same hint of something unfamiliar plays behind her eyes. "I saw the photo from dinner. I take it the reunion was more than professional?"

"On his end." I grind my teeth and pull my hair back into a ponytail.

Any reminder of his lips on mine makes me want to scrub my skin clean off.

"And yours?"

"Why? Would that make you happy?" I snap, feeling myself slipping. The look on Mom's face shows she's as surprised as I am. "That's what you wanted, right?"

Mom and Dad were the ones to introduce us—to encourage us. She was the one heartbroken when we split.

So I'm not sure why she looks almost unhappy at this conversation.

"I did," she says, not offering much more.

But then the most surprising thing happens. Mom's lips turn down in a frown, and it's the most genuine expression I've seen on her in years. Reminding me of a version of herself she was when Dad was still around.

"We'll talk more later," Mom says, walking past me without a hug.

Every time she does that it widens the hole inside me because even if I should be used to her unaffectionate nature by now, it doesn't make me stop wishing someday it will change.

"Lili." Mom pauses at the door but not turning to face me. Her back is stiff, and her fingers are tight on her purse. "Let me know if there is somewhere you want to go next. I'll talk to Vaughn."

She disappears, leaving me feeling like the air has been kicked from my stomach. What I want has never mattered before, and that one statement is the most care she's shown in years. Plus the fact that she offered herself up to talk to Vaughn. In the past, she'd be anxious for the opportunity to put me face-to-face with him for any reason.

But today I get the strange impression she's acting as a barrier.

Doesn't she want us back together?

I'm still trying to wrap my head around my strange interaction with her as I gather my things and make my way out of the building. Mom almost looked like she cared, and I can't help but replay the past week in my head. How she's kept her distance, even after rehearsals. How she hasn't commented on my meals or the circles under my eyes. How I caught her in more than one tense conversation with Vaughn across the room.

What have I been missing?

I push open the theater door and am met with a familiar figure standing across the street, leaning against his Range Rover. My insides flutter at how casually his smile crosses his face. At how it grows with every step I walk toward him.

Even if I know Mom has seen him picking me up after practice, I don't care anymore. I'm already running on borrowed time with him.

"Hey, sweetheart." Rome smiles, cupping my jaw as I reach him and pulling my face to his.

Two words and I don't care if other dancers are leaving the building or if I know Vaughn's men are watching at a distance. I don't care about being caught or chastised. I don't care about anything that isn't Rome.

Two words and I know exactly what I want when this performance ends. If only that meant I could have it.

32

LILI

Waking up in Rome's arms makes it feel impossible to leave. Whoever I was before meeting him in Denver isn't the same person I am right now.

She was imaginary, going through the motions. It wasn't until Rome dug his hands in the pit of my stomach and pulled the real me out that I finally saw the real girl beneath my molded clay version.

A girl with no strings.

A girl less agreeable.

Enjoying, feeling, *existing*.

Rome peppers a kiss on the back of my neck, telling me he's awake.

"Good morning." I nuzzle against him.

He wraps his arms around me tighter and presses his hips against my ass, digging his hard dick into it. "Morning, sweetheart."

I roll until I'm facing him, and he pulls my leg up over his hip.

"Can I ask you a question?"

He holds me close, cupping my face with his hand like he does often, rubbing his thumb over my lip and toying with my reactions. "Anything."

I pull my lip between my teeth and bite the spot he was just toying with. I swear I can taste him on me. I smell him in my pores. Spice, danger.

Sacrifice. One I'd willingly make if I thought it could change things.

Rome's eyebrows pinch, and he pulls back slowly as he tries to read my face. His hand falls to my hip, and he runs his thumb in the sweetest circles over it.

"Do you ever get tired of music?" I ask, letting out the sigh I've been holding.

"Music, no." He leans in and gives me a kiss on the forehead, brushing my hair off my face. "It's in my blood. It's my home. I don't know where I'd be without it."

"What do you mean?"

Rome pauses with his hand on my shoulder, watching me, and even if he's still right here, I feel his eyes become distant as he travels somewhere in his mind that doesn't seem to bring him much comfort.

"My mom was a singer for a local band," he says. "I've only heard a couple of really old recordings, but they were good. If things had gone differently for her, she might have been able to make something of it."

He's absentmindedly tracing circles on my shoulder, and his eyes are fixed at the spot on my skin, like he's making a pattern of his memories on me.

"She met my dad and got pregnant. And from what he said, she was happy about it, even if she shouldn't have been. She was willing to give it all up for me. Not that she knew it'd also take her life."

I open my mouth to say something but think better of it, snapping it closed when his eyes focus on mine. Hurt swirling with loss, still fresh in the wounds deep inside him.

"My father hated me for killing her, even if it was just a *complication*." He says the word like even he doesn't believe it. Like his father convinced him that his birth and his mother's death are his fault. "He made sure to remind me of that every way he could. Said if she had to suffer for me, he'd make sure she got her justice. He was a drunk, and a druggie, and a piece of shit."

Rome shakes his head and my hand trails down his chest, over the ink laced with scars. And even if I've seen them before, now they seem to cut deeper into his flesh. They leak into the places Rome doesn't talk about. But while he seems to think it makes him impossible to love, I can feel his heart beating through them.

I trail down until I place my hand over the most ragged scar that stretches the length of his side and stomach.

"That was when he pushed me into a glass table," Rome says, nonchalantly, like it's nothing out of the ordinary for a parent to do that to their child.

I may not be emotionally close with my parents, but they would never physically hurt me.

Rome pulls me closer and looks me dead in the eyes. We're so close I can feel the pain spilling out of him.

"He tried every way possible to break me. But you can't break something that was never together in the first place. I've always been pieces since the day I was born. Never meeting the only person who might have given a shit about me. So I held onto the only things I could—and music was that. It was in her blood, and if it was in mine, then I still had something in me that wasn't him."

Reaching up, I cup his jaw in my hand. "She isn't the only person to give a shit about you. The band does. And… me."

He places his hand over mine, and we're in the bubble of pillows and blankets and morning sunshine streaming through the window. A scene that makes even Rome Moreno appear reachable.

"You," Rome says, looking into my eyes with such intensity I can hardly stand it. "You're like music. Something good in all this fucked up chaos."

"I'm not all good," I remind him.

There's darkness swimming inside me that I don't talk about. A few times over the years I almost gave into it. At least then I wouldn't have to feel the restriction, and I could just be free. Rome's been the first person to quiet it in a long time.

Rome smirks, bringing my vision back into focus. It's a beautiful mix of wicked and playful, and I want to keep his smile in my heart for bad days. Something to look at when things don't feel worth getting through.

"You're good for me," he says.

"You're good for me."

He frowns. "I'm not good for anyone."

I press my lips together, tracing the hard lines of his face with my gaze, trying to read the softness in his expression because he fights so hard to hide it. I graze my thumb up over his cheek and brush the stubble that rubs the pads of my fingers roughly.

"Then why did you tell me all that?" I challenge him. "Why do you let me see some of the good if you don't believe it exists?"

"Because I can't help it."

My heart tightens in my chest, but I try not to let it show on my face because he'd see me falling so hard for him it's going to break every bone in my body when I hit the ground.

"People always look at me like I'm broken, or fucked up, or whatever I let them see." He chokes on the last word. "But that's the surface, Underneath is so much worse. I'm a fucking mess, and all I want to do is show that to you for some reason."

"To scare me away?"

"Maybe hoping it doesn't." Honesty and fear flash in his eyes.

And I understand what he's saying more than he realizes. Because I don't show people my sharp edges either. Except with him, I offer them just to see if he can handle it.

I hold his face in my hands as he holds my body in his, but it's so much more than our flesh and bones in this bed. We are raw hearts laying beneath the blankets. We are bleeding out all over each other, and it stings, and it swirls, and it's beautiful.

"I get tired of dancing," I admit. "Not the dance part, necessarily, just everything that comes along with it. But it's all I've had for so long; I don't know who I am without dance."

Rome rakes my hair back and leans in to plant a kiss on the apple of my cheek. It's so sweet and intimate, I bask in it.

"You're more than what you do, Lili."

I can't help the unamused chuckle that breaks out of me.

"I'm serious. You're so much more than just a dancer." He pulls my hand to his mouth and kisses the back of it. "You're smart and inquisitive. You see past everyone's bullshit. You're darkness, but you're also light. A yin and yang always a fraction away from tipping too far from one to the other. And you're wild. Beneath the facade they've made you into, you're actually someone else entirely. It's beautiful."

Rome sees right through, carves me open and places the parts I've feared to have on display between us.

"They don't see that."

He holds my hand against his mouth. "I do."

Something too close to peace coats this moment. Silence sits between us and with the thick windows in his house, we can't even hear the sounds of the forest stirring. There's nothing but me and Rome in this room, bare for each other in all the ways that matter. Numb and broken and not fearing the other one seeing it.

I've always worried about what someone would think if they could see the real me. The twisted parts that tangle deep. I wondered if there was anyone who could dip their heart in my darkness and still love me.

Why is it the right person comes at the wrong time? Or that the right person is also the wrong person entirely?

Because there is no time or place where Rome Moreno and Lili Chen make sense. There is no world where the two of us fit. We barely fit in the confines of our own lives, much less each other's.

I pull my hand from his mouth and rake it into his hair, moving my body flush against his as we stare into each other's eyes. His skin warms with my own, and I wonder if fusing us together can prevent them from ever tearing us apart.

Rome closes his eyes and tips his forehead so it's touching mine. He lets out a deep breath, and I feel the entire weight in his chest release as he whispers, "If I had a heart, I'd give it to you."

"You do." I nudge him with my nose, and he looks into my eyes. "And you already have, just like I've given you mine."

We shouldn't have. It's an error in judgment from two people who know better than to play in games like love. But it doesn't mean we could avoid it, either.

"I told you I'm not the man to own your heart, Lili."

"Too late." I tip my chin up to press my lips against his.

Rome's fingers tangle in my hair and he rolls, pressing me onto my back. I open my legs to make room for him between them. And without so much as breaking the kiss, he reaches down and lines himself up, thrusting inside me and fueling himself with the air that escapes from my chest.

He takes my body like he took my heart—completely.

I hold onto him, dig my nails in, claw like there's a chance I'll get out when I already know there isn't. And he thrusts into me like he's mad at me for the fact that he let me fall for him.

We fight this battle with our hearts, our teeth, our flesh. We fight this battle with our souls and with each other. It's hard and fast and angry. It's all things him and me, playing a reckless game of mercy with the universe and asking it how far it's willing to let us get. Seeing how long it takes before we're begging to stay in or get out.

A man who doesn't love.

A girl who can't.

But I feel them both disintegrating.

He props up on his elbows so he can look down at me as his thrusts intensify, and it's his eyes that draw out the last bit I'm holding back. He hits me deep and it's like he wills my climax to destroy him. And I swear I almost do. Because I burst into pieces at the feel of him inside me, carving a place only he'll ever fit.

Rome chases my orgasm with his own, so hard it hurts the way I need it to. It feels good enough to break me in two.

When we come down from the rush and he relaxes over me, he brushes my hair off my face. Leaning in, he plants the simplest, warmest, most perfect kiss on my lips.

"You can keep my heart, Lili," Rome says, kissing me again on the side of my temple and resting his forehead on the pillow beside me. "Once you leave, I'm not going to need it, anyway."

33

Lili

How can a soul hurt?

It's not an actual piece of you the way an arm or a leg is. Yet, somehow, it's more. And as Rome climbed off me this morning, I swore I felt it. It was hurting and breaking and beating like its own life force.

Rome disappeared into the shower, and I felt the air change like the seasons are about to. Fall fading and snow is on the horizon. The crisp air giving me the sense of a cold winter.

What started as fun, a challenge, a test, became something else. And while we entered this game with our bodies, our hearts ended up on the table.

It's too cold to ride the motorcycle back to my house, so Rome drives me in his Range Rover. Something about the large interior is unsettling. Instead of being pressed against his body, I'm a seat away. And I feel every inch of space the music tries to take up as we drive.

Rome is quiet, and it makes me wonder if he regrets what he admitted. Not that I'd hold it against him. Sex with him makes me spill out all over the place, so if he was just talking nonsense in the heat of the moment, who am I to judge?

But I hope he wasn't.

My fingers dig into my thighs as I stare out the window at the passing trees. It looks colder somehow. Leaves are changing color, and the Denver I showed up to a couple of months ago is being replaced with a shadow of itself.

Warmth encompasses my hand, and I look down to see Rome has reached out and placed his over mine, relaxing me. His tattooed fingers graze over my leg, and it fills me with an ease I shouldn't allow.

On the backs of his knuckles on one hand he has tattooed the word *pleasure*, and the other is *pain*. And when he touches me, I feel both, so it's strangely fitting.

"What are you thinking?" he asks, not looking at me as he casually holds the steering wheel with one hand and leans back in his seat.

"I don't know," I admit; because I don't. It's a mess in my head. Thoughts moving in and out so quickly that I can't make sense of them. "Everything."

He nods slowly, and his tongue runs between his lips, wetting them. His gaze flicks in my direction for a fraction of a second, but it feels like an eternity.

Why do moments have to be so temporary?

"Do you regret this?"

His hand squeezes mine. "No."

It shouldn't put me at ease, but it does. "Me either."

The faintest smirk ticks up at the corner of Rome's lip, and I love it so much. Love *him* so much, not that I'm brave enough to admit it.

"Something going on today?" Rome's eyebrows pinch as he turns into my driveway.

I follow his gaze and see two cars sitting there, making my heart plummet in my chest.

"Crap." I pull my hand out of Rome's and plant my palms over my face.

This can't be happening after our morning together was so perfect. Because these cars sitting here might as well be the first flakes of snow in a blizzard that's about to cause a whiteout.

"What's wrong?" Rome comes to a stop in the driveway and puts the Range Rover in park.

"Nothing," I lie, shaking my head, hoping to get him out of here to avoid whatever is about to happen. "I'll call you later, okay?"

His jaw ticks as I hurry to open the door, but I'm already too late. The front door to the house is opening, and I feel two halves of my life about to collide.

No, no, no.

This can't be happening right now.

Every good moment from this morning feels like it's running away. The memories fading into a dark place; I don't know if I'll ever be able to unbury them. I watch my mom step out the front door of the house with a cold expression, followed by Vaughn.

"Lili?" Rome plants his hand on my leg before I can climb out of the car, and it pulls my attention. "What's wrong."

"I—" but I can't finish the sentence because I'd be caught between a lie and the truth, and either of the two would hurt him.

My fling with Rome was meant to be temporary, made clear in this moment with reality approaching us. Mom and Vaughn head toward the car, and I feel time slow while it also seems to speed up.

If this day were paper, I'd tear it in two. I'd crinkle one half and keep the other. But with Mom and Vaughn watching me, I know the truth. Rome isn't my future, and even if he handed me his heart, I sold my soul years ago to pay the debt for my dreams. And payment is due.

Mom stops a few steps away from the car, but Vaughn doesn't. With a smug expression, he comes all the way to my door and grabs onto it, holding it wide open.

"There's my fiancé," Vaughn says with a wicked smile, looking at me, then over my shoulder. "And the man she's been fucking."

Rome's hand pulls away, and I feel the emptiness on my skin like there's a hole in it. I turn in time to meet an expression I've never seen on Rome's face. Shock, hurt. It's like those words just ripped out his insides, and he doesn't know how to put them back in.

"Rome." I reach for his hand and am surprised when he lets me take it. "It's not like that."

His eyes cut to mine, and they're so dark they're nearly black.

Rage.

Something I've never fully seen from him, even if I've always known it existed right beneath his surface. And right now, it's all he is.

"He's my ex, that's it."

"You hurt my feelings when you say things like that, Lili," Vaughn says, reminding me he's standing right there with the door open. "We're working things out, remember? We talked about it."

I feel the bile rising in my throat, my stomach trying to jump out. Turning to face Vaughn, I'm met with what can only be described as pure evil, and he's amused.

"Fuck you, Vaughn," I say, and he actually seems surprised by my harsh words. "You talked, but I never agreed to it."

I shake my head as my throat closes in, and I feel like I'm about to suffocate. The sides of the car are trying to close in on me. I need to get away from Vaughn, from my mom, even Rome before I explode. Because I swear that's what's about to happen. I'm going to burst, and maybe if I'm lucky, it'll all be over.

I jump out of the car, but as I try to step away, a hand catches my arm and stops me.

"Do I need to remind you who you're talking to?" Vaughn's playfulness has all but faded, and he's looking at me with the controlling expression I've seen on his face many times.

He opens his mouth to say something else, but he's pulled backward before he gets the chance.

I'm not sure when Rome got out of the car, but he has Vaughn by the shoulder, and then Rome's hand is wrapped around his throat as he pushes him against the car.

"Don't you dare put a fucking hand on her." Rome's gaze is murderous.

"I could charge you with assault." Vaughn smirks, like this is the reaction he was hoping for.

He must not see what I'm seeing because when Rome smiles back there's nothing gentle about it. It's a warning, like he is seriously considering snapping Vaughn's neck.

Walking up slowly, I place my hand on Rome's shoulder. "He's not worth it."

The muscles in Rome's forearm flex as he tightens his grip, holding it like that for a long moment before dropping his hand. I sense it took everything in him to do it as Vaughn tries to catch his breath.

Rome steps back, but he keeps his body between Vaughn and me as Vaughn stands up tall and starts laughing. It's not playful or amused, it's maniacal. And it gives me a sinking feeling in my stomach.

"Cute," Vaughn says, catching his breath, and I realize Mom has come up beside him, but she's quiet.

Mom is an opinionated woman, except around certain men—Vaughn is one of them. She wants their money and their status. So she allows them the guise of feeling like they're in control if it means staying in their good graces.

But right now, when I meet her stare, she looks worried. I'm not sure she's seen this side of Vaughn before, and Rome's protective actions aren't de-escalating the situation. I feel her thinking the same thing I am, *how far is this going to go?*

"You've had your fun." Vaughn's looking at me again, ignoring Rome between us. "Strip clubs and bars and God knows whatever else."

"How do you—"

"I know everything you do, Lili." Vaughn cuts me off. "And this ends now."

"It's adorable you think that's your decision," Rome says, narrowing his eyes at Vaughn.

In my social circle, Vaughn is a powerful man. People don't talk back or stand up to him, but Rome is Rome, and he doesn't care. He is who he is, and he says what he wants. And he's standing up for me.

It's almost... *romantic*?

"It is my decision," Vaughn's eyes snap to Rome. "Who do you think runs the company that owns her career? One word and I could end it."

Rome's jaw hardens at the realization. He and I haven't talked about the fact that my ex-boyfriend has complete control over my future in dance. He made me who I am, and he could take it all away if he wanted. It's how he's kept his place in my life this long.

When you sell your soul to the devil, he usually intends to keep it.

"Trust me when I say, you don't need this trouble." Vaughn might still be talking to Rome, but his eyes scan me like I'm nothing, an object in this conversation. "I've heard about your reputation, anyway. You won't be lonely for long. Lili is mine."

"Wrong again. She's not anyone's but her own because she's a fucking person." Rome takes a step toward him.

"And if you say that shit again, I might be tempted to show you the parts of my reputation that are less known by the press."

His fingers flex, and I can sense him holding back, but the dam is so close to breaking. Water beats on the wall, and he's begging Vaughn to do one thing to push him over the edge.

"She is mine," Vaughn says, stepping in. "From her career to her fucking virginity, you piece of rock star trash."

I don't know who moves first, but Mom steps back as chaos unfolds. It's like watching lightning strike a foot away from you and seeing it split the world open where it once was whole.

Except this is skin, blood, and bone.

They're on each other, then apart. I can't tell who is winning or losing as they tumble around. I reach in and try to break them up, but it's no use, and Rome tries to get between me and Vaughn when Vaughn's fist almost connects with my jaw in the midst of it.

Rome hits Vaughn in the face so hard I'm sure it breaks his nose, but Vaughn retaliates by shoving Rome against a tree.

"Stop." I grab onto Vaughn's arm and try to pull him off, even if I know Rome doesn't need the help as he's already recovering.

But Vaughn swings his arm back, shoving me hard.

And time slows as I fall.

Down.

Down.

Down.

I really am weightless, but somehow, gravity still manages to pull me to the ground. And I hear the snap before I feel it, so loud it echoes through the empty forest. And then there's only pain.

34

ROME

My face aches, my body aches, but from the moment I heard the snap, none of my pain mattered. Because he fucking pushed her.

It took everything in me not to murder him on the spot for it because when Lili screamed, I lost all sense of sanity.

I looked over to see Lili on the ground, her leg twisted beneath her where she'd tripped over a rock as she fell backward. And for some reason, instead of reaching for her leg, she was holding her stomach. Like everything inside her hurt in that moment.

I've felt all kinds of pain—knives, burns, knuckles, and broken bones. But watching her face twist in unrecognizable anguish was the worst.

"What happened?" Adrian stops in front of me.

He's definitely pissed, not that I blame him. I'm sure getting a call from jail to come pick me up wasn't how he planned on spending his day.

"Assholes," I say, tipping my head back. "Please tell me you're getting me the fuck out of here."

"Just posted bail, let's go."

He doesn't say anything else as we make our way out of the police station. And as much as it hurts biting my tongue, I don't say shit because I don't need anyone to overhear something and decide to hold it against me later. It isn't until we get in the car that I finally let out a breath.

The fucker actually had me arrested. If I thought being a celebrity gave me some kind of sway with law enforcement, it's nothing compared to what Vaughn's money can do. The second he saw me try to get in the ambulance to go with her to the hospital, the asshole said I assaulted him.

Technically true.

But semantics. The bitch hit me first. I made sure of it. I always do because I'm not going to waste my money and reputation on fights.

Although, I would for Lili.

Because the fucker. Pushed. Her.

"What the fuck happened?" Adrian asks me again, pulling out of the station.

"Her ex showed up, that's what." I rake my hands through my hair. "He's a fucking dick."

"So you hit him?"

"He hit me first," I say, noticing Adrian about to turn down the wrong road. "Wait, turn right. I need to get to the hospital."

In my five-second phone call to Adrian, I didn't get to explain what was happening, but now that I'm out, there's no way I'm not going to where I should have been in the first place—with Lili.

I'm done denying that I've fallen hard for this chick. Whatever started as sex or obsession has become something deeper, and I need her to know that.

"The hospital? Are you okay?" Adrian's eyes skim me.

"It's not for me. Lili's there."

He shakes his head. "Back up. Why is Lili in the hospital?"

I explain the whole thing and watch Adrian's face change. He might be frustrated with me for getting arrested for fighting, but the second he hears about Vaughn pushing Lili, his entire demeanor shifts. The same murderous rage welling inside me seems to surface within him. If there's something that pisses Adrian the fuck off, it's someone putting their hands on a woman.

"Fuck, Rome." He grips the steering wheel.

"Yeah, and the fucker has the cops in his back pocket. They laughed when I tried to tell them he was the one who hurt her."

He shakes his head. "Why didn't she?"

"I don't know." I rub the heels of my hands over my eyes. "Maybe she did. It all happened really fast once they arrived. I wasn't around her long enough to know what she did or didn't say. But Adrian—she was in so much fucking pain."

My stomach is trying to claw itself out of my body at the thought. I want to scream or puke or break something.

"We'll get to her."

Adrian is a man on a mission. We might have been at odds many times over the years he's managed the band, but right now, we're on the same page. And I'm thankful for him in ways I can't find the words to express.

It feels like it takes hours to get to the hospital, even if it's probably thirty minutes max. Every stoplight. Every car in the way. I want to push them aside and tell them to fuck off.

By the time we pull up, Adrian barely has time to park before I'm getting out of the car.

"Rome, wait." He jogs up to my side. "Let me do the talking. We don't know what's gone down after he had you locked up."

As much as I hate it, Adrian's right. Vaughn had the nerve to get me locked up for a fight he started, so I don't know what I'm walking into. It takes all my strength to compose myself as we walk into the hospital.

And the second we do, I realize what a shit show this is going to be because Vaughn is standing in the waiting area with three guys who look just like him—assholes with power.

"Shit," I say under my breath.

Adrian's eyes follow my line of sight. "Let me guess. Dick who likes to hit women?"

I nod, and I feel Adrian tense. I might be the one who needs to be kept on a leash to make sure I don't go straight back to jail, but I get the feeling Adrian isn't far behind me if something goes down.

Vaughn watches us walk up to the desk, and he looks almost amused, but he doesn't approach us, which only adds to my unease. He's not even trying to stop me, like he already feels like he's won and is enjoying watching me figure out the reason.

We get to the desk and Adrian asks what room Lili's in. I wait to be turned down and am surprised when the nurse tells us.

Vaughn's eyes don't leave us as the nurse points down the hall and offers directions. Somehow, the fact that we aren't being turned away from seeing her is unsettling.

As I follow Adrian, Vaughn finally turns away, moving back into whatever conversation the group around him is having.

I try to ignore the sinking feeling in my gut. The same one that used to tell me when Dad was on a bender, and I was about to have a really bad day. I try to ignore the mouth of hell opening beneath me as Adrian leads the way down the hall. I try to ignore Lili's mom's eyes as they connect with mine when she steps out of the room. I try to ignore her unflinching expression as she passes me like I'm nothing to her.

I've always known I don't belong in Lili's world but never felt it more than in this moment. It's how they're acting with utter disinterest. Like they don't even need to bother. A reminder of how unimportant a guy like me is to the people in Lili's life.

Adrian turns, pausing at the door to her room and planting a hand on my arm. "I'll wait here, okay?"

I nod.

"Let me know if you need anything." He looks me over. "And Rome, this right here, is about her. Just be there."

I swallow, feeling like my soul is stuck in my throat as Adrian steps aside and Lili's face comes into view through the glass door that leads to her room. She's looking out the window with an unreadable expression on her face. It reminds me of the one I was used to seeing on her in the beginning—numb.

Adrian steps aside, and I walk up to the door, taking a breath before grabbing the handle and pulling it open. I step inside and it's quiet, apart from the machines beeping.

She doesn't immediately turn to face me, and when she does, I wait for her expression to change.

It doesn't.

Her eyes are distant, and her lips don't so much as part or lift. Nothing shifts. She's cold like the girl I met, who I wanted to read more than anything. The girl I was in bed with this morning is almost entirely gone.

Lili's leg is in a cast and hung up on a sling to elevate it.

She watches me cross the room, and I sink into the chair beside the bed. I want to reach out and grab her hand, but something about her demeanor stops me from doing it. I can't tell if she even wants me here, and it reminds me of the look on Vaughn's face when I walked into the hospital.

He'd already won.

"How are you?" I look at her leg and know I'm seeing a lot more than a broken bone. I'm seeing a broken girl, a dancer about to miss out on a performance she's spent months—years—preparing for.

"It's a clean break," she says, almost clinical.

I nod, looking back at her. "That's good."

"None of this is." She wraps her arms around her stomach like she did in the forest. Like she's trying to comfort herself or hold herself in.

I can't help it, I reach out and take her hand, needing to feel her skin and offer her whatever I have left. But even though she doesn't pull away, she doesn't squeeze or return the comfort. Her fingers stay relaxed as I stroke the back of her hand with my thumb.

"I'm glad they let you out," she says, but there's not much emotion behind it.

"Yeah." I swallow. "But why wasn't he locked in there with me?"

"What are you asking me, Rome?" It's snippy, like she's already on the defense. I can feel her walls building, even though they aren't physical.

"He did this." I look at her leg. "He fucking put his hands on you."

"It was an accident."

"I'd never accidentally do anything like this."

She pulls her hand away. "That's because you're you and he's—he didn't mean to."

"Fuck that."

"Just stop it," she almost yells, but her voice is raw and croaks on the end. "It's complicated."

"Because he's your boss?" I ask her, clenching my hands into fists. "Or because he's your ex?"

I don't know what answer I'm looking for because none of them are going to comfort me, but I'm pissed off, and I hate seeing her like this. It's drawing out everything bad in me.

I wait for Lili to answer, watching her eyes close for a moment before she opens them again.

"You and I are over," she says.

At least, I think that's what I hear. It's less words and more a blade slicing my chest open.

"Why?"

I just can't help myself, so I open myself wider and see what more damage the girl can do. I've always been curious to test my limits on pain, and Lili seems to be the only one with the ability to bring me to the brink.

"What do you mean, *why*?" She's cold in her posture, her delivery, her expression. She's frozen. "We shouldn't have done this in the first place. We don't fit into each other's lives. And Vaughn will—"

"I don't give a fuck what he'll do."

"He had you locked up."

"Not the worst thing I've ever been through, remember, sweetheart?"

Lili's face softens, but it's not with hope, it's something else. She reaches out her hand, but somehow it feels distant when her fingers touch my skin. "I can't be your sweetheart, Rome. No matter how much I want to."

"But—"

"I'm sorry." She squeezes my hand. "I need to heal. And you need to go. And we both need to leave this as what it was, something that felt good in the moment, but now it's over."

She pulls away and turns her torso as much to the side as she can without moving her leg in an effort to turn away from me. She wraps her arms around her center and closes her eyes. She shuts me out in every way I can see and feel.

I stand up and hope she'll look at me, but she doesn't. Lili sighs, and I feel the pain radiating out of her.

"I'm sorry, too," I say, turning to walk away.

I brush past Adrian as I leave her room, but even if he follows me, I don't say anything.

I've had my share of broken bones in my life. They're worse than broken flesh. Deeper, more painful. But in this moment, I learn a cold hard truth. None of it comes close to a broken heart. Those hurt like a fucking bitch.

35

ROME

"Trying to forget or trying to feel?" Noah stops in front of me, and I almost don't hear him over the people and music.

I look up and see him standing there looking like he just rolled out of bed. Hair tied back and wearing a T-shirt and sweats.

"What are you doing here?"

Noah crosses his arms over his chest. "Adrian was worried about you."

"Not sure why." I stretch my arms across the couch and sit back. "I'm all good."

"Clearly." Noah's eyes drop to the coffee table in front of me where there's a buffet of drugs just waiting for me to pick my poison.

I still haven't decided what sounds more appealing because if I'm being honest with myself, none of it does.

"You shouldn't be here."

Not only because I don't feel like a fucking pep talk right now, but because this isn't the kind of party Noah needs to be at when he's a recovering addict. The entire scene is sex and drugs and all the stupid shit I've spent years surrounding myself with.

Distractions that used to seem more appealing than they do right now.

"Walk with me," Noah says, turning away and not waiting to see if I'll follow.

I'm not sure what compels me to follow him, but I get up and do. None of this shit is doing it for me anyway. I'm trying to drown out the thoughts in my head but everyone's too fucking loud and annoying. And then there are the girls who keep coming up to me with their tits out.

I used to want to fuck them, right?

Because now all they seem to do is make me want to scream. So I ignore them and sit by myself trying to forget what's raging in my chest.

Noah leads me to the backyard and it's cold this late—or early. I'm not sure what time it is. Or what day it is. I left the hospital and stepped into a black hole where nothing really exists—not even the people in my house.

I'm pretty sure I invited them here, but who knows? I stopped caring who was coming and going. I can't even tell if they're the same ones or rotating. All I know is I can't seem to be here without them because then I'd just be alone.

Noah spins when he closes the back door behind us. "What are you doing, man?"

Good question. The lights from the house make the forest strobe, and it's a little intense. I'm not sure if it's waking me up or putting me to sleep.

"Partying." I shrug.

"But are you?" Noah narrows his eyes, and I kind of hate him for reading me.

I didn't invite anyone from the band over for this very reason. I don't need people actually seeing through whatever's going on inside me right now.

"You're sober." It's not a question. "And you look miserable. Not to mention, you're sitting alone on the couch. Since when is that how you party?"

"I don't need this right now."

"Or maybe you do." Noah grabs my shoulder when I try to walk past him, forcing me to stop. "Remember when I was all fucked up about Merry, and you were a total dick to me about it?"

"So?"

"Beneath all that, you also said a lot of shit that made sense because deep down, this isn't who you are, Rome." He shakes my shoulder like he's trying to shake some sense into me. "You've used all this shit as a barrier for years, but finally you didn't need it anymore."

"Well, maybe now I need it again."

"Why?"

"She fucking broke me, man."

That wasn't what I was supposed to say. I was supposed to be fine. No one needs to know that for once I let someone in, and all they did was play more games, leaving me more broken than my father ever did.

And what sucks is deep down, I get it. I always knew Lili was too good for me. That she'd realize it at some point. I just didn't expect to feel this way when it happened.

"Good." Noah lets go of my shoulder.

I laugh really loud, not sure I heard him right. "Good?"

Noah smirks. "Yes, good. She broke you because you let her. You've never let anyone that close."

"So, this is a good thing?" I might have lost my mind. Or maybe he has because he's not making any sense.

"Love isn't easy, Rome. I mean look at me and Merry. Falling for someone is hard enough, but the shit you're gonna go through with the person afterward is even worse."

"And this is you trying to convince me of what?" I drop down into one of the lawn chairs, and he sits opposite me.

"I'm reminding you of what you said to me when I wanted to give up." Noah's expression is no longer light. "You said I needed to decide if it was worth all the pain. And at the time, I wasn't sure because it can be really hard to see the light at the end of the tunnel. But I didn't give up, and now look where I am."

"It's not the same," I argue. "Lili isn't like Merry."

"Don't I fucking know it." Noah tilts his head back and laughs. "Merry's a pain in my ass."

I shake my head and can't help but smile. The cheeriest fucking dude on the planet had to go and fall for the most difficult chick. But he doesn't seem the least bit regretful about it.

Noah stops laughing and leans forward on his elbows, looking me directly in the eyes. "Is she worth your pain, Rome? Is she worth hurting over?"

I rake my hands through my hair and think about that. About her smile, her energy. How she makes me feel like I'm not dead when I'm around her. "She's the only thing worth hurting over."

He nods, a smile ticking in the corner of his lips. Dude is fucking sunshine and it's annoying, if not comforting right now.

"I hate to break it to you, man..." He slaps a hand on my leg. "But you're in love."

I lay back on the lawn chair at his statement and let out a groan. Like maybe if I don't look at him, I can avoid his comment. Because I've had that thought and decided it was impossible. I'm not a guy who falls in love.

"Shouldn't love feel good?" I cover my face with my hands.

After all, they write books and movies about that shit—people head over heels and acting ridiculous. Love is supposed to be all rainbows and roses, but here I am, a mess and alone.

"Fuck, no," Noah says. "Love is painful."

I sit up and look him in the eyes. "Then why the fuck do it?"

Noah rests his hands behind him and leans back. He looks up at the sky, even if the stars are hidden behind clouds. Winter's closing in faster this year, and I feel it in the air—in my bones.

"Remember when Merry lost the baby?" Noah's voice cracks a little at the question.

"Yeah."

I remember Noah went through hell after that. They didn't know she was pregnant when they found out she was having a miscarriage, and it really fucked him up in the head. I remember him telling me he didn't know if he was allowed to feel sad over something he didn't know existed, and I've never seen him so broken.

"That was…" He pauses, biting his lower lip. "Unbearable."

I nod, not sure what else to say. As bad as I think things are for me right now, I realize there are things that could hurt more. The idea of Lili being pregnant with my baby and losing it. I can't handle the thought.

"Merry tried to pull away after."

"I remember." We had to follow Noah to Seattle because he refused to let her go. I thought it was a bit of a punk move at the time, but now I kind of get it.

"We all deal with things in different ways. She was hurting and that was her solution to the problem. But love isn't about backing off when shit gets hard. It's about working it out together."

"Yeah, well it must not be love then because Lili backed the fuck off real quick." So fast I've still got whiplash from it.

"And you didn't try to stop her," Noah argues.

"What was I supposed to do, man, tie her down and make her hear me?" Not a terrible idea now that I think about it.

Noah shrugs. "That's for you two to figure out. But all I can do is remind you of what you told me when shit hit the fan in my life. You need to decide if it's worth all the fucking pain. And if it is, then you need to decide if this is how you should be dealing with it."

He waves his hand to the glass wall beside us where a party rages on inside my house. People are trashed. I'm not sure I noticed when I was sitting there earlier. But they're stumbling and vacant. A couple is fucking on my kitchen table.

Is this what my life has become? Some random couple fucking in the middle of my house? I know at one point it would have been me because I didn't care where I was or who I was with. I didn't care about anything more than the exact moment I was in.

But all I can think about now are my moments with Lili and how I felt in them. How when she pushed me away, I swear she cut the beating heart straight from my chest.

I never wanted to love her, and I hate her for making me. But I hate her for ending it more. And I hate myself for letting her.

I'm not a punk. Pain doesn't scare me. So why am I still acting like that kid who drowns his problems in booze and women the moment they arise? I could be better than this if I let myself.

It's like Eloise said, sometimes you have to jump in the deep end, and maybe I'm ready.

I face Noah again. "Can I crash at your house tonight?"

"Not even going to kick 'em out?" He laughs.

"Let them have their fun." I stand up.

He shakes his head. "Whatever you say, man."

We walk toward the door, but I stop before opening it. "So why were you the sacrificial lamb coming out here tonight? Did you guys draw straws, and you got the short one?"

"Nope." He shakes his head. "I offered."

"Why?"

"Because a year ago you reminded me that we all deserve to be happy. That some things are worth the trouble and the pain. And I owed you for that."

He claps me on the back and heads inside. I follow him, ignoring the mess of people that are destroying my living room.

I'm not sure what I did to make the band care about me as much as they do, or why they always have my back. Especially when I haven't done much to deserve them.

Maybe meeting them was destiny, even if I told Lili I don't believe in that shit. Because even if my father convinced me no one could love me, they took me in.

And right now, I couldn't be more thankful for them.

36

LILI

"What do you think you're doing?" Mom walks into the room, stopping when she sees the burger on my plate.

"Eating." I take a bite and try to ignore the deep frown that forms wrinkles on her face.

"Just because you're recovering doesn't mean you can let yourself go." She stops in front of me and places her purse on the table. "If you can't train or practice, you need to be following a stricter diet to make sure—"

"What?" I set the burger down. "That I can perform again eventually?"

"Well... yes." She nods her head.

I laugh really hard because I can't stand this anymore. "My leg is broken, Mom. Snapped. I won't be performing for a very long time, so whatever ideas you have in your head, you might as well cancel them."

"The doctor said—"

"I know what they said." I cut her off for the second time in this conversation, and she looks surprised by it. Surprised is something Mom never looks. "They also said the reason my leg broke so easily from a simple fall is because I'm malnourished. Years of starvation will do that to you."

I pick up the burger again and take another bite, even if it's small. Breaking a lifetime of disordered patterns isn't as easy as I wish it was. And as much as I want to fill myself up, there's a voice in my head fighting me.

Still, I chew and swallow, letting it fill the holes and hoping over time I won't look at food and do a calorie count in my head.

"Don't be dramatic," Mom says as she begins straightening up the mess in the room. "You're not malnourished. You watch what you eat. There's nothing wrong with that. You've been on a diet."

"Since I was seven."

"It comes with the business."

"And what if I'm done with it?"

She pauses with her hand a fraction away from grabbing a glass. Her eyes drift to me, and instead of anger, I'm met with confusion.

"Done with what, exactly?"

"All of it." I sigh, setting the burger on my plate.

I'm not sure how long I've been feeling this way, but it wasn't until I met Rome that I realized it. Something about the way he loved music like it wasn't his job made me realize how dance had become something I dreaded.

Mom walks back over to the table and sits in the chair directly across from me, folding her hands in front of her.

"You don't want to dance anymore?" she asks, with a pinched expression, like she can't fathom the words coming out of my mouth.

If she thought I actually enjoyed this, I should have been an actress. Because every performance has eaten a piece of me for years, and I don't know how many bites of me there are left.

"I love *dance*," I tell her, and it's the truth. "But this job has taken the joy out of it for me. And now I just feel tired."

As painful as it was breaking my leg, once I left the hospital, I was flooded with a surprising amount of relief. It was over. The excuse couldn't be argued. There would be no show or plans in the foreseeable future.

I was free.

I'd cut a tie I didn't realize was holding me back.

"Does this have anything to do with Rome?" she asks, and I'm surprised she's able to say his name without frowning.

I close my eyes and take a deep breath. The mention of him sends me straight back to the only good thing I regret destroying.

"Yes and no." There's no point lying to her if I'm laying all of this out there. "I stopped loving this long before I met him; he's just the one who helped me realize it."

And I pushed him away.

I broke his heart.

I broke my own.

I didn't know how to deal with the loss of my career or the fact that Vaughn had him thrown in jail. I couldn't handle the fact that my life was going to hurt him, so I pushed him away before it could get worse.

Vaughn could destroy me all he wanted, but I couldn't let it happen to Rome.

So I let him go. Closed my eyes and felt him walk away. I swear the space stretched the further he got, but all it did was make me feel him more.

When he said he'd handed me his heart, I don't think he was lying because I still feel it in my hands, bloody and broken.

Looking at my mom, her face is blank, and it's hard to read anything in her expression. Her eyes are at a distance, and I'm reminded of how she looked at Dad's funeral. Almost as if a piece of her had broken off and floated away, and she was staring out at the ocean, watching it drift until it disappeared.

"Mom, are you okay?"

Her gaze flicks to mine. She drops her stare to my broken leg and back up again. She inspects the burger on my plate and my face, but I can't tell what she's thinking.

"Your father was right," she says, finally. "He said we were losing you. That he thought you were done dancing. He said your heart wasn't in it anymore. But I was so insistent."

"You couldn't have known."

"I could have." She shakes her head, and there's a softness I don't think I've ever seen in my mother starting to overcome her expression. "I didn't want to see it. You had so much potential, and I couldn't let you pass it up."

"It's not that I hate it, you know."

She nods, and I can see her thinking. "Vaughn wants you to commit to a European tour next year."

"And you want me to go?" Just the thought of Vaughn makes my stomach curl.

"I always thought he was good for you," Mom says, and when I open my mouth to argue, she holds up a hand, stopping me. "I know men can be difficult, and he struggled with fidelity."

She says it like an excuse, like I should expect it and accept it, but I'm not sure why.

"But after this..." Her gaze moves once more to my broken leg, and this time I realize there is pain in her expression.

My mother, who doesn't show affection, who acts like she doesn't care, seems bothered by the fact that my leg is broken. And it isn't because I can't dance. It's because Vaughn caused this.

She was there, she knows the truth just as I do. I might have tried to deny it with Rome, but I know Vaughn pushed me. I was just too brainwashed and broken to do anything about it at the time.

So I hid from the reality of the situation, and I walked away from the only man who ever mattered to me.

"Do you want to do the European tour?" she asks.

I shake my head. "I don't know what I want to do anymore. I know I need to figure out something—"

"Lili." She reaches across the table and puts her hand over mine. I'm not sure she's ever touched me in a way that didn't feel like her picking me apart, but there's care behind her gesture. "Just heal. We'll talk about it later."

I don't know how to respond to her statement. It throws me completely off balance. She isn't berating me or making me feel guilty about this decision. She's accepting it, and for the first time in my life, I feel like she's accepting me.

"Thank you." I almost choke on the words.

Mom nods, looking around the room. I follow her gaze and realize what a disaster it is. I got discharged from the hospital a few days ago, and I've been a mess ever since. Between takeout deliveries and movies, I've barely moved from this room.

Luckily, Eloise hasn't come by to see what I've done to her house.

"Here, let me clean up," Mom says, standing and starting to straighten up again.

I'm not sure who this woman is who showed up today, but she doesn't feel anything like the person I've spent my life with. She feels like the person Dad used to tell me she was when he met her.

"Have you heard from him?" Mom asks, not looking at me.

"Vaughn?"

She shakes her head, and I realize she means Rome.

"No." Not that I should have.

After what I did, he probably never wants to speak to me again. Rome doesn't open up to people. I'm still not sure why he opened up to me. But he did. He laid there and handed me all of him, hours before I told him I didn't want it.

"Your father and I were very different." Mom wipes down the counter. "My mother hated the idea of us dating. She said we came from different worlds, and it would never work out."

"I didn't know that." She's never opened up to me about the exact reasons for the rift with her family. I've only ever assumed.

Mom shrugs like this isn't something important. "I tried hard to prove her wrong, but over time, I just had to come to terms with the fact that she would never see it."

"Why are you telling me this?"

She pauses, looking up at me from the other side of the counter. "Because I shouldn't have cared so much about appeasing her when it was my happiness on the line. And I'm sorry if I made you feel that way."

Mom turns back to cleaning like she's not standing here dropping bombs on my views of her left and right. I'm not sure how to process all these revelations. Or the fact that my mother could have ever felt insecure herself. She's not someone who lets that show, so I didn't think it was possible.

"Mom," I say, and she looks up at me. "I love you."

I've never said that to her, and she doesn't return it, but she does smile the slightest and nods at me before turning back to cleaning. It feels like we're crossing a bridge I didn't think was there.

The doorbell rings and my stomach sinks. It was only a matter of time before Eloise came to check in. She's been texting me and asking how I'm doing, offering to bring me food. I've been putting her off because even if she's my friend, she reminds me of *him*. And it hurts to think about Rome.

"I'll get it," Mom says. "You go sit on the couch."

She disappears around the corner, and I grab my crutches and ditch my food. I've only had three bites of my burger and I'm not full, but I'm trying to mentally overcome these hurdles, even if it's a slow process.

Obstacles made further difficult without Rome. He made me feel hungry for life again. Hungry for food again. With him gone, I'm struggling to find the point in any of this.

I make my way to the living room and sink onto the couch, bringing my leg up and setting my crutches aside. It still hurts, but at least I'm feeling things. It's been too long since that's happened.

Resting my head back, I close my eyes. Maybe I can sleep these feelings away, then I can forget that even if I'm making decisions for myself for once in my life, I've still lost him.

But I hear Mom walk back into the room before sleep claims me.

"Who was it?" I ask, letting out a sigh.

When she doesn't answer, I open my eyes, and I'm met with my imagination. Or maybe I did fall asleep after all, and this is a dream. Because he wouldn't be here otherwise. He'd know better.

"Hey, sweetheart." Rome's lip ticks up at the corner.

I see him. I hear him. I smell him. And I can't breathe.

37

ROME

I wasn't sure what to make of the fact that Lili's mom answered the door and actually let me in, but I was thankful. Even more so that she left when I showed up.

I feel like enough of a pussy showing up here when the girl flat out rejected me. I don't need an audience for round two.

But walking into the room and seeing her on the couch with her broken leg lifted on a pillow and her eyes closed, I realized there was no use fighting it. I'm a punk, a pussy, a bitch—whatever they want to call me.

I can't stay away from her even if she wants me to.

When her eyes open, I'm sure that I'm staring into the gates of hell because it feels so good to be looking in them that it can't be right.

"Hey, sweetheart."

She takes in a sharp inhale at the sight of me, but she doesn't immediately tell me to go away.

I sit on the coffee table facing her, so as not to disturb her setup on the couch, and I hope she doesn't come to her senses.

She looks so innocent like this, like an angel made to tempt the devils of this world, and I'm one of them. Her long black hair is tied off her face, and she's not wearing a dash of makeup. Her big brown eyes are wide, and they might as well be lips because they drink me in at a glance. I'm tempted to crawl under the blanket and hold her, but I'm terrified to put myself out there again when it comes to her.

After Noah showed up at my house, I couldn't get what he said out of my head. I know Lili pushed me away, but it's only because I let her. I know what I saw when we were together. She didn't want to let go any more than I did. I just need to stand here and hope she sees it.

"How is it?" I look at her leg, still hating that she's going through pain. I'd happily be the one to experience it for her if I could.

"You're here," she says, not answering the question.

Her voice is the sweetest sound to my ears, and hearing it now, I realize how much I've missed it.

Yep—I'm a punk ass and totally whipped. The guys are going to give me so much crap about this.

"Thought you could scare me away, sweetheart?" I lift an eyebrow in a challenge. "I don't remember either of us calling *mercy*."

Her eyebrows pinch, before softening. "You're here."

She repeats it like she can't believe it, and then her entire face fills with so many emotions I don't think I've ever seen a person wear that many at once. Her hands come to her face and her eyes seal shut and tears start falling out of them. She sobs so loud it fills the entire silence of the room.

"Hey, hey." I drop to my knees on the floor beside the couch and hold her cheeks.

At the feel of her warm skin, I'm not sure how I ever walked away from her or let her push me. I swore I was done letting her run, and then I went and let her do it anyway.

"Why are you crying?" I rub my thumbs over her cheeks, and it smears her tears across them.

She blinks her eyes open, looking at me like I'm not real. But I've never been more real for someone. She asked me once to tell her something real, and instead, I've shown her.

Every bit of me.

"I pushed you away," she says, choking on the words as they come out. "You were the only one who saw me, and I went and pushed you away. I'm so messed up."

"That makes two of us."

She laughs through her tears, and it's a beautifully painful sound. "So now you're a masochist?"

I run my thumb along her cheek. "Only for you."

Lili blinks as her laugh fades, and she just looks at me. Like she's seeing so many things in my eyes. And I want to know what all of them are. Lili's the only person who has come face-to-face with the demons inside me and made them quieter. She's the only one who has accepted their existence and not tried to fix me.

She understands what it's like to feel broken, and she's okay with the fact that sometimes people will always be pieces. She understands what it means to exist as someone permanently broken.

"I shouldn't have pushed you away."

I shrug. "I shouldn't have left. But we're both bad at this, so…"

The smallest smile creeps up her face, and I'm tempted to capture it with a photo. Or better yet, my lips.

"If I'd have stayed, I would have told you to stop shutting me out because you're the only person I've never closed off." I trace a tear on her cheek and then plant my hand over her heart. "I'd tell you there's no use fighting this."

"I know," she whispers, and it sounds like a confession.

"Then tell me, does this heart belong to someone else, Lili?" I ask her, like I did before but with different intentions.

She shakes her head.

"Then make room for me."

I'm already on my knees, and even if it makes me everything I said I'd never be, I'm not opposed to begging.

Lili reaches up and traces her fingers on my throat. She traces every lash on the third eye. She must feel me watching her like the tattoo does, but she doesn't look into my eyes until she traces it fully.

"Not a room," Lili says, cupping my jaw in her hand. "You can have all of it. Make it your home."

I can't help the stupid smile that climbs my cheeks, or the fact that her face mirrors mine when it happens. She drags her hand down my face, down my chest, and rests it over my heart.

I feel it racing for her like it's been running a marathon my whole life in an effort to get to this moment. I feel it jump out of my chest and into her hands. Into her chest. I feel it pump with her blood.

Planting my hand over hers, I squeeze and want to keep her like that forever, even if I know we're both a little difficult, and I'm sure there's more to come.

"I fell for you, Rome," she says quietly, looking at our hands on my chest. "You warned me not to, and I did it anyway."

"I love your defiance," I say, and it makes her smirk. "I love you."

It slips out, or I let it. I don't know. She pulls things out of me I didn't think existed before she made me see them.

My confession makes her eyes go wide.

"Rome Moreno." She pulls her hand away and lifts up onto her elbows, bringing her face closer to mine. "Did I just hear what I think I did? The infamous Riff King is off the market?"

I lean in and wrap my hand around the back of her head. "Has been since he met you."

She bites the corner of her lip, but I bring my free hand to her jaw and peel it out with my thumb.

"I feel like I've been *on* the market until I met you, if that makes sense," she says with a laugh, and I know what she means. "I love you, too."

She tips her chin up, but doesn't lean closer for the kiss. She makes me chase it. Why is that such a turn on? I'd chase her to the ends of the earth, and it's not a way I've felt about another person.

Closing the distance, I press my lips to hers and enjoy the moment her breath escapes them. She makes the most delicate sounds when we're kissing. Half moans and exhales I want to consume me.

I hold the back of her head and part her lips with my tongue, remembering every bit of how she tastes and feels. I thought I knew pleasure, but it wasn't until Lili that I actually felt it. She exists in the only place where there's so much pain it kills me, and somehow there's also none at all.

Her hand wraps in my hair, and she bites down on my bottom lip, toying with it as she runs her tongue over it. I pull away and love the little smirk she wears like a dare she can't live up to right now.

"Keep that up, and I'm going to carry you to the bed." I look down at her laying on the couch. "Or here works."

I reach for the blanket, and she laughs, pushing me off. "Rome, you know I'm not cleared for any kind of *activity* yet."

"Activity?" I tease her. "Are we talking about mini golf or fucking, sweetheart? You'll have to clarify."

"Either." She swats at my arm, and I sink back on my heels. "I have to keep it elevated, and I'm not allowed to move it too much."

"Who said I need you to move anything?" I stick my tongue out, wiggling it at her, and she gets a full body blush that runs from her chest to her cheeks.

"Rome, my mom is here." She looks around frantically. "Wait, where is she?"

I laugh and shake my head. "She left when I got here. Didn't even frown at me. What was that about, anyway?"

"She's being..." Lili thinks her words over, biting her lip. "I don't know—different. She didn't even argue when I told her I think I'm done with dancing."

"Done?" I tip my head to the side.

"My hearts not in it anymore," she says, looking a little nervous to admit it to me for some reason.

"Wait, so if you're done dancing... at least for the time being... does that mean you aren't leaving Denver?"

She shakes her head, fighting to hold back a smile. "Not anytime soon. Although, my lease runs out on Eloise's house in a month, so I'll probably have to head into the city."

"That's it." I wrap my arms under her and pick her up, being careful not to hurt her leg, even if she shrieks in surprise.

"Rome, what are you doing? Put me down. I have crutches." She's swatting at my chest, but I ignore her and carry her back to the bedroom.

"Nope." I shake my head. "What did I tell you about running? I'd catch you. This is just making it easier."

"And I told you we can't have sex yet."

"Lili, I'm not here to have sex with you." I set her on the bed and pull out my phone to cast a movie.

Her eyes furrow as she watches me. "What are you here for, then?"

I drop down onto the mattress beside her and slip my arm under her head, loving that she nuzzles against my body and gets comfortable.

"I'm here to take care of you. To cook for you. And to love you."

"Love me, huh?" She looks up at me through her thick lashes.

I lean down to kiss her on the forehead. "Even if it hurts, sweetheart."

Epilogue

Lili

Five Months Later

"Do they bother you?" Cassie's eyes drift to the stripper poles in the middle of Rome's living room.

"They're unusual, but they're Rome." I tip my head back and laugh. "Besides, we have our fun with them."

Cassie, Eloise, and Merry burst out laughing, and it throws me into a fit of giggles.

I honestly wasn't sold on the idea of moving into a house with stripper poles in the middle of the living room, but I've learned to have fun with them. Besides, I'll be the only one dancing on them now.

"More power to you." Merry holds up her water glass in a cheers with mine. "Gotta fuel those kinks."

"I don't want to know," Cassie says, looking at Merry.

Merry bites her lip. "No, you don't."

Eloise shakes her head and smiles.

I'm still adjusting to being a part of this group, but I'm thankful for them. It's nice to actually have friends of my own. People in my life who aren't here just because of something I can offer them. And even if we're different in almost every way, I manage to fit in.

"What does your mom think of them?" Cassie nudges my arm, looking at the poles once more.

"I'm pretty sure she was mortified when she saw them," I admit. "She made sure to sit facing away from them the entire time she was here, and she didn't say anything."

"So, you guys are good?" Eloise asks.

I nod. "Yeah, she even got a place in the city to stay close."

Once my leg healed, and I got the all-clear to start practicing again from my doctor, I expected her to start pushing for me to take Vaughn up on his offer, but she didn't. In fact, she was the one to stand up to him when he tried to push my contract at us to force me to keep dancing for the company.

Mom hired a lawyer and brought to light some behind-the-scenes dealings Vaughn has been up to, threatening to out him if he didn't leave us alone. I always knew Vaughn wasn't a good guy, but apparently, his business has been built on bribery and blackmail, so it's worse than I thought.

I was also able to convince him to drop the charges against Rome once I said I would go to the police about what really happened if he didn't. Now he's finally out of my life for good.

"What are the four of you cracking up about?" Rome asks, walking into the room in a chest-hugging T-Shirt and sweats. Looking like sex, comfort, and danger all rolled into one. My eyes dip to the bulge prominent in his sweats and when I look back up, I realize he caught me.

He always looks sexy as hell, so I'm not sure I'll ever get used to the sight of him.

Leaning against the counter, he crosses one ankle over the other and ticks an eyebrow up at me. "See something you like, sweetheart?"

"On that note." Eloise hops up and shakes her head.

Sebastian, Noah, and Adrian follow Rome into the room.

"Don't even try and play innocent, princess," Rome says to Eloise. "I know you and Adrian are into some freaky shit."

Her eyes go wide, and she looks at Adrian, who laughs and shakes his head.

"He's fucking with you." Adrian walks up to her and wraps an arm around her shoulders. "I don't kiss and tell."

"This would be *fuck and tell*." Rome shrugs. "Doesn't matter, her face confirmed it."

Rome is definitely the troublemaker of the band, and he can't seem to help starting shit just to see how far he can push them.

"Leave my friend alone," I say, walking over and wrapping my hands around his waist to look up at him.

"Now you're on their side?"

"When you're picking on them, yes."

He leans down to bring his lips close to my ear. "You're going to pay for that later, sweetheart."

His teeth graze the shell of my ear before he bites down on the lobe, and I feel all the blood in my body rush between my legs. I try to wiggle away, but he wraps his arms firmly around me and holds me tight.

"We're taking off," Sebastian says, and it finally draws Rome's attention. "Have fun."

"Thanks again." He waves but doesn't stop looking at me as the band leaves.

"Is your secret project done yet?" I ask, looking down the hallway to a room he hasn't let me inside of for a month while he and the guys worked on something in there.

"Maybe." Rome grabs the front hem of my cropped T-shirt and pulls me to him. "Want to find out?"

He gives me a quick dirty kiss before pulling me behind him down the hallway. I'm reminded a little of the first night we did this. Feeling like I was falling into an alternate universe with him. Knowing if I went too far, I'd never get out. And I never did, but I also don't regret it.

Rome stops in front of the door and pauses, turning to face me. "For you, sweetheart." Then, he opens it.

It takes me a moment to process what I'm looking at because the room is empty. But the floors that were carpeted have been replaced with smooth wood planks, and the walls on three sides are mirrors, while the fourth is windows.

"A dance studio?" I step inside, noticing how the lights on the ceiling are small and dim like stars, and how the room has a quality that feels almost magical.

Rome stands behind me and pulls my back to his chest. "Just because you're done with it professionally for now, doesn't mean you can't fall in love with it again, even if it's just for you."

I blink back the tears forming in my eyes. It's the sweetest gesture from a man who doesn't like to show this side of himself to people.

"It's…" I spin until I'm facing him and wrap my arms around his neck. "It's absolutely perfect. Thank you."

Lifting up on my toes, I kiss him.

I hold the broken man with the torn heart and put him back together with my lips. I try to show him he's enough in the way that he's shown me. I want him to know that no matter who he is or what he's done, I love him how he is, and I would never want him to change as long as I can be his.

Rome drags his hands down my back and over my ass. "Not perfect yet."

He slides his thumbs into my leggings and peels them down my legs with my underwear, kneeling before me as I step out of them.

"Fuck," he says, looking from my eyes to my pussy. "You bring me to my knees."

"Literally." I smile at him.

He leans in and kisses my pussy slow and soft, like he did my mouth, running his tongue over me like he can't get enough of the taste of me. But he only gives me a rush before he's gripping my thighs and standing, wrapping my legs around him.

Carrying me across the room, he slams my back into one of the mirrors.

"Take my cock out, sweetheart." He leans in and bites the side of my neck. "We're going to christen this room."

I can barely contain myself when he gets commanding and dirty. I love every bit of it. Reaching for the band of his sweats, I reach in and wrap my hand around his thick cock.

Rome groans, pressing his hips into me as he holds my back to the mirror, and I can't help but tighten my legs around him. I tug his sweats down enough to free his dick, and he uses the opportunity to lift me up and slide my pussy along him.

"Fuck, you're so wet." He slides me along him again.

I almost black out from the feel of his piercing hitting my clit. That thing was made to drive me insane because I can barely stand the sight of it, much less the feel.

"Now who's teasing who?" I ask him, resting my forehead in the crook of his neck.

Rome tightens his hold around my thigh with one arm and releases the other so he can bring it up to my throat. The pressure pushes me further into the cool mirror.

"Teasing would imply I'm not planning to fuck orgasms out of you all night." He tightens his grip, and it makes me lightheaded. "Now be a good girl and put my cock inside you."

He pulls his hips back enough for me to get him in position, and as he thrusts in, he releases my throat. Air fills my lungs as he fills me, and I'm in the stars of this room—the stars in the night sky. With Rome buried inside me, I'm in another universe altogether.

His hands once more grip either thigh, and he starts to pound in harder. He's thrusting so hard it slaps my back against the unforgiving mirrors. Across the room, I can see him fucking me and it's the sexiest thing. He's still fully clothed and my bare legs are around him. But through his T-shirt I can see his back flexing from holding me in his grip, and his ass flexing with every thrust.

"You like watching me fuck you?" He asks, catching me watching him in the mirror.

"This might be my new favorite room."

He slows his thrusts, and I moan in disappointment as he lowers my feet to the floor and slips out of me.

Leaning down, he whispers in my ear. "Turn around and put your hands on the mirror, sweetheart."

I bite my lip as I do, and he grabs my wrists to slide them lower until I'm bent in front of him.

"That's a good girl," he says, smacking my ass so hard my scream fills the room.

"Nice acoustics." He grins at me in the mirror and smacks my ass again, and again, filling the room with my screams. His hands rub the raw spot on my ass gently before he slips a finger between my legs. "You get so fucking wet when I spank you."

Before I can think about it, he shoves his dick in me again. From this angle it hits deeper, and I have to lift up on my toes to take him.

Rome's arm wraps around my waist, and he holds my hips to his while his other hand plants over one of mine on the mirror, and his lips dip low by my ear. "Scream for me while I fuck you. I want to hear it."

He thrusts into me, and I do just that. I scream so loud it must fill the entire house. It probably echoes through the forest. I scream and I shake, and Rome holds me through every ruthless thrust of it. He plays me like his guitar. Like he's writing music with my body.

Building to the chorus.

Our eyes connect in the mirror, and it rips me apart. I feel myself gripping him so tight I see the pain in his eyes mixed with the pleasure. I can't help but feel the warmth in my chest as my climax pulls his out of him. I can't help that I love watching him fall apart like me.

My legs almost collapse, but Rome catches me. He pulls out and lifts me up so I'm standing with my back to his chest. I'm naked from the waist down, and he's looking me over, appreciating the sight.

"You're so beautiful, Lili." He runs his hand over my stomach and up to the center of my chest. "Tell me who you belong to, sweetheart."

I smile, looking up at him, holding my hand over his on my heart. "I'm yours, Rome. My heart belongs to you."

EPILOGUE

ROME

Eight Months Later

LOVE IS STRANGE. IT'S not what people say it is—all fairytales and fluffy things. It's painful. It *hurts*.

It's everything good and hard, and I'm in so deep that when our eyes connect through the crowd, I swear hers peel the flesh from my bones. She makes me strong and vulnerable all at once.

Lili's sipping water, sitting at a table to the side of the room, and I love that she's just watching me from where she is. I feel her eyes roam me every so often and it might as well be her hands. Or her mouth. I'd go for either.

"You and your chick seem happy," Jude says. He lifts his drink and I tip mine against it.

"Hard to not be happy when you're with the hottest chick on the planet."

He laughs, but I'm being serious.

"It's good to see you, man. Long time," I say. "Didn't know if you'd make it."

"Sebastian threatened my nuts if I didn't make it to his wedding. Although he failed to mention there'd be so much fucking pink." Jude looks around the reception, frowning.

"They're fucking weird."

"Says the dude who can't go five seconds without staring at his chick?" He nudges my arm, and even in a suit, his tattoos peek out from every corner.

I shrug, not bothering to explain it. Jude isn't the kind of guy who'll be caught dead in a relationship. Sage told me it has something to do with Jude's past, and that he doesn't talk about it. All we know, is there's no getting beyond those walls with him, no matter how close a friend you are.

"How are things at the shop?" I ask him.

Jude shrugs. "Fine. Busy."

Jude, Sage, Crew, and Echo took over Twisted Roses when Blaze stepped back, and I hear from them less and less lately.

Not that I'm one to talk. The band has been so occupied with the label; we're swamped with meetings every time we're in Los Angeles.

But he's here now, and it feels good to see a friend who knows me from when the band was living in California recording our first album. That's the only good thing about weddings, I guess, catching up with people you wouldn't see otherwise.

"Rome, where the fuck have you been?" Sebastian comes up to me, looking out of breath.

"Here?" I quirk an eyebrow at him.

"Alright, well Cassie wants to get the wedding photos done, and I want to fuck my wife, so let's get on with this shit."

Jude laughs and drains his drink. "You two have fun with that. Catch you next time you're in LA."

I nod at Jude before he retreats into the mass of people around the dance floor. He says he's in town for Sebastian's wedding, but I know better. Something's up with him, and I make a mental note to check in when everything settles.

Turning to Sebastian, he looks stressed as fuck. I'm sure this is supposed to be a special day, but I don't understand putting yourself through this kind of stress. Maybe Lili and I will end up at the courthouse someday, but this crap is ridiculous.

"I'll grab Lili," I tell him, and he relaxes the slightest.

"Thanks, man." Sebastian claps me on the shoulder before disappearing through the crowd, and I make my way to Lili.

Sometimes I think there are magnets inside the two of us because the closer I get, the stronger the pull is.

I used to think it was crazy to settle down. The idea of fucking one chick for the rest of my life sounded like a waste of time for my dick. But the second she comes into view, I'm reminded all over again how it was only because I hadn't met her yet.

"Picture time, sweetheart." I hold out my hand and she takes it. "Your feet feeling up to it?"

"My feet, yes." She grips my hand and lets me help her to stand. "But I swear there's no room left inside me. How do I still have two more weeks?"

I plant a hand on Lili's round belly and smile at her, knowing better than to actually answer her question. If there's anything I've learned since Lili got pregnant, it's that if I don't watch my tongue, I'll be sleeping on the couch because her hormones have made her savage. Not that I mind it.

Lili's always been hot, but seeing her belly grow with my baby has got to be the sexiest thing I've seen in my life.

We weren't planning it, but we weren't really stopping it either. Lili didn't like how the pill made her feel, and I didn't want to stop coming inside her, so we kind of threw caution to the wind, and I knocked her up.

Best not-planned thing I've ever done. Even if at first it made me a little nervous.

I didn't grow up with the best example of a parent. And even if I know I'm nothing like that piece of shit, I don't know how to be a good dad either. Lili says I'll figure it out, and I keep waiting for her confidence to rub off on me.

But even if it does, nothing erases the looming stress of knowing she'll be going into labor soon. And with what happened to my mom, the thought of that alone is a level of fear I've never experienced before.

I can't lose Lili.

"Do I look okay?" she asks, brushing her dark hair back. Pregnancy has made her ask that question a little more frequently, which baffles me since she's never been more beautiful.

"Perfect."

Leaning down, I plant a kiss on her forehead before leading her in the direction of the photographer. We swing through the crowd and grab Noah, Merry, Adrian, and Eloise on the way. And by the time we all find Sebastian and Cassie, they don't seem the least bit worried about pictures.

The two of them are standing in front of a wall of white roses, her in his arms. He's looking at her like his world would fall apart without her, and she can't tear her eyes off him. Basically, how they've been for the past two years.

Her white and pink lace dress flows out like a river toward the photographer, and they lean in for a kiss.

The photo snaps, and I realize maybe I do want this sappy shit after all. I'd love to see Lili in a white dress just for me.

"There you are," Cassie says with a big smile on her face.

She waves us over and we all gather in front of the wall of flowers. Noah's making jokes to pick at Adrian, who looks like he really doesn't want to smile. And Merry's still frowning about the fact that Cassie dressed her up in a pink bridesmaid dress.

We're all so fucked up and perfect.

"Smile," the photographer says, and the lights are flashing.

When you've been in the spotlight as long as we have, you get used to having your picture taken. You're used to it not meaning anything. But then there are those rare moments, like this one, where it feels like it does again.

I spent my entire childhood feeling like I didn't have a family, but I made one with this band, and now I'm creating another with Lili.

I'm no longer alone.

"Ah," Lili winces beside me, and I look down to see her holding her stomach with one hand.

"What's wrong?"

She looks up at me. "Nothing."

But her face winces, and she flinches again in my arms.

"Lili?"

Her eyes go wide then, and she looks down, where my gaze follows, to find a puddle of what looks like water at her feet.

"Oh my gosh," Cassie squeals so loud half the room turns to look at us. "You're having the baby."

She jumps up and down with excitement, and Eloise grabs onto my arm, smiling, while Merry and the guys stand there looking terrified at the prospect of a baby falling out of Lili at any second.

"Holy shit," I say, holding Lili's arm. "We need to get to the hospital. We need a car. Crap, I don't have our stuff here."

"Rome." Lili plants her hand on my cheek and it settles me back in place. "It's going to be okay. We've got this."

The brightest smile stretches her face. It lights up her cheeks and brings light to her eyes. She might as well be glowing from the inside out.

"You're going to be a daddy."

Those words knock me in the stomach like a physical thing because I feel it slamming through me. I'm going to be a dad. Of all the fucking guys in the band—of all the guys in the world—Rome Moreno is going to be a father.

"And you're going to be wonderful," Lili says, grazing my cheek. "Now let's go and have a baby."

I thought nothing could compare to the decimation of falling in love with Lili Chen, but when I hold my daughter in my arms, something officially shatters beyond repair inside me because I know I'll forever be hers.

"Nera Serene Moreno." I named her.

My light.

Like her mother, she shines bright enough to lead me out of the tunnel I've spent my life in.

I hand her to Cassie, who's still in her wedding dress as she stands in the hospital room.

The entire band was in the waiting room the whole time, missing the rest of the reception. I told them they didn't need to, but that's family for you.

I sit down next to Lili on the bed, and she curls into my arms.

Watching her give birth was the single most terrifying event in my life. I tried to tell myself things would be fine, and that she's not my mother. But I couldn't help but watch her eyes the whole time, making sure she didn't leave me too.

It wasn't until it was over that I was able to breathe a sigh of relief. And now, as Cassie passes our baby back to Lili, and she holds her in her arms, I feel complete.

"We'll let you two get some alone time." Noah plants a hand on my shoulder. "Happy for you man."

Merry curls into his side, and I'm worried that it's bittersweet for them. She must read it in my face because she shakes her head.

"Don't look at me like that, Rome," Merry says. "I'm happy for you. Noah and I aren't ready for this, anyway. But soon enough..."

Noah looks down at her and smiles, like they're already planning their own little family, and I really want that for them.

"Thanks, guys."

They all give final hugs before leaving the room. And it's just us. Me, Lili, and the tiny person we created.

"She's beautiful, isn't she?" Lili says, brushing her small fingers along Nera's cheek.

"Perfect," I agree.

She has dark hair and even darker eyes. A mini version of her mother. It's terrifying looking at her little face and feeling something so big in my chest I don't know how there's space for it. Holding her in my arms, I can't imagine how a parent could hurt their child, or abandon them, or do anything close to what my father did to me.

I'll do everything in my power to make sure Nera never feels pain.

Running through women never made me think twice, but now looking at the women sitting in this bed with me,

I kind of hate myself a little because I don't want anyone to hurt either of them.

"I can't believe we're here, Rome." Lili rests her head on my shoulder.

"I can." I brush her hair out of her face, and she nods sleepily. "Here. Get some rest."

I hold my hands out and take Nera from Lili, giving her a kiss as she closes her eyes. It's been a long day, so I'm not surprised when she immediately falls asleep.

I take Nera and settle in a rocking chair in the corner where I've got a clear view of Lili and can keep an eye on her.

My girls.

My life.

Nera squirms, and I look down at her scrunched face as she stretches.

"Shh," I whisper, running my finger over her forehead to her nose until her face relaxes. "I've got you, lovebug. If it's the last thing I do, I'll make sure nothing bad ever happens to you."

She settles in like her mother and falls asleep. The sounds of their breathing fill the room. After so many years in purgatory, I never expected a chance at peace. I was prepared to live in the in-between and never feel it. But sitting in this room with the first hint of morning coming through the window, I'm there.

I've found what makes me happy.

I've found what feels like home.

Catch up with Rome and Lili seven years later! Download their **FREE bonus epilogue** now!

Ready for Jude's twisted tale? Start the Twisted Roses series with ***Lies Like Love***.

BOOKS BY EVA

Series Starters

Seattle Singles
(Billionaires, Bad Boys, Big City)
Start with **Miss Matched**

Enemy Muse
(Damaged Rock Stars with Dark Pasts)
Start with **Heart Break Her**

Twisted Roses
(Morally Gray, Taboo, Dark Fairytale themes)
Start with **Lies Like Love**

Find a complete book list at www.evasimmons.com

amazon.com/Eva-Simmons/e/B07MMX2MLB?ref_=dbs_p_ebk_r00_abau_000000

facebook.com/AuthorEvaSimmons/

- goodreads.com/author/show/16225312.Eva_Simmons
- bookbub.com/profile/eva-simmons
- instagram.com/evasimmonsbooks/
- tiktok.com/@evasimmonsbooks
- twitter.com/evasimmonsbooks

Acknowledgments

There's something to be said about love that doesn't try to fix us. Love that understands scars form a foundation that will always house a few demons. Love that is truly unconditional. This is what makes Rome and Lili's story truly special to me, and I hope you enjoyed it.

Rome's evolution through this series will always be one of my favorite things I've written. He had so many walls around his heart, he no longer believed it existed. All it took was the right person to uncover it.

If anyone was going to bring the Riff King to his knees, it had to be a girl like Lili. Someone delicate enough to balance Rome's rough edges, but strong enough to meet him toe to toe every time he pushed and challenged her. The energy they share is magical, and I love them so much for how they draw out the best in each other.

As this series comes to a close, I'm incredibly sad to say goodbye to the band. Each story has a piece of my heart tucked between the pages, and walking away is harder than expected. But I'm so grateful you have shared in this journey with me. And I promise you'll be seeing the band again through cameos in future projects.

Chris, what a journey this has been. You've seen it all as I immersed myself in this series and barely came up for air. Thank you for standing by my side through all of it. The writing process can be all consuming. I appreciate you supporting me when I needed space to write, and reminding me when it was time to surface. Thank you for keeping me grounded, listening to every thought, and for your unconditional love.

For my boys, never stop dreaming and reading. You are, and will always be, my whole world. I love you more than anything.

Mom, what's the final verdict? Do you love Rome yet?? Joking aside, I love every ounce of commentary and feedback. I love that you read these stories, even if I cringe a little thinking *my mother is going to read this*. When I think back to why I didn't start writing romance sooner, it had a lot to do with worrying about judgment from others. I wish I hadn't let that hold me back as long as I did because you raised me to always be proud of my work. When I say I truly have the most wonderful mother in the world, I mean it. You are there through it all, and I can't begin to express what your support means to me.

Mikki, my sister, my sounding board... how do I sum this up? You've listened to every little thought I've had about this series. You talked through the tough moments. You cheered on the exciting ones. There's a lot I'm thankful for, but most of all, I want to thank you for November and December of last year. I'm not sure you realize how important your support during that time was. Our daily chats kept me going mentally and creatively. Those conversations kept me afloat, and in turn, made these last two books in the series possible.

Alba, I'm starting to think my notes to you in these books are going to become a series of couch stories. Because, as I start to write this, all I can think about is us on the couch talking about acknowledgments. There's a lot I could say, but it all boils down to this... thank you for the small things that don't seem big, but really are. The flowers, the red bracelet, the memes on rough days. You're the most thoughtful friend, and I'm so lucky to have you in my life.

Ally, I look forward to the calls and texts I get from you each time you finish one of these books. Thank you for loving the heart of these stories.

To my beta readers, you guys have seen it all. I distinctly remember Rome not being popular with the group at the start of this series, and I felt like it was my mission to change your minds. Thank you for giving feedback on the messiest versions of these books, and for seeing the heart in them before they were fully realized.

For my editor, Kat—it almost seems like fate that I stumbled upon you when I needed an editor for these four books. Only you could have done them justice. I'm so thankful for the many chats we've had over the course of this series. Thank you for understanding my chaotic thoughts and making them seamless.

Vanessa, I appreciate your final set of eyes on these pages. Thank you for catching all the little things that are seemingly unimportant but become the elephant in the room if they aren't cleaned up before the book is published.

A giant thank you to my ARC and promo teams! Many of you discovered my books through this series and have helped it grow in ways I didn't expect. Thank you for taking a chance on a newish romance author and for falling in love with these books enough to want to spread the word. Your messages, posts, shares, and videos are what keep me going when I start to get cold feet about hitting the publish button. Thank you for believing in my stories before they see the light of day. For loving these characters at their rawest moments. And for supporting my work with your time and energy.

And finally for my readers... a thank you that is never big enough. I save it until the end each time, like maybe I'll figure out how to properly put my appreciation into words once I get here. But nothing captures how thankful I truly am. We've been through it with this series. The tears, the stories, the emotions. The way you have embraced the band fills my heart with so much love, and has surpassed anything I expected. I can't wait to share more stories with you soon. Thank you a million times over. I'm beyond grateful for you.

About the Author

Eva Simmons writes hot, heartbreaking romance with complex heroines, and broken, dirty-talking bad boys who fall hard for them.

When Eva isn't dreaming up new worlds or devouring every book she can get her hands on, she can be found spending time with her family, painting a fresh canvas, or playing an elf in World of Warcraft.

Eva is currently living out her own happily ever after in Nevada with her family.

Printed in Great Britain
by Amazon